EAT CROW AND DIE

A P.J. BENSON MYSTERY

EAT CROW AND DIE

MARIS SOULE

FIVE STAR
A part of Gale, Cengage Learning

GALE
CENGAGE Learning·

Farmington Hills, Mich • San Francisco • New York • Waterville, Maine
Meriden, Conn • Mason, Ohio • Chicago

GALE
CENGAGE Learning·

LIBRARY OF CONGRESS CATALOGING-IN-PUBLICATION DATA

Soule, Maris.
  Eat crow and die : a P.J. Benson mystery / by Maris Soule. —
First edition.
    pages ; cm
    ISBN 978-1-4328-3076-2 (hardcover) — ISBN 1-4328-3076-7
(hardcover) — ISBN 978-1-4328-3080-9 (ebook) — ISBN 1-4328-
3080-5 (ebook)
    I. Title.
PS3569.O737E2 2015
813'.54—dc23   2014047833

First Edition. First Printing: May 2015
Find us on Facebook– https://www.facebook.com/FiveStarCengage
Visit our website– http://www.gale.cengage.com/fivestar/
Contact Five Star™ Publishing at FiveStar@cengage.com

Printed in the United States of America
1 2 3 4 5 6 7 19 18 17 16 15

To
Climax, Michigan.
Thank you for 27 wonderful years.

ACKNOWLEDGMENTS

Many thanks go to Captain Robert E. McAlear, a member of the South Haven Coast Guard Auxiliary, for taking the time to "talk" me through what would happen—who would be involved—if a boat exploded on Lake Michigan near South Haven.

My thanks, also, to Retired Detective William Lux of the Van Buren Sheriff's Department for telling me how the sheriff's department would proceed with the investigation, especially since a deputy from another sheriff's department was involved.

And a big thanks to retired Lt. Patrick J. Doolan of the Saginaw Police Department for not only answering my questions about impounding the victim's car, but for going to others and getting additional information for this story.

I also gleaned a lot of information for this story from the law enforcement personnel (retired and active) on the online Crimescenewriters Yahoo group. Those men and women willingly answered a multitude of questions.

If I messed up on any law enforcement procedures or information, I apologize.

My critique partners, Dawn Bartley and Julie McMullen, were wonderful. Online and in person, they diligently caught my typos and other mistakes and kept reminding me to add in the five senses. I treasure our critique sessions. Also, thank you Gordon Aaalborg for taking what I send you and making it a better book. I may silently grumble when I get your edits, but you're usually right, even though I hate to admit it.

And thanks to the fans who kept asking if P.J. was pregnant and what happened next. They kept me at the computer so I could answer their questions.

And finally, thank you, Bill, for answering all the crazy questions I throw your way, for helping out around the house when I'm too tired to cook or clean, and for constantly believing in me. The day we met was the luckiest day of my life.

CHAPTER ONE

The telephone rang, jarring me out of my misery. I started to stand up, but just as quickly changed my mind. The answering machine could get it.

This was the third time in the last half hour I was kneeling in front of the porcelain throne, trying to convince my stomach to calm down. I simply didn't have the energy to talk to anyone. Or the desire.

Here it was one o'clock in the afternoon. That meant I couldn't be suffering from morning sickness. Right? It had to be a bug. Something I ate. A germ. The stomach flu.

I couldn't be pregnant. I was on The Pill.

The phone kept ringing, and I squeezed my eyes shut. My head ached, my mouth tasted like garbage, and I was exhausted. Too tired to move. Besides, who would be calling me on a Saturday afternoon? I'd already talked to my grandmother. She'd said Mom was off with her boyfriend, attending the Rib Fest at Arcadia Creek. And Wade was on his boat on Lake Michigan, with his six-year-old son Jason, Wade's ex-wife, Linda, and her new husband. It was supposed to be just a fishing trip with his son, but his ex had insisted on going along. I think maybe she thought Wade would try to run off with Jason.

Anyway, Wade had said not to expect a call until tomorrow, and my regular clients know I don't work on weekends. "Too taxing" I like to tell them, playing on the fact that, as a certified public accountant, taxes are my job. That meant whoever was calling my home phone number was either a new client or a salesperson.

If they left a message, I would know.

The phone stopped ringing. I expected my answering machine to click on, and that I'd hear my message and then the caller's response. But the answering machine didn't come on. For a moment there was silence.

I sighed in relief.

Then my cell phone started ringing.

Baraka howled.

My dog always does that when my cell phone rings. Rhodesian Ridgebacks have floppy ears, but they hear quite well, and there's something about the ring-tone I picked for my cell phone that sets my dog off. I know, I could change the ring-tone, but when I'm away from the phone, such as outside or working in a different part of the house, his howling alerts me to any incoming calls.

At the moment, his howling grated on my nerves, but since I only give that number out to a select few, I decided I'd better answer the phone.

"Okay, okay," I said, pushing myself to my feet. I just hoped my stomach stayed calm long enough for me to tell the caller I couldn't talk.

I stumbled into the dining room and grabbed the cell phone from the table as it began to ring again. "What?" I practically yelled.

"P.J.?"

I recognized Wade's sister's voice immediately. Ginny has a sexy, throaty way of talking that always reminds me of Marilyn Monroe. She's also a very nice person and certainly didn't deserve to be yelled at. I softened my tone. "Yeah, it's me."

"I tried your home number. I don't know where you're at, but there's been an accident."

"Accident?" I sank onto the nearest chair. "What kind of an accident?"

"Wade's boat," Ginny said. "It's . . . it's blown up."

"Oh my God." I've been on that boat, fished off it, gone swimming off it. Wade and I have made love on it. *The Freedom* is Wade's pride and joy. But it wasn't the boat I was worried about. "What about Wade? Was he on it? Jason? The others?"

"I think so. I mean, I think Linda and her husband were on it."

"But not Wade?"

"Yes. I mean, yes, he was on it. And so was Jason. I don't know about Linda and her husband."

Wade's boat blew up, and he was on it. Wade and Jason. I hated to ask the next question. "Is Wade dead?"

"No," Ginny said. "Damn, why do I always get behind a slow car when I'm in a hurry?"

"Where are you?" I asked, hearing a horn blast.

"On East Michigan, heading for Kalamazoo. Listen, one of Wade's friends from the marina called me just a while ago. He said he was out fishing when Wade's boat exploded. He and some other boaters helped fish Wade and Jason out of the water and got them to shore. He said Wade and Jason are being airlifted to Bronson."

"They're taking them to the hospital?" That didn't sound good. "How bad are they?"

"I don't know. The guy said Wade was unconscious when they pulled him out of the water, but he was talking by the time they put him on the helicopter."

"And Jason?"

"He seemed to think Jason was okay. Shaken up, but okay."

"And you said they're taking them to Bronson?"

"That's what I was told."

Bronson Hospital was located in downtown Kalamazoo,

roughly thirty miles from my house. I could be there in forty minutes or less. But first I needed to change clothes, put the dog out, brush my teeth . . .

"I'm at home," I told Ginny. "I'll be there as soon as I can. Call me on my cell if you find out anything."

CHAPTER TWO

It took me longer than I expected to get ready and drive into Kalamazoo. By the time I arrived at the hospital, Ginny had called twice. The first time was to tell me both Wade and Jason were in the ER, the second time she said they'd moved Wade to a room, but she was still with Jason in the ER. I decided to go there first.

Ginny had already told them at the reception desk to send me back when I arrived. I found the two of them in one of the exam rooms, Jason sitting on the table and Ginny standing next to him. At the moment, the two were alone, not a doctor or nurse in sight.

Ginny looked as if she'd received the call about Wade and Jason right after stepping out of a shower. Normally she reminds me of a model, not a hair out of place, her makeup perfect, clothes color-coordinated and stylish. I would hate the woman if she wasn't so nice, but it was rather comforting to see she could look disheveled, that even though she was still pretty without makeup, she wasn't drop-dead gorgeous. With her hair pulled back in a ponytail, she looked young, and I could tell she'd been crying.

Wade's son, Jason, was leaning his head on her shoulder, his eyes closed. His unruly brown hair still looked a little damp, and he had a blue-and-white checked blanket wrapped around him that covered all of his body except for his bare feet. "Hey you two," I said as I entered the room, not quite sure how Jason was going to react.

He blinked his eyes open and stared at me. He has the same beautiful, blue eyes and long brown lashes as his father, but this afternoon there was a sadness in those eyes that I'd never seen before.

"Hey, P.J.," he said back and sat a little straighter. "Did you hear? Daddy's boat exploded."

"Yes, I did hear that." I looked at Ginny for guidance, not quite sure how much Jason knew or understood.

"Daddy hit his head," Jason continued before Ginny had a chance to respond. "And they sewed him up, just like Grandma Healy sewed up my teddy bear, and then he started yelling, so they made him leave."

Ginny chuckled and nodded. "That about sums it up. I guess if you want to get out of the ER quickly, you start making a fuss."

"They sent him home already?"

"No, they want to keep him overnight for observation, so he's already in a room." She gave me the number. "As soon as we get the results back from some tests they ran on Jason, we're going to go up and see him. Aren't we, Jason?"

"Yeah, because he's real worried about me. And about Mama, too." Jason frowned. "I don't know where Mama is."

"We haven't heard anything," Ginny said, rubbing a hand over the blanket where it covered Jason's shoulders. "We're hoping real hard that she's all right."

"Yeah. Both Mama and Daddy Michael," Jason said.

"And what about you?" I asked Jason. "Are you all right?" With so much of him covered by the blanket, I couldn't tell.

"I'm okay," he said.

I looked to Ginny for confirmation, and she nodded. "The tests are just precautionary. I don't think they're going to find anything wrong with this little rascal. In fact, from what I've heard, he saved his daddy's life."

" 'Cause Daddy hit his head," Jason said and pointed to his own forehead. "Right here. And there was blood in the water, so it's a good thing there's no sharks in the lake. And he went under water once. He had his life jacket on—we both did—but you needed to pull a piece of yellow plastic to make his inflate, and he couldn't do it."

"So somehow Jason managed to swim over near Wade and pulled the tab for him." Ginny gave her nephew a hug. "You saved my brother's life."

"Yeah." Jason grinned. "I did, didn't I?"

Talking about his father seemed to help Jason forget that he didn't know what had happened to his mother, and I hoped for his sake that Linda and her new husband were okay, but the fact that Linda wasn't here with her son didn't bode well.

I think Ginny knew what I was thinking. "Go see Wade," she said. "Let him know Jason's fine, and we'll come see him as soon as we can. Tell him to stop being a pain in the rear."

As I headed for the room number Ginny had given me, I thought back over the four months I've known Wade. The first time I saw him, he reminded me of Nicolas Cage and Tom Cruise wrapped up in one man. He certainly didn't look like a homicide detective. Back then he thought I'd murdered someone. That or I was crazy, like my mother. We've had a couple more misunderstandings since then, but for the most part we've gotten along quite well—in bed and out. On the other hand, there are times when he can be stubborn, irritating, and unreasonable. As I neared his room, it sounded like he was being all three.

"I'm fine," he bellowed. "I do not need to be in bed."

"Until the doctor releases you," a feminine voice said, "you need to stay put."

"Damn the doctor. I told them downstairs I need to get back to South Haven."

"Are you giving the nurse a bad time?" I asked as I entered the room.

Wade made a grunting sound as he looked my way. "They're treating me as if I'm sick. I hit my head, that's all."

The poor nurse looked at me and shook her head. "He's supposed to rest."

"Be a good boy, Wade. Do as she says. Put your legs back up on the bed and rest."

He glared at me—at both the nurse and me—but he put his legs back up on the mattress and allowed her to pull a sheet up to his waist. He didn't lay back, so I asked, "Can he have the bed cranked up, so he can be in a seated position?"

"If it will keep him in bed, I guess so."

She didn't make a move, and neither did Wade, so I stepped closer and pushed the button that raised the back so Wade could be in a fully seated position. "That better?" I asked.

He grumbled, but gave a slight nod, then winced.

He had a four-inch square bandage on his forehead, and I could see some discoloration along the side of his face, but it wasn't until he went to lean back against the pillow behind him and grimaced that I knew it wasn't just his forehead that had been injured.

"If you need anything, press that button," the nurse said, indicating the red one on the corded remote.

Wade grunted, and she quickly left. I'm sure she was glad to leave him to me. He clearly wasn't in a good mood.

"You seen Jason?"

"I just left him. He's with Ginny."

"He's okay?"

"He seems fine. They're waiting for the results on a couple of tests, then, Ginny said, she'll bring him by your room."

"That or I'll pick him up as I leave."

"I don't think they want you leaving today."

Again the glare. "I'm fine. I hit my head, that's all."

"Uh-huh. And how many stitches?" I asked, pointing at the bandage on his forehead.

"I don't know." He gave me a crooked smile. "Maybe fifteen."

"And the back of your head?"

"I have a little goose-egg, that's all."

I reached behind his head, but I'd barely touched his scalp before he let out a yelp. From what I could feel, his "little goose-egg" was more like an ostrich egg. "How did you hit both the back and the front of your head?"

"I don't know." He let out a deep sigh. "I don't remember anything from the time Linda and that arrogant bastard she married finally arrived at the boat with Jason until I found myself on a stretcher, being lifted into a helicopter." He narrowed his eyes. "I don't even remember that very well. It wasn't until they poked my head with a needle that I really started focusing on what was happening."

"You don't remember taking the boat out on Lake Michigan?"

He started to shake his head, but immediately stopped. "Not a thing."

The pupils of his eyes were dilated, and since Wade doesn't do drugs, and it was fairly light in the room, I figured the doctors were right, he did have a concussion. I'd heard how people who had concussions often couldn't remember what happened before or even after the accident. Some lost entire days. Sometimes the memories came back; sometimes they never did.

"I do remember Linda said they didn't want to fish," Wade grumbled. "Here she insists she wants to go on this fishing trip with Jason and me, that both she and Brewster want to go along, and then as soon as she arrives—an hour late, at that—she starts making a fuss about going fishing. I'd even brought fishing poles for the two of them."

"But they did go out on the boat with you? With you and Jason?"

"They must have." Wade looked out beyond the end of the bed, and I could tell he was trying to remember.

"Do you have any idea where you and Jason were when the boat blew up?"

"No." Wade looked back at me. "You haven't heard anything about Linda?"

"Nothing."

"So they're not here, not in the hospital?"

"I don't know for sure, but I don't think so."

From his expression, I knew what Wade was thinking. If Linda and her husband were on the boat and had been thrown to safety, Linda would be with Jason now. The woman had become paranoid since telling Wade that she and her new husband were moving to California and taking Jason with them. She was sure Wade was going to do something to stop her.

"If she was on the boat . . ." I started to say, but didn't finish. The thought of what might have happened to Linda—to both Wade's ex and her new husband—caused my stomach to lurch.

I knew what was coming, and as much as I hated to leave Wade at this moment, I knew I had to. "I'm sorry. I need to go to the bathroom," I said, already heading for the door. "I'll be right back."

CHAPTER THREE

I could have used the bathroom in Wade's room, but I didn't want to be throwing up where he could hear. Luckily, on my way to see him I'd noticed there was a woman's bathroom only a few yards away from his room. I made it to a stall just in time. Leaning over a stool, I emptied what little food I had in my stomach.

I thought I was by myself, but when I stepped out of the stall, I saw a middle-aged woman standing near the wash basins. Her pale-blue scrubs, along with the ID tag that gave her name as ANN M., RN, indicated she was a nurse. She was watching me, not washing her hands, and her expression reminded me of my grandmother's looks when I was a kid and did something wrong.

"If you're sick, you shouldn't be visiting patients," Nurse Ann said.

"I know, but . . ." I started, not sure how to explain. "My boyfriend . . ."

Jeez, calling a thirty-four-year-old man a boyfriend sounded stupid, but I didn't know what else to call him. Friend wasn't strong enough, and lover implied he loved me, and though I hoped he did, he'd never actually said so.

I started again. "His boat blew up, and he may have a concussion, and his sister called me . . ."

Shoot, if I were truly sick, none of that should matter. I stared down at the floor, hating to say aloud what I feared, but hoping maybe she could assure me I was wrong. "I may not be sick. Lately I've been waking up feeling sick. It usually lasts a couple hours, and then I'm fine. Today it's lasting longer, but between bouts, I feel fine. A little tired, but otherwise fine."

She frowned slightly. "You say you've been feeling tired lately?"

"A little. Yes." I wasn't sure what she was getting at, but I hoped nausea and tiredness weren't the symptoms of a serious disease.

"And what about coffee?" she asked, stepping closer. "Does the smell make you nauseous?"

"Yes. Oh, yes." I was amazed that she knew this. "I love coffee. At least, I used to. Now—" I shook my head. "I made a pot of coffee yesterday morning and just the smell as it was brewing made me sick. I had to dump it. Same thing this morning."

Nurse Ann's frown turned into a grin. "That's normal, honey. When you're pregnant smells intensify. It's because your body is now producing more estrogen."

"But I can't be pregnant." This wasn't what I wanted to hear. "I've been on The Pill. I mean, my period's late, but that's happened before."

"Can't be?" The lift of her eyebrows said she didn't agree. "I'd suggest you buy one of those pregnancy tests."

I sighed. "I suppose I'd better."

Nurse Ann must have sensed my fear because she came even closer and slipped an arm around my shoulders. "Do you know who the father is?"

I nodded. "The guy with the concussion."

"Are you afraid he'll be upset?"

"I don't know." I hadn't thought that far. "He . . . We . . ."

She glanced down at my left hand, and I knew what she was wondering.

"No, I'm not married . . . and neither is he."

"Sometimes children come whether you're ready or not."

Well, I certainly wasn't ready. Deep down I've always thought it would be nice to have a baby, but I've also always told myself I shouldn't. It would be too dangerous. Like tempting fate. "You don't understand," I finally said. "My mother's a schizophrenic."

"Oh," she said, and I knew she did understand.

What she "understood" was offspring of schizophrenics have a one in ten chance of also being schizophrenic. If both parents are schizophrenic, those percentages go even higher. "My mother didn't show any signs of the disease until she got pregnant with me," I said. "I'm twenty-eight, going on twenty-nine, the age when schizophrenia often shows up in females."

Nurse Ann nodded, and then asked, "What about your father? Is he schizophrenic?"

"He's dead," I said, understanding why she'd asked. Two schizophrenic parents would definitely increase my chances of having the diagnosis. "He was never diagnosed as such, but there were things he did in the past that I would certainly consider crazy."

"And you've never been tested."

"For schizophrenia? No." Scientists have discovered certain genes might play a role in a person being schizophrenic, and I'd thought about being tested, but so far I'd put it off. "I guess I should, especially now."

"Maybe . . . or maybe not," she said. "That research is still in its early stages, and the genome scans available now don't provide a complete picture of a person's risk. But if it would make you feel better . . ."

She let the idea hang in the air, and I knew it would be my decision, but I wasn't sure knowing I would become schizophrenic would make me feel better.

"Meanwhile," she went on. "I think you should buy one of

those home pregnancy tests. If you are pregnant, you need to make an appointment with your doctor, get on some prenatal vitamins, and start taking care of yourself. There's no cure for morning sickness, but try drinking ginger tea. That seems to help a lot of women. Get plenty of rest, avoid stress, drink lots of water, and eat small meals." She checked each suggestion off on her fingers, then laughed. "Do whatever works for you."

"Sounds like you work for a baby doctor."

She shook her head. "Nope, but I have three children." She gave my shoulders another affectionate squeeze. "It will get better, dear. I know that for sure. Try carrying around a slice of lemon. Sniff it whenever you start to feel nauseous. Some women find that helps. And if you keep throwing up while you're here, have one of the nurses bring you a soda or a sports drink."

She left the bathroom then, and I took a few minutes to wash up and compose myself. *Pregnant?*

Damn. What was I going to do now?

Chapter Four

I almost ran into a man coming out of Wade's room. Short and squat, he looked like he might have been a wrestler in his youth. I guessed his age around fifty or sixty. He didn't have the usual paunch middle-aged men carried around, but his head was as smooth and shiny as a billiard ball, and crow's-feet etched the corners of his eyes. He had on a short-sleeved black silk shirt, black slacks, and black shoes. His clothing reeked of cigarette smoke, and his lack of a tan indicated he probably worked inside. Maybe even at the hospital.

He walked by me without saying a word, but just before I stepped into Wade's room, I heard a sharp, "Hey! You, Lady!"

I paused and looked back. He was staring directly at me.

"You know him?" the man asked, motioning toward Wade's room.

"I do," I said cautiously, not sure what was up.

"How about Brewster? You know Michael Brewster?"

"No." I've met Wade's ex-wife, but not her new husband.

"Your friend says he don't know what happened to them. Do you? Was Brewster on the boat when it blew up?"

"I think so, but I haven't heard for sure."

"They're sayin' the boat sank. You think he's dead?"

"I have no idea." This was the first I'd heard that Wade's boat had sunk. "Try calling the Coast Guard. They should know."

"Yeah, I might just do that. Meanwhile, if Brewster is alive and you see him, tell him I still want my money."

"Money? How much does he owe you?" I asked, curious. From the little Wade had told me about Linda's new husband, I thought Brewster was loaded with money.

The man started to walk away without answering my question, so I called after him, "What's your name? In case Mr. Brewster asks."

Baldy paused to look back. "He'll know who I am."

"But I . . ."

What I thought or wanted didn't seem to matter. Without another word, Baldy headed down the corridor. I watched for a moment, and then I went into Wade's room.

"Who was that?" Wade asked when I reached his side.

"I have no idea." I glanced back toward the door. "What did he say to you?"

"He asked me where Brewster was, if he was on the boat when it blew up."

"Same here. He also told me to tell Brewster that he still owes him money."

"You're kidding. How much?"

"I asked, but he didn't say. I got the feeling it's quite a lot. Did he tell you his name?"

"No." Wade smirked. "So Linda's rich hubby owes someone money. Maybe she didn't find the perfect man after all."

I doubted there was such a creature, but I understood Wade's meaning. From what he'd told me, Wade's ex-wife considered Michael Brewster to be exactly the man she'd been looking for: intelligent, ambitious, and well heeled. At least she'd told Wade that Michael Brewster made a lot more money as a financial advisor than Wade had or ever would have earned as a sheriff's deputy.

But what, I wondered, *if Michael Brewster wasn't as well off as Linda had thought*? "Do you think Brewster was moving to California to get away from that guy?"

Wade scoffed at my question. "What, you think that guy is a hit man?"

"I don't know." I had no idea what a hit man might look like, other than the ones I'd seen on TV and in the movies. "Probably not."

"He's probably someone Brewster worked with."

I didn't think so, but I didn't know that for sure, either. "Did he tell you your boat sank? At least, that's what he heard."

"Damn." Wade squeezed his eyes shut. "Why can't I remember anything?"

I didn't have an answer, and the arrival of two men—one young, tall, and slender and wearing a deputy's uniform with a Van Buren County Sheriff's Department patch, the other older, heavy-set, and in a brown plaid sports jacket, tan shirt, and slacks—eliminated the need for me to respond.

"Are you Wade Kingsley?" the plain-clothed man asked. "Deputy Sergeant Wade Kingsley?"

I stepped back, away from the bed, as Wade answered yes.

The one in the sports jacket identified himself as Sergeant Milano of the Van Buren Sheriff's Department and the uniformed officer as Officer Blair. Then Sergeant Milano looked at me. "And you are?"

"P.J. Benson. And yes, just the initials." I've learned if I don't say that right away, they always ask.

"And your relationship to Sergeant Kingsley?"

"We're friends." And a lot more, I hoped. Especially if I was pregnant.

"Were you on the boat with him today?"

"No." I shook my head, silently thanking whatever power above had made me decide to stay home. "I just heard about the explosion a short while ago. Is it true that Wade's boat sank?"

"That's what we've heard," Sergeant Milano said, then motioned toward the door. "Miss Benson, would you mind stepping outside for a moment or two? We have a few questions we'd like to ask Sergeant Kingsley."

I looked at Wade and he nodded, so I did as told and stepped outside of the room. The uniformed deputy closed the door, but I stood next to it, and I could hear some of what was being said inside. In a way the questions asked by Sergeant Milano reminded me of the questions Wade asked me the first time we met back in April. That day I'd found a man dying in my dining room, and Wade was the homicide detective who responded to my nine-one-one call. His were the basic "who, what, where, and why" questions. What had bothered me the day Wade questioned me—and bothered me now, listening to this detective question Wade—was the repetition. Same questions over and over but asked in different ways.

"How many people were on the boat when it exploded?"

Wade wasn't sure.

"How many were on the boat when it left the marina?"

Wade thought four but he didn't know, not for sure.

"Why did you choose that location to set anchor?"

"How the hell should I know?" Wade finally shouted. "I don't even remember going out on the lake."

Wade's response was loud enough that time for me and anyone else in the hallway to hear, and I think the deputies decided they'd better try another angle because the next time I heard Wade's voice, he was complaining about how late Linda and her husband had arrived with Jason. "She blamed it on last-minute packing," he said. "Didn't have time for this fishing trip. I told her to leave Jason, that I'd bring him back to her place after we went fishing, but no, he wasn't going anywhere without her. She acted as if I'd kidnap him. Kidnap my own son."

I could just imagine Linda's attitude. The one time I'd met her, she'd been snippy and accused Wade of trying to undermine her relationship with Jason. In my opinion, if anyone was doing the undermining, it was her. She was the one who kept coming up with reasons why he couldn't see his son, and Jason once said his mother didn't have anything good to say about Wade . . . or me.

"No, I wouldn't kidnap my son," I heard Wade tell the deputies, but I remembered a conversation Wade and I had had a few days before. "I'd like to take Jason somewhere where she would never find him," he'd told me. "Where she'd never find either of us."

But, of course, he wouldn't.

At least, I'd never seriously thought he would.

After that I think the deputies asked Wade some questions about his boat because the little I did hear of his answers involved the boat's size and age. I did hear Sergeant Milano ask Wade about the engines and the equipment he had in the cabin, and if the stove was electric or propane. I could have answered that. The boat had an electric stove that wasn't working, so I'd bought Wade a fancy Coleman's grill stove, one of the big ones that used the larger propane tanks. That was what we'd been using when we cooked on the boat. Last time I'd seen it, Wade had latched the grill on the top of the old stove and secured the propane tank on the floor next to the stove so neither would bounce around if we were out on rough water.

Soon enough the deputies went back to questions about what had happened just before the explosion. They wanted to know why both Wade and Jason were wearing life jackets, which I thought was a pretty stupid question. By law, kids Jason's age should wear a life jacket when on a boat, and the type of life jacket Wade has must be worn to be legal. He always wears it when we go out, and he makes me wear mine.

Thank goodness he had his on. If he hadn't, and Jason hadn't known enough to pull the tab that inflated the life jacket, Wade would probably have drowned.

I'm not sure how long the two deputies questioned Wade because after a while I wandered down the hallway and got a drink of water. My stomach seemed to have calmed down and I was getting hungry, so I also went down to the gift shop and purchased a package of crackers and cheese. By the time I returned to Wade's room, the door was open, the deputies were gone, and Ginny and Jason were in with him.

"I'm fine, Daddy," Jason said. "Really. Aren't I, Aunt Ginny?"

He looked up at Ginny and she nodded. "Doctors said he's their little hero."

Jason beamed for a moment, and then his smile turned into a frown. "But they said they don't know where Mama is. Do you know, Daddy? I've been looking for her, but I haven't seen her anywhere."

"I haven't heard where she might be." Wade reached out and took his son's hand. "I'm just glad you're all right."

"I think she's all right, too," Jason said, seriously. "She's a good swimmer. Grandma told me Grandpa Healy made her take swimming lessons when she was little. She's probably worried about me."

"She probably is," Wade said, though I could tell from his expression that he didn't think his ex-wife was alive, much less worried about her son.

"Tonight I'm going to stay with Aunt Ginny," Jason said. "She said I can feed Spike, and then I can play with the boys."

The boys were Ginny's two Siamese cats, and I doubted they'd let Jason anywhere near them, much less play with him. However, Spike, her miniature poodle, was a different matter. The dog should help keep Jason's mind off his mother and what had happened.

Wade didn't make a fuss, so I thought he approved of the situation, but as soon as Ginny and Jason left the room, Wade pushed back his covers and started to sit up. "Find me some clothes, P.J. I'm getting out of here."

CHAPTER FIVE

I tried talking Wade into staying overnight, but he wouldn't listen, and I finally gave in. Getting out of a hospital, however, isn't a simple endeavor. The moment I asked the nurse at the desk where I would find Wade's clothes, that he was leaving, there was a flurry of activity. First the nurse marched down to his room and for five minutes lectured him on why he could not leave. That didn't go over well, and Wade demanded to see a doctor.

"Now, now, Mr. Kingsley. You need to rest. The doctor will be by later."

"Forget later," Wade said and started for the door wearing the skimpy gown he had on. He was halfway into the hallway, his butt cheeks showing, when, with a sigh, the nurse made the call.

The doctor gave Wade a dozen reasons why he needed to stay in the hospital and in bed. None of them worked. Finally, after Wade promised he'd spend the night at my place, and said he would take it easy and wouldn't drive until he was sure he was all right, the doctor relented. A nurse had Wade sign a release promising he wouldn't sue the hospital if anything went wrong and that his leaving was against doctor's orders. Only then did a plastic bag with Wade's wet clothing appear.

The nurse tried arguing that he should wait until they had a chance to dry his clothes, but he told her to forget it, he was leaving, wet clothes or no clothes. I think for a moment she considered seeing if he would walk out naked, but then, with a shake of her head, she started helping him dress. While they worked on pulling a wet T-shirt over Wade's head without causing him more pain, another nurse took me outside the room and gave me instructions. "He should take it easy for the next forty-eight hours, but if he goes to sleep, you'll have to wake him every so often. If he starts complaining of a really bad headache or pressure in his head, or if he seems confused and starts slurring his speech, get him back here immediately. Call nine-one-one. Let the paramedics deal with him."

"I live out in the country," I said. "If he does start slurring his speech, what should I do while waiting for the paramedics to arrive?"

A shake of her head and the lift of her eyebrows were the nurse's initial response, then she shrugged. "Get him to lie down, if you can. Make him comfortable if he starts throwing up, and try to keep him from losing consciousness."

I didn't want to think of the mess there would be if both Wade and I started throwing up. Playing nurse has never been one of my favorite roles. Give me a list of numbers or a column of debts and credits, and I'm happy. Not once while growing up did I consider studying medicine. Now, it seemed, I was going to be Wade's nursemaid. At least for a while.

"Anything else I should be aware of?" I asked.

"Keep that bandage on his forehead dry and check that area for any signs of infection. He'll need to come back and get those stitches out in ten days." She glanced into Wade's room. "Looks like he's almost ready. I'll be right back."

She took off for the nurses' station, and I knew Wade wasn't going to be happy when I saw her come back with a wheelchair. She pushed it into Wade's room, and he roared, "I do not need a wheelchair!"

For the next five minutes the two nurses tried to convince

him that he was not leaving the hospital unless he was seated in a wheelchair. I stayed out of the argument until I started to get a headache. Only then did I speak up.

"Get in the damn wheelchair, Wade. Do it now, or I'm leaving and you can find someone else to bail you out of here."

He looked at me, his mouth slightly open, and then with a huff he settled himself in the wheelchair.

The nurse handed me his discharge papers and a sheet with after-care procedures, and everything went smoothly until we reached the main floor of the hospital and ran into Linda's parents. I'd never been formally introduced to Frank and Jean Healy, and it didn't look like that was going to happen this time either. As they neared us, Jean Healy's eyes narrowed and her features hardened. "You!" she practically screamed, pointing a finger at Wade. "Linda said you'd do something to keep her from taking Jason to California, but I never thought—"

She didn't say what she'd thought. She simply started crying. Her husband, however, didn't hesitate to share his thoughts.

"You killed her. You killed both of them. She'd finally found a good man, a man who could give her the life she deserved, and you couldn't stand it."

"They're dead?" Wade asked. "They found the bodies?"

Linda's mother shuddered, releasing a shaky moan.

Frank Healy glanced at his wife, then back at Wade. "Don't you mean body parts? The officer I talked to said they had an arm."

It was my turn to shudder as I pictured a disembodied arm being fished out of Lake Michigan. Manicured fingernails or hairy forearm? If the deputies who'd visited Wade told him they'd found an arm, he hadn't shared that with me.

To my relief, my stomach didn't turn over. Perhaps because what Linda's mother said next took priority over a severed arm. "Where's Jason?" she demanded. "I want to see my grandson."

"He's already been released," Wade answered. "They checked him over, and he's fine."

"Fine?" She made it sound like a four-letter word. "His mother's dead, and you say he's fine?"

"He doesn't know his mother's dead . . . We don't know if she *is* dead. At least not for sure."

Linda's father shook his head. "The officer I talked to didn't sound hopeful."

"I want my grandson," Linda's mother demanded, ignoring the possibility of her daughter's survival. "We're taking him home with us."

"No you are not." Wade responded.

"He's my grandson."

"And he's my son."

Wade started to stand, but the nurse and I both put a hand on his shoulders, keeping him in the wheelchair. I was pretty sure getting into a fist fight with his ex-in-laws wouldn't be good for him. "Stay where you are," I ordered. "I'm going to go get my car. I'll be back in a second."

A nod from the nurse indicated she'd do her best to keep him in the wheelchair, and I hurried to my car. All four—the nurse, the Healys, and Wade—were on the sidewalk when I pulled up to the curb. Wade was still in the wheelchair, the nurse seeming to hold him there with a hand on his shoulder, and Linda's father was shaking a finger at Wade. The moment I shifted into park, the nurse started rolling the wheelchair toward my car, and the Healys had no choice but to move aside or be rammed.

As I pushed the passenger-side door open, Linda's father spun around and yelled, "We'll see who has custody."

"You do just that," Wade fired back and climbed into the car.

The nurse quickly closed the car door and backed away with the wheelchair. I think she was glad to see Wade gone. He certainly wasn't going to win any "Congenial Patient" award. I just wanted to get him home.

I said nothing as I drove off. The flare of Wade's nostrils and rigid line of his jaw told me he wasn't in the mood for conversation. Only when I was on King Highway, heading for I-94, did I hear him give a deep sigh and saw him lean back against the seat and close his eyes. "You okay?" I asked.

"Yeah. Sure."

"Headache?"

He didn't answer right away. When he did, it was a grumbled, "A little."

I decided to leave it at that. I wanted to get him to my place as soon as possible. Although it had been quite warm all day, the temperature was dropping, and I knew sitting around in wet clothes wasn't good for Wade. He didn't need pneumonia as well as a concussion.

We were about five miles out from Zenith when Wade finally said something. "I used to like Jean. Linda's father and I never hit it off, so his attitude doesn't surprise me. From the start I was never good enough for his daughter, but Jean and I got along pretty well . . . even after the divorce."

"She's upset," I said. "You'd act the same way if you thought Linda had done something to Jason."

"Yeah, I guess."

"Did you tell them Jason's with Ginny?"

"No, but they'll figure it out. I'd better call her." He put his hand in his pocket, then pulled it out empty. "Damn, I lost my phone. It's probably at the bottom of the lake."

"Use mine." I pointed at my purse on the floor by his feet.

He grunted when he leaned forward to reach into my purse, then grumbled when he pulled out my flip-phone. Someday I'll get one of the newer smartphones, but until my accounting business picks up, my old one is all I need. This one's already smarter than me most of the time.

From the corner of my eye I saw Wade punch in a phone number. He again leaned back in the seat and closed his eyes. The doctor had said Wade might be sensitive to light and noise. I'd left my radio off, but I didn't have any dark glasses he could use.

"Ginny," Wade finally said, sounding tired. "Linda's folks are down here. They're going to try to get Jason. Maybe you should bring him to P.J.'s place."

I could hear Ginny's voice as I drove, but not what she said. My mind had already jumped to wondering what I had in my refrigerator and cupboards that would interest a six-year-old boy.

It seemed I didn't need to worry. The moment Wade ended the call, he filled me in. "She's at the store with him right now," Wade said. "Buying Jason dry clothes. Then, she said, they're getting something to eat. She said they'd take Jason over her dead body, and not to worry about it." He sighed. "If Frank and Jean think getting Jason away from Ginny will be easy, they're in for a big surprise."

CHAPTER SIX

As soon as we were back at the farmhouse that I'd inherited from my grandfather, and Wade had put on some dry clothes, he turned on the television and began surfing the channels for news about the explosion. What he wanted to know—what we both wanted to hear—was if either Linda or her new husband had survived.

Being a Saturday, the only news on at five o'clock was national, and a train wreck on the West Coast topped a boat explosion on Lake Michigan. Local channels had golf and baseball, so I tried the computer, hoping I might find something there.

No such luck.

Finally, at six-thirty, Wade called to me. "They're talking about it."

I made it into the living room just as the station ran a video clip. I could hear a man's voice in the background describing what he was filming as his camera scanned South Beach, the pier, and the lighthouse. Finally, he zoomed in on the boats out on the lake, first focusing on those nearest the beach, then capturing one farther out.

The scene was tranquil, an image of people enjoying a Saturday in August.

The explosion came as a total surprise.

The cameraman gasped and jerked the camera upward before bringing it back to focus on the now-burning boat. It was then that the station's newscaster took over, explaining the video clip had been provided by a tourist who just happened to be filming when the boat exploded. So far the television station had identified the boat as *The Freedom,* a thirty-two-foot cruiser owned by a Wade Kingsley, a deputy with the Kalamazoo County Sheriff's Department.

Other stills flashed on the screen as the reporter spoke, pictures of boats and jet skis heading out to the burning boat, boaters rescuing Wade and Jason, and Wade and Jason being loaded onto a helicopter. "Two other passengers" the reporter said, "are still unaccounted for. The Van Buren County Sheriff Department's marine dive team has been called in to search for their bodies."

"Bodies," Wade repeated, sounding deflated.

"They didn't say anything about finding an arm," I said. "Maybe Linda's parents were wrong."

"No. It's more likely they're not saying anything about that because it might discourage people from going to the beach. Would you want to be swimming and run into an arm or leg?"

"Gotcha." Simply thinking about swimming with body parts bothered me.

The TV station again showed the video clip, starting at the point when the camera was focused on the boats. That was when I noticed Wade and Jason on the bow of the boat. "What were you doing?" I asked, not quite sure why both of them were bending forward, as if ready to dive into the water.

Wade frowned and leaned closer to the television. "I need a copy of that video."

"Were you going to go swimming?"

"Huh?" He looked at me as if I were crazy. "We were going fishing, not swimming. I would have taken the boat down to the dunes if we were going swimming."

"Maybe so, but it sure looked like the two of you were about to dive off the boat."

Wade sat back on the couch, and I could tell he was trying to remember. I felt sorry for him. How terrible to have a period in your life where you didn't remember anything.

"I don't know," he finally said. "I don't know what we were doing or how we even got there."

Baraka must have heard the sadness in Wade's voice. My dog got up from where he'd been sleeping and ambled over to put his head on Wade's knees. Without even looking down, Wade began stroking Baraka's head.

"He's feeling sorry for you," I said.

"I'm feeling sorry for myself. I just wish I could remember what happened after everyone got on the boat."

"You need to talk to Jason." Wade's son might be only six, but he was a smart kid. Being tossed in the water didn't seem to have affected him. "He can tell you what happened. Do you want me to call your sister?"

"No." Wade's response was immediate and forceful. "I don't want him thinking about what happened. Not tonight. If he thinks about it, he's going to realize his mother's dead."

"You don't know that for sure."

Wade gave me a withering look. "Come on, P.J., you saw those pictures. Do you really think she could have survived that explosion?"

Call me an optimist, but I hoped she had . . . for Jason's sake. "I'm just saying, you don't know for sure that she's dead. After all, you and Jason survived that explosion."

"Because we happened to be on the bow of the boat. I didn't see Linda or Brewster anywhere on deck. Not in any of those pictures. If they had been, if they'd been thrown into the water like Jason and I were, I'm sure someone would have noticed. Would have picked them up."

I hated to admit he was probably right. "Sometimes miracles

do happen."

"The miracle is Jason and I are alive. P.J., you heard the reporter. They're sending dive teams to look for the bodies." Wade looked back at the TV. "I wish they'd show that clip again."

The news, however, had moved on to the weather.

"I need to know where the center of the explosion was located. I couldn't tell if it was in the cabin or the engine compartment. I know I needed gas." He stopped petting Baraka and looked at me. "I remember that. I remember I'd planned on filling up on our way out to the lake."

"There should be a record if you did." Whenever we went out with the boat and Wade got gas, he used a charge card.

"You're right." For a moment his expression brightened, but then he sighed and leaned back. "But that doesn't tell me anything. Even if, for some reason, I didn't vent the gas fumes, we never would have made it to the lake before there was an explosion."

So we were back to square one. "You want anything?" I asked, noticing Wade looked as tired as I felt. "Something to eat? Drink?"

I hoped he wouldn't ask for coffee.

He merely shook his head, then grimaced.

"Do you feel sick? Feel like you're going to throw up?" I was probably being overly concerned, but the nurse had made me nervous with her list of symptoms to look for.

"I'm fine," he said and patted the space on the couch beside him. "Come sit by me."

I switched from the chair to the cushion next to Wade, and he slipped an arm around my shoulders and gave them a squeeze. "I'm glad you weren't on the boat."

I wasn't sure what to say. *So am I?*

"So glad."

"I'm so sorry for you." I reached up and gave the hand on

my shoulder a squeeze. "For you and Jason."

"I didn't want her taking Jason," he admitted. "But I wouldn't have hurt her. I'm sure I wouldn't have." ·

I heard the uncertainty in his voice and glanced at his face. He'd closed his eyes, his mouth a tight line. More than once I'd heard him cuss his ex. Never in front of Jason or others, but often when we were alone. He'd called her unflattering names and questioned why he'd ever married her. But murder? No, I'd never heard him say he wanted her dead.

"I don't know why we were on the front of the boat," he finally said and leaned his head against mine. "No idea at all."

I checked on Wade several times during the night. By Sunday morning I was exhausted, but he looked better. He said even though he still had a headache it wasn't as bad as before. His eyes were focused and his skin had lost its chalky pallor. He had me take a peek under the bandage on his forehead, and other than the bruising around the stitches, the cut looked okay. No red to indicate infection.

He wouldn't let me touch the goose-egg on the back of his head.

By nine o'clock the outside temperature was pushing eighty and the humidity was rising. Wade put on a pair of tan shorts and a blue Polo shirt he'd left at my house, but he was stuck with the still-damp sneakers he'd had on when he went into the lake. I also chose a pair of shorts to wear—my white ones—and a red T-shirt that I think enhances my brown hair and eyes. I'd just slipped into a pair of rainbow-colored sandals when Wade asked if I was going to make coffee. I lied and said my coffee maker was on the fritz. I then took Baraka outside for his morning exercise.

My mistake was forgetting you never tell a man something isn't working and think he'll simply go without. The moment I stepped back into the house, I could smell coffee brewing.

"Works fine," Wade proudly announced. "Want a cup?"

I dashed for the bathroom.

He looked concerned when I came out. "You sick?"

"Must have been something I ate last night." I grabbed my purse. "If you're all right, I need to go into town. I'll be back in a couple hours."

"But . . . ?" I heard him say as I stepped out on the porch.

"Oh, can you feed Baraka? Please?" I called back, hoping I could reach my car before my stomach decided to give a repeat performance.

I stared at the drug store's display of pregnancy tests. They all promised the same results. Ninety-nine percent accurate. Early detection. Easy to use.

A salesclerk coming down the aisle paused next to me. "Do you need help?"

"No," I said and grabbed one of the boxes. *Yes,* my mind cried. *I need this to be all a dream.*

I bought a Sunday paper as well as the pregnancy test and then headed for my grandmother's house. I wanted to be with someone who would understand my fears when I read the results, and if anyone would understand, it was my grandmother.

For almost thirty years Grandma Carter has been the mother of and often the caretaker of a schizophrenic. Even now my mother lives with Grandma. For the last few months that arrangement has gone smoothly, but we never know when Mom might decide to go off her meds.

It scared me to think I might soon be like Mom, seeing things, acting weird, and making foolish decisions. Who would take care of me? Certainly not my mother. That would be double trouble. And not my grandmother. As spry and sharp as she is, Grandma's in her seventies. I know she's already worried about my mother's future care. She doesn't need my welfare to worry about, too.

On the other hand, if the test showed I was pregnant, I hoped she'd have some sound advice.

I called her before I arrived. "I'm about five minutes away," I said as I waited for a traffic signal to change. "Mind if I stop by?"

"I'll put some coffee on," she said.

"Please don't."

"Don't?" Her voice rose slightly.

"I'll explain when I get there."

Actually, I didn't explain. The moment I saw Grandma, I burst into tears and showed her the pregnancy test. She scooted me up to the bathroom and embraced me when I came back downstairs, a slight nod on my part the only communication we needed.

She took me outside to sit on the front porch steps, which I appreciated since both Grandma and Mom smoke and the house reeked of the smell. Only then did we talk. "So how are you feeling?" she asked.

"Miserable. For several days now I've been throwing up."

"Your mother was the same way when she was pregnant with you."

That wasn't what I wanted to hear. Mom getting pregnant with me was what triggered her schizophrenia. Once again I started crying. "I don't want to be like Mom."

"Oh, honey." Grandma put an arm around my shoulders. "Just because you have morning sickness doesn't mean you'll end up like your mother."

"But you and I know—"

She stopped me. "Hush. Probabilities are probabilities, not certainties. You've made it this far without any problems. Don't go looking for trouble."

I wiped away my tears and smiled. "I haven't been looking for trouble. I think it found me."

"What's that hunk of yours think about this?"

Grandma likes Wade, which surprised me since the times law enforcement has come to the house because of my mother's wild assertions, Grandma hasn't been the most cordial to them. "He doesn't know," I said. "And this doesn't seem like the right time to tell him."

"Because of what happened yesterday?" she asked. "I just read about it in the paper and was going to call you when you called me. The boy's all right?"

"Shaken up and confused. I haven't seen him since yesterday."

"The mother's dead?"

"Wade's sure she is, along with her new husband."

"What exactly happened? The paper was pretty vague."

"Wade doesn't know. He doesn't even remember taking the boat out on the lake."

"Sounds like a concussion." Grandma rubbed my shoulders. "I've heard some people never remember what happened when they have one of those. Was he hurt badly?"

"Other than a cut on his forehead and a bump on the back of his head, he seems all right. He was up making coffee this morning."

"You need to tell him."

I said nothing.

"You're not thinking of having an abortion, are you?"

The rise in Grandma's voice conveyed her thoughts about that. I shook my head. In truth, I hadn't thought much about what I was going to do. I was still in shock.

"Will he marry you?"

I looked at Grandma. "I don't know."

CHAPTER SEVEN

The house I've been living in for the last eight months is over a century old and belonged to my grandparents, Mamie and Harlan Benson. I was surprised when I learned Grandpa Benson had willed the house and forty acres of woods and tillable land to me, along with enough money to start my own home-based accounting business. The house is a two-story-high rectangle, with a small wooden porch on the front and crumbling concrete steps leading up to the back door. Upstairs there are two bedrooms that I never use, and a storage area mostly filled with my grandparents' things. One of these days I'll get around to cleaning that out.

On the main floor there's my bedroom, a large living room and dining room, a laundry area, bathroom, and kitchen. The house also has a Michigan basement, which is no more than a dug-out area under the house with a dirt floor, cinderblock walls, and a ceiling made up of exposed floor joists and supports. My furnace and hot water heater are down there, along with a shelving unit my grandfather made to hold the jars of canned goods my grandmother put up during the summer. The whole area has a musty, mildew smell, and harbors spiders and mice. I don't go down there unless it's absolutely necessary.

Since moving in, I've added an office area at one end of the living room, and a fence around the perimeter of the house. I needed the fence to keep my dog from running out onto the road. Rhodesian Ridgebacks aren't cheap to begin with, but more than that, Baraka has become part of my family. I love that dog.

He's also part of the reason I've been cleaning out the chicken coop behind the house. My grandfather was a hoarder. He never took anything to the dump, just shoved it into one of the outbuildings or tossed it out in the woods. Since I don't want Baraka stepping on broken glass or a nail, I've been working on cleaning up the place ever since I moved here. The chicken coop is now in pretty good shape, so my next project is either the woodshed or the woods.

Maybe.

There's a lot of junk in both of those places, and if I'm going to have a baby, should I be hauling old tires, boards, and wire to a dumpster? Should I even lift some of that stuff?

Those questions were running through my head when I opened the back door and stepped into my kitchen.

The first thing that greeted me was the smell of old coffee. I quickly took a sniff of the sliced lemon Grandma Carter had given me. That quelled my initial feelings of nausea, and I hoped it would keep working since Wade did like his coffee in the morning.

Baraka came trotting into the kitchen, tail wagging. He's almost nine months old and just over twenty-seven inches at the shoulders. That's on the tall side for a male Rhodesian Ridgeback, but not overly so. I don't want him to grow any taller, though I know he'll fill out as he matures. In Africa, the Rhodesian Ridgebacks were originally bred to run in packs and corner lions. They needed to be fast, agile, and strong, and Baraka certainly is.

As he sniffed my legs and shoes, his sensitive nostrils telling him where I'd been and who I'd been with, I patted his back. I could hear male voices in the other room. One was Wade's, the other belonged to Howard Lowe, my closest neighbor. When I first moved to Zenith, Howard and I didn't get along, mainly because I posted "No Hunting" signs on the woods behind my grandfather's house. As far as Howard and his coon dog, Jake, were concerned, I had no right taking away what had been one of their favorite hunting spots. It wasn't until last April, when I found Howard injured behind my house and called nine-one-one, that he became friendlier. However, since people keep dying around me, Howard is convinced I'm the Jessica Fletcher of Zenith Township.

"Was worried about you," Howard said when I entered the dining room, Baraka by my side. "Saw the video about the Sergeant's boat exploding. They said two people were still missing."

"When he didn't see your car this morning," Wade added, watching me walk toward the bathroom door, "he was afraid one of the two might have been you. You feeling better?"

"A little," I said and smiled at Howard. As usual he was dressed in denim overalls, a ragged cotton T-shirt, and scuffed work boots. He's always reminded me of a blend of Rambo and Willy Nelson, and he acts more like a hillbilly than a retired contractor who was in Special Forces during the war in Korea. He's still connected with a militant group known as CROWS, which stands for Civilian Resistance Opposing Wayward Science. He says he's just a listener, but I'm not convinced.

"I'm touched that you were concerned about me," I said.

" 'Course I'm concerned." He grinned. "Somethin' happens to you, Nora might actually end up with those woods, then I wouldn't dare hunt them, or she'd shoot me."

I grinned. Nora Wright's house and farm are almost directly behind my property, on the next road to the north. Ever since I inherited this place, Nora has tried to get possession of the ten acres of woods between our places. She's shot at me, fed me poison, even threatened my grandmother and another woman taking a walk in my woods . . . which is why she's now in jail, awaiting trial.

"I'm sure she wouldn't hesitate to shoot, but you're not supposed to be hunting there now," I reminded him.

"Well, having your crazy mother as a neighbor wouldn't be any better."

"So I'm the best of the worst?"

"Naw, I didn't mean that." Howard glanced out the window facing the road. "Looks like you got company," he said and stood. "Think I'll just mosey on."

Wade also stood and looked out. "Shoot," he said with a tired sigh. "It's those two deputies from the Van Buren Sheriff's Department."

Howard went out the back door as the two deputies, who yesterday had come to Wade's room in the hospital, came up my front steps and onto the porch. Baraka barked a deep, guttural warning, the hairs on the back of his neck bristling so it looked like the ridge on his back extended from the top of his head to his tail. I quickly went up beside him and placed a hand on his collar. "It's okay, boy," I said, hoping it was.

I opened the screen door and smiled at the deputies. "Hello again," I said and motioned with my free hand for them to come in, then remembered Wade once told me I should never willingly invite law enforcement into my house. This from a man in law enforcement.

Sergeant Milano hesitated, his gaze on Baraka. "Is it safe?"

I glanced down at my dog. He was no longer bristling, but a lot of people see the ridge on his back, where the hairs grow the opposite direction, and think it indicates he's angry and might attack.

"I bite, but my dog won't," I said and waited for him to process that.

For a moment Sergeant Milano stared at me, a slight frown

crossing his brow, then he stepped into the room, Deputy Blair following. Wade hadn't moved from where he stood. He also didn't say anything, which I thought was a bit strange. After all, these were sheriff's deputies. They might work for a different county, but they were comrades in arms, so to speak.

"We have a few more questions," Sergeant Milano said, then glanced at me. "If you don't mind."

"She stays," Wade said before I even realized the sergeant was asking me to leave.

Sergeant Milano hesitated, then shrugged. "Fine with me." He walked over to the chair that Howard had recently vacated. "Mind if I sit down?"

"It's her house," Wade answered, indicating me.

Again I was surprised by the hostility I heard in his voice. "Go ahead," I said, pointing at a second chair for the uniformed deputy. "I'll be in the living room."

I moved over to the recliner by the arched opening between the two rooms and sat, keeping Baraka with me as the three men settled into chairs. I was curious to hear what was up.

"Have you found my ex-wife and her husband?" Wade asked.

"Not yet," Sergeant Milano said. "Water's too rough today for the divers to go down."

"Where the boat sank, how deep was it?"

"You don't know?"

Wade slowly shook his head. "I watched the video they've been showing on the news, but I couldn't tell how far out we were."

"I've heard forty feet," the sergeant said. "You're saying you still don't remember anything?"

"Nothing from the time my ex arrived at the marina."

"What about your son?"

"What about him?"

I could hear the tension in Wade's voice and remembered

how he'd reacted when I suggested talking to Jason. He's always been protective of his son, and I wouldn't want to say anything that might upset Jason, but if I were in Wade's position, I certainly would want to know what happened.

"We'd like to talk to him." Sergeant Milano looked around. "Is he here?"

"No, he's not here, and I don't want him questioned, not until we know for sure what happened to his mother."

Sergeant Milano looked directly at Wade. "I think it's obvious what happened to your wife, Sergeant. She's dead."

"Ex-wife," Wade reminded the man. "And I'd like to hope . . ."

Wade didn't say what he hoped, and Sergeant Milano's grunt indicated his disbelief. "From what I've heard, you and your ex weren't on the best of terms," he said. "In fact, some of your friends said you'd do anything to keep her from taking your son to California."

"Who said that?" Wade demanded.

"Do you deny it?"

"I never said 'I'd do anything.' " Wade shifted position in his chair. "I did say I wished there was something I could do to stop her." He kept his gaze locked with Milano's. "Something legal is what I meant, just so we're clear about that."

"I understand you purchased some gasoline Friday."

Wade didn't answer right away, simply sat twirling his empty coffee cup in front of him. Finally he gave a slight nod. "Yeah, I guess it was Friday. I filled my Jeep."

"Along with a couple gas cans?" Milano added.

"For my lawn mower."

"And where are those gas cans now?"

"In my garage."

"We've looked in your garage. We only found one. Where's the other one, Sergeant?"

"You've looked in my garage?" I noticed Wade's nostrils flared, and he leaned back in his chair, his eyes narrowing. "And do I assume you've been in my house, too?"

"You know the procedure, Sergeant. Now, where is the other gas can?"

Wade didn't respond immediately, and I could see the tension in his jaw. Finally, he swallowed hard and took a deep breath. "The other gas can," he repeated, "is with my next-door neighbor. He and his wife were taking their RV up north and into Canada. He said he was worried about running out of gas. Said the gas gauge on the RV was broken, and he had to guess how much was in the tank. He figured it would be safer to have some extra with him, so I let him take one of the cans."

"And how do we get in touch with this neighbor?"

"How the hell should I know?" Wade almost shouted. "I don't have his phone number. We're not buddy-buddy, just neighbors."

I grimaced. Wade was definitely getting hostile, but I didn't really blame him. Milano's questions would have made me hostile.

"And this neighbor's name is—?"

"Jones. Arthur Jones."

Sergeant Milano's eyebrows rose slightly and I groaned internally. The name Jones was almost as common as Smith.

"And his wife's name is Helen," Wade added, almost with a sigh. "They own a Winnebago. I don't know what year."

Milano nodded and looked over at Deputy Blair, who had pulled out a notebook and pencil and had been taking notes. "And how long will Mr. and Mrs. Jones be gone?"

"No idea."

"I see." Milano didn't bother to hide his smile, but it was gone when he looked back at Wade. "I also understand you arrived at your boat after dark Friday night and made several trips back and forth between your vehicle and the boat."

"So?"

"Trips in the dark."

"What the hell are you getting at?"

"Just trying to understand what you were putting on your boat that you didn't want others to see."

"Nothing," Wade ground out. "I was putting nothing on my boat that . . ." He didn't finish whatever he was going to say. Baraka had risen to his feet and started for the door, tail wagging.

CHAPTER EIGHT

Jason ran from Wade's sister's car to my front porch, Ginny trailing behind the boy. His shorts, T-shirt, and flip-flops all looked new and expensive, which didn't surprise me. Wade's sister only bought the best.

Tail wagging, Baraka whined in anticipation of a playmate, but I knew this wasn't the time for a romp. Moving quickly, I had Baraka in his crate by the time Jason entered my house. "Daddy!" the boy shouted, "Did they find Mama? Is she okay?"

Wade had stood and gone toward the door the moment he saw Jason coming; now he knelt and embraced his son, hugging him close.

"Is she, Daddy?" Jason asked, pulling back slightly, his question more tenuous.

"We don't know," Wade answered.

I saw the look he gave the two deputies, a plea for them not to say anything about the possibility—or probability—of Linda's death.

Ginny came into the house then, looking glamorous but tired. She glanced at the two deputies, who had also stood, and at Wade, and then she silently moved over to stand by me.

Sergeant Milano cleared his throat, and Jason twisted in Wade's arms to look up at the deputy. "We're still looking for your mother," Milano said. "And you can help us find her by telling us what happened yesterday."

"But if you don't feel like talking about it, that's okay," Wade said quickly.

"It's okay, Daddy," Jason said and freed himself from Wade's embrace. With no hesitation, he stepped closer to the table and the two men. "We were on Daddy's boat, and there was this really big boom, and it made Daddy and me fall into the water."

"That's what we heard." Milano motioned toward the chair closest to where he had been sitting. "Can you sit down and tell me where your mother was when the boat exploded?"

"She was with Daddy Michael, down in the cabin," Jason said, and then frowned. "Haven't you found him either?"

"Not yet, but we're looking."

"Aunt Ginny said it's a big lake." Jason looked over at Ginny. "Right, Aunt Ginny?"

"Right," she said. "And someone may have picked up your mommy and not even know we're looking for her."

"Because maybe she can't remember things," Jason added, looking back at Sergeant Milano. "Just like Daddy can't."

I'm sure Jason was echoing what Ginny had told him, and I wasn't surprised when Jason looked to Wade for reassurance. "Right, Daddy?"

"Right," Wade agreed and smiled at his sister.

"But *you* remember what happened, don't you?" Sergeant Milano said and sat down, patting the chair close to him.

"Kinda." Jason scooted up on the chair Milano had indicated, wiggling to find a comfortable position, his legs not quite reaching the floor. Deputy Blair also sat, but Wade remained standing. He moved closer to his son.

"It was really scary," Jason said. "Daddy and me was lowering the anchor when all at once there was that big boom, and I fell in the water, and so did Daddy, only he hit his head on something because he was bleeding, and he wouldn't answer me when I called his name, and then he went under the water, and I was scared, and—"

Jason's words were coming faster and faster, his voice rising and his body tensing. Wade placed a hand on his son's shoulder. "Thank you for saving my life," he said softly.

Jason looked up at his dad and took in a deep breath. "I was really scared," he said.

"I know, but you did everything right."

"Jason," Milano said, bringing the boy's attention back to him, "can you tell us everything, starting with when you and your mother and stepfather first arrived at the boat?"

"Sure." Jason glanced back up at his dad. "When we got there, you were really mad at Mama, weren't you?"

Wade nodded, but said nothing.

"She was late," Jason told Milano. "Mama's always late. And she didn't want to go, but she was afraid Daddy would try to steal me."

"She said that?" Milano asked.

"Uh huh." Jason smiled. "She was mad at Daddy Michael, too, 'cause some man called the night before and said nasty things to her, and then another man called in the morning, and he said something Mama didn't like. They yelled at each other." Again Jason looked at his dad. "She was even madder than when she gets mad at you. She called him a liar and a thief."

"She said that to the man on the phone?" Wade asked and sat back down on his chair.

"No, to Daddy Michael. For a while I didn't think he was going to go fishing with us, but then he said he didn't want her talking to you."

"Okay," Milano said, glancing at Deputy Blair, who had been writing as Jason spoke. "So your mother was angry with both your father and your stepfather. Is that right?"

"And with me," Jason admitted, looking down at the table. "I kinda forgot to put the milk away after I got myself a drink."

For the first time since he'd arrived, Sergeant Milano smiled.

"So your mother was in a really bad mood when she got on your Daddy's boat?"

"Yeah, but Daddy Michael said she'd forget being mad at us once we were out on the lake and she had a couple glasses of wine."

"They had a picnic basket with them," Wade said, looking at me, then at Milano. "I remember that. Brewster said his coworkers had given him the basket as a going-away gift, that he had all sorts of goodies for our lunch, and a couple bottles of homemade wine."

I knew the excitement in his voice was because he remembered something from the day before, but I wasn't sure how a picnic basket would explain what had happened. On the other hand, if he remembered the basket, maybe he would remember more.

Milano picked up the questioning. "Once everyone was on the boat, then what happened?" he asked Jason.

"We had to wait until the bridge went up so we could go under. I got to wave to the bridgeman." Jason smiled. "And he waved back. Then we stopped and got some gas." He looked at his dad. "You don't remember that?"

Wade shook his head.

"You let me turn on the bilge fan," the boy said proudly.

Which I realized meant they had vented the boat after filling up, eliminating gas fumes as a possible cause of the explosion.

"And then?" prompted Milano.

"Then we went out on the lake, and it was kinda rough, but not too bad, and Mama said she didn't want to go out too far, and that if we were gonna do any fishing, we'd better get started. So Daddy said we'd stay fairly close to the shore, and Daddy Michael said he didn't want to do any fishing 'cause he was hungry, so Daddy and I went up to the front of the boat, and then—" He looked at the two deputies and threw up his hands. "Boom."

"So you and your father were on the bow of the boat, and your mother and stepfather were in the cabin fixing lunch. Is that right?"

"Uh huh." Jason nodded and looked at Wade. "You and me were gonna lower the anchor. Remember?"

"No, I don't remember," Wade said with a sigh.

"Jason, tell me," Sergeant Milano said, "before the explosion, did your daddy make a phone call?"

Jason looked confused. So was I. What did a phone call have to do with what happened?

Wade, however, seemed to understand. "I did not trigger that explosion," he ground out, then looked over at his sister. "Ginny, take Jason outside. Have him show you where he found an Indian arrowhead."

"I'm not finished," Milano said.

"Yes, you are."

CHAPTER NINE

Ginny ignored both Sergeant Milano's and Jason's objections and escorted the boy outside. I let Baraka out so he could join them, and then sat back down. Only when Wade was sure his son was out of hearing distance did he speak. "You are not going to accuse me of murder in front of my son."

Milano's response was as firm. "Are you afraid he's going to tell us something incriminating, Detective Kingsley?"

"I don't know what happened on that boat, but I do know I didn't plant a bomb in the cabin."

"You have motive. You didn't want your ex taking your son to California."

"Do you think I would have chanced killing my son as well as my ex with a bomb?"

"You made him go to the bow of the boat, made sure he was as far from the center of the explosion as possible. Made sure he was wearing a life jacket, that you, yourself, had on a life jacket."

"You heard him. We were lowering the anchor."

Milano grunted. "You're telling me your son, who weighs what, maybe fifty pounds, could handle an anchor?"

"I'm sure I was holding onto the rode, that Jason was merely guiding the anchor into the water."

"But you don't remember," Milano reminded him. "And, according to witnesses, your cell phone holder was clipped to your belt when you were pulled out of the water, but there was no cell phone in it. How do you explain that?"

Wade said nothing, so I spoke up. "That holder's old," I said. "His phone could have been knocked loose when Wade hit the boat or the water."

Both deputies turned to look at me. I think they'd forgotten I was in the house.

"Just how sure are *you*, Sergeant, that it was a bomb?" I asked and stood. "There was a propane grill in the cabin, right next to the table where Michael Brewster and Linda would have been fixing lunch. A propane tank on the floor. What if Wade's ex or her husband did something to make that tank explode?"

"And just what would make a propane tank explode?" Milano snapped back.

"I don't know. I'm just saying it's another possibility."

"She's right," Wade said, far more calmly than I felt at the moment. "Save your accusations until you have some evidence."

"We are not making any accusations," Milano insisted and looked back at Wade.

"Sure sounds like you are," I said, wishing the two deputies would simply leave. Disappear. Or better yet, that we could go back two days in time, and none of this would have happened: no boat exploding, no injuries, and no possible deaths. "First you question him about a can of gas, then you ask about his cell phone. Sure sounds like you're trying to pin this on Wade. Well, let me tell you, he didn't do it."

Milano scoffed. "And you know this because . . . ?"

"Because I know Wade. He solves murders; he doesn't commit them."

Both Milano and Blair smiled. I guess I did sound naive, but darn it all, I do know Wade. As upset as he was with his ex-wife and with the idea of having his son taken two thousand miles away, he never would have done anything to harm Linda.

"I think what she's trying to say," Wade said, "is I'm more than willing to help you discover what happened yesterday, but until those divers find the cause of that explosion, don't go jumping to conclusions." He rose from his chair, walked over, and held the screen door open. "Have a good day, gentlemen."

Sergeant Milano stared at Wade for a minute then he also rose from his chair. Deputy Blair glanced up at Milano, received a nod, and closed his notebook. The interview was clearly over.

On the way out, Milano paused in front of Wade. "We'll be talking again. Soon."

Wade grunted. "Fine."

I walked over to stand beside Wade, and together we watched the sergeant and deputy walk toward their cruiser. Baraka somehow knew the men were leaving and came dashing around the corner of the house. I smiled as both men picked up their pace, and Blair quickly closed the gate behind him.

Ginny and Jason also came into view as the men backed their cruiser onto the road and then drove off. "We found another arrowhead," Jason shouted, waving his hand in the air. He held something, though I couldn't tell what it was.

"Good for you." Wade waited until his son, sister, and Baraka entered the house before closing the screen door. Then he carefully examined the small black stone Jason handed him.

The shape did resemble an arrowhead, but I had a feeling it was merely a piece of black rock, one that had broken off in a triangular shape. Wade kept his response vague. "Sure looks like it could be one."

"I'm going to add it to my collection," Jason said and took the rock—or arrowhead—back. "P.J., can I have something to drink?"

"Please?" Wade and Ginny said in unison.

I laughed and said, "Sure, what would you like, orange juice, water, or soda?"

"Soda . . . Please," he said and grinned.

I'd known he'd pick soda. I always keep a can or two in the fridge for him. The non-caffeine type, of course. Wade insisted on that. Jason is hyper enough without adding a stimulant. I was on my way to the refrigerator when Wade said, "And I'll put another pot of coffee on."

"No! Don't!" I cried out, my stomach turning at just the idea of coffee. "Please, no coffee."

Wade frowned. "But . . . ?"

"Not today."

Ginny cocked her head slightly. "Why not today, P.J.?"

"My . . . my stomach," I said and brought a small can of Sprite to Jason. "It's been upset lately."

"And the smell of coffee makes it worse?"

The way she said it, I knew she knew. Slowly I nodded my head.

She grinned. "So when are you due?"

Wade looked at her, and then back at me, frowning the entire time. "Due?"

"I'm not sure," I said, avoiding Wade's gaze.

"Have you seen a doctor?"

I shook my head. "I just kinda found out today."

"Found out what?" Wade demanded, still frowning. "What are you two talking about?"

"Found out she's pregnant," Ginny answered. "You're going to be a daddy again, big brother."

"You're pregnant?" Wade looked directly at me. "But I thought you were on The Pill."

"I was. I am." I had no explanation.

Ginny helped. "Sometimes it happens."

"But . . ." Wade stared at me and then slowly shook his head.

Chapter Ten

I wasn't sure if I wanted to hit Wade over the head or run for my room. I decided neither alternative would solve the problem. "But nothing," I said. "It is what it is. And I think," I added, looking down at Jason, "this is something we should discuss later."

"Mama's pregnant," Jason said and held his can of Sprite up toward Wade. "Can you open this for me?"

"What did you say?" Wade asked, his attention switching to his son.

"Mama's gonna have a baby."

"A baby?" Wade stared at Jason for a second, then took the can and popped the tab open. "I didn't know that."

"Daddy Michael said he's a stud." Jason frowned and shook his head. "I don't know what that means. Can we go back to the lake and look for them?"

"No, not today. Today we need to let the Coast Guard and the sheriff's department look for them."

"But you're with the sheriff's department," Jason said, tears beginning to well in his eyes. "And I really miss Mama. Why can't you look for her?"

I could tell Wade wasn't quite sure how to answer that question, so I spoke up. "Your daddy needs to rest today. He needs to let that bump on his head get better. Maybe tomorrow. Meanwhile, are you having a good time with Spike and the boys?"

"The boys don't like me. They run and hide when they see me."

"They do that when they see me, too," I said, though lately Ginny's two Siamese cats had become more curious. The last time I visited her house they'd actually come over and rubbed against my legs. "What about Spike?" I loved that Ginny had named her miniature poodle Spike.

"He's neato," Jason said and grinned. "Last night Aunt Ginny couldn't find him, and she got all worried. And you know where he was?"

"No," I said. "Where?"

"In bed with me." Jason giggled. "He crawled under the covers, and she couldn't find him."

"Until he poked his head out," Ginny added.

" 'Cause he had to breathe," Jason said and took a gulp of his Sprite.

I thought we'd successfully gotten off the subject of the boat explosion and Mama, but the moment Jason put the can down, he looked up at his dad and asked, "Why did those men want to know about your phone?"

For a moment Wade said nothing, then he touched Jason's hand. "I don't know. What do you remember? Did I have my phone out?"

"Uh huh. You said you were going to take my picture lowering the anchor." Jason faced me and grinned. "He said he wanted to show you how it's done."

I understood why Wade would have wanted such a picture. The last time we'd gone out on his boat, I'd tried to lower the anchor and had ended up nearly tossing myself overboard. I also understood how bad it would have sounded if Jason had told the two deputies from the Van Buren Sheriff's Department that Wade had his phone in his hand when the boat exploded. Cell phones could be used to trigger bombs.

Ginny also understood. "Oh dear," she said and grimaced. "That's not good, is it?"

Wade shook his head.

"What we've got to do," I said, "is prove you didn't do it."

"P.J.," Wade's voice had a warning tone. "This is not a matter for civilians."

"Oh, and you're going to leave it up to Milano and Blair to prove you're innocent?"

"Innocent of what?" Jason asked, looking at his father, then me.

"Of killing—" Wade stopped himself.

"Of killing fish," I said quickly, hoping Jason's six-year-old mind would accept that answer. "Boats blowing up isn't good for fish."

"Oh, well Daddy didn't do it on purpose, did you, Daddy?"

"No, I didn't." Wade looked at his sister. "Would you mind keeping Jason with you one more night? I'll get my car tomorrow, then I'll pick him up."

"Tomorrow?" The way Ginny rolled her eyes I could tell she'd hoped her nephew-sitting time was over. Finally, she nodded. "Yeah, sure."

"And will you be a good boy for your Aunt Ginny?" Wade asked Jason. "I promise I'll come get you tomorrow."

"You or Mama, right?"

"Right."

I didn't say anything, simply watched Wade hug his son. Although there was a chance Wade's ex might be alive, the longer we didn't hear anything from or about her, the less that was a possibility. Call me a chicken, but I didn't want to be around when Jason learned his mother was dead.

I was ten when I was told my father was dead, killed in an attack on a foreign embassy. Irrational as it might be, I blamed myself for his death, even though I was thousands of miles away. How would Jason feel having been on the boat with his mother? How would he feel if his father was accused of her murder?

I didn't care what Wade said, I was going to make sure he was cleared of all responsibility or culpability. I just had to. After all, he was also the father of my unborn child.

I think that was the first time I actually thought of the baby growing inside of me as an actual living being. I was going to have a baby. A child of my own. Scary as the idea was, I also liked it. For that reason, after Ginny and Jason left, and just Wade, Baraka, and I remained in the house, I wasn't ready when Wade turned toward me and said, "What are you going to do about this pregnancy thing?"

"Pregnancy thing?" I repeated, glaring up at him. "It's a baby, not a thing."

"You know what I mean." He let out a sigh of frustration. "How did it happen?"

I almost said something smart-mouthed, and then decided he wouldn't find a lecture on the birds and bees funny. "I don't know," I admitted. "It's not something I planned."

He started to raise his eyebrows, then stopped himself, probably because of the cut on his forehead. Let him feel pain, I thought.

"You know I didn't want to get pregnant," I said. "You know my fears."

"That you'll end up like your mother. So why didn't you do something to make sure you didn't get pregnant?"

"I thought I had."

I was practically yelling, tears forming in my eyes. Turning away from him, I walked into the living room. Baraka followed me, staying close by my side.

"What if I'm arrested for Linda's murder, accused of blowing up my boat?" Wade called after me. "What if I'm convicted?"

I turned toward him. "We have to make sure that doesn't happen."

He shook his head. "You shouldn't have this baby."

"What alternative do I have?"

He didn't say the word *abortion,* but the way he looked at me, I knew he was thinking it. My hand dropped to my still-flat stomach, and I slowly shook my head. Wade turned and walked out of the house.

CHAPTER ELEVEN

When Wade returned he didn't say anything about an abortion or my being pregnant, just that he had a bad headache and was going to lie down for awhile. I checked on him around dinner time. As far as I could tell, he was breathing normally. I touched his forehead, and he moved slightly, but his skin wasn't hot or clammy. I called his name, and he grunted.

"Are you hungry?" I asked.

I'm pretty sure he said no. At least, he said something, and then he started to snore. Not a loud snore. More like a purr. I covered him with a spare blanket and let him sleep. Around nine o'clock I looked in on him again. He'd changed position and tossed off the blanket, but otherwise he seemed fine, so I grabbed my nightgown and another blanket. I would sleep on the couch.

The next morning Baraka had been fed and let out, and I'd just fixed myself a bowl of cereal when Wade came out of the bedroom. Although he keeps his hair cut short—military style—it was pressed flat on one side of his head and sticking out on the other. Add the stubble of beard on his face, his mussed, slept-in clothes, and that bandage on his forehead, and he looked more like a vagrant than an officer of the law.

"You okay?" I asked, trying to decide if his pupils were dilated.

"Yeah." He rubbed a hand over his chin and grimaced. "I guess I was tired."

"I guess so. You slept at least eighteen hours. Hungry?"

"Not really."

I saw him glance at the coffee pot on the counter. I hoped he wasn't going to want to make some. So far my stomach had been okay this morning, and I wanted it to stay that way.

He must have decided the same thing. He gave a slight shake of his head and said, "After I get cleaned up and you finish breakfast, think you could drive me back to South Haven so I can get my car?"

"Are you sure it's okay for you to drive?"

"I'm fine," he practically growled.

"Okay then." Eighteen hours of sleep evidently hadn't improved his mood.

To be honest, I was more than willing to drive Wade over to South Haven. So far I hadn't heard anything about Wade's ex and her new husband being found. I wanted to talk to some of the boaters who'd been around on Saturday, people who might know more about what had happened than what they were showing on TV. I also hoped, during the drive to South Haven, that Wade and I could talk about the baby growing inside of me and what that meant as far as our future.

I was wrong about us getting a chance to talk. As soon as we got in the car, Wade turned on the radio and started looking for news. He picked up a Chicago station, and we heard there was a traffic jam on I-90, but the only local news was about the weather. The wind had died down overnight and the temperature was expected to reach the high 80s. Although it was Monday, I had a feeling there would be a lot of people heading for the beach, especially since school would be starting in a couple more weeks.

Wade kept flipping from station to station as I maneuvered around Kalamazoo, dodging semis, late-to-work speeders, and the usual idiot drivers. Once we were on M-43, I knew I was right about the hordes heading for Lake Michigan. In addition to passenger cars, traffic was slowed by vehicles pulling boats.

Now that I only had to worry about the car in front of us, I reached over and clicked off the radio. "About the baby," I started.

"I don't want to talk about that," Wade snapped. "Not now. Not until I know what happened to my boat."

"But . . . ?" That wasn't the response I expected. Or wanted.

Wade gave me a quick glance. "Later, okay?"

He clicked the radio back on and looked out the side window. I decided there was no sense in arguing. He wasn't going to talk about it. Not yet.

My sigh must have conveyed a message to my dog. We'd taken Baraka with us, and from the back seat he poked his head between Wade and me and licked my bare shoulder. His way of saying he was there for me.

Some days I wondered why I even wanted a man in my life. Dogs were obedient, loving, faithful, and forgiving. Men— especially men like Wade—were stubborn, moody, domineering, and often irrational.

I glanced over at Wade and knew why I wanted him in my life. In spite of his failings, he was a good man: caring, dependable, and sexy as all get out. He definitely looked and smelled better after a shower. Even wearing the faded T-shirt and worn jeans he'd left at my place last month, when we worked on cleaning out the chicken coop behind my house, he looked good. Thank goodness I had washed his clothes since then or the smell would have gagged us and we would have been driving with the windows down, not up with the air conditioner on.

I was getting a little cold with the air blowing on me, even at the low setting, and I wished I'd worn long pants instead of shorts and had brought along a sweater to put on over my yellow tank top. I thought about turning the air conditioning off and rolling down the window, but it had already been sticky hot when we came out of my house.

The closer we came to South Haven, the tenser Wade became. Finally, he switched off the radio. "All they talk about is the weather," he grumbled. "You'd think they'd have something about the accident." He turned in his seat so he was looking at me. "Was there anything new on the eleven o'clock news last night?"

"I don't know," I admitted. "I fell asleep before the news came on."

"This morning?"

"Just the same clip they've been showing. Same information they've given before."

Wade let out a frustrated sigh. "When I called in this morning, Dario said he hadn't heard anything."

Dario Gespardo was another detective with the Kalamazoo Sheriff's Department. He and I had bumped heads back in June when he accused me of stealing a dog. He wasn't my favorite deputy, but he and Wade had been friends for a long time.

"Why did you call in?" That surprised me. "Were you thinking of going in to work?"

"I was scheduled to. I felt I should let them know I wouldn't be in." He scoffed. "I guess I didn't need to. Seems I've been put on leave. Suspended duty with pay. Even my own department thinks I'm guilty."

I glanced his way. "Oh, come on, Wade, that can't be true."

"Oh no?" He looked back out the side window. "I'm to come in and hand over my badge and service weapon."

I heard him take in a deep breath and slowly let it out.

"They didn't even have the balls to call and tell me."

"Maybe they tried." I hated seeing him feeling so dejected. "Would they know to call my number?"

Wade's silence told me he hadn't listed my number as an alternative contact. That didn't make me happy. If he hadn't told his boss about me, it must mean he didn't see our relationship as permanent.

"Well," Wade said, his attention again focusing on the road ahead, "at least now I can do my own investigating." The moment he said that, he scoffed at himself. "What am I thinking? I don't even know where the boat went down."

I could answer that, at least in part. "From the video they've had on the news, it looked like you were to the left of the lighthouse."

"Drive me to South Beach."

No "Please," or "Would you, please," or any softening of the order. I glared at him, but Wade was once again staring out the side window, his mouth a tight line and his jaw rigid. Even his breathing was shallow.

I decided I could handle a little bit of being ordered around. Not knowing what happened had to be much worse.

I probably should have taken one of the side streets instead of driving down Phoenix. As I'd expected, the town was jam-packed with tourists, all of the parking spots filled and cars making left turns holding up traffic. By the time we were on Water Street, driving parallel to the river channel, Wade was on the edge of his seat, looking down the road, and grumbling at the slow car in front of us. Baraka, on the other hand, seemed to be enjoying the slow speed. Sitting up, he kept a silent watch over all the dogs being paraded by the Municipal Marina and channel, heading for the pier and lighthouse.

Once we reached the beach area, the car in front of us stopped to let passengers out. The delay allowed me to look out over the sandy beach. Masses of people had already claimed spots along the water's edge, colorful towels and umbrellas marking their territory. In the water some adults and children were wading and swimming while others gawked, all looking westward. Watching the video had given me a rough idea of where Wade's boat had been when it exploded, but even if I hadn't seen the video, I would have known. Boats were clustered in that area—a Coast Guard boat, the Van Buren County Sheriff's boat, fishing boats, pleasure boats, kayaks, jet skis, and dinghies.

"So that's the spot," Wade said softly. "I wonder what they've found."

"You want me to take you over to the Coast Guard auxiliary? Maybe someone there can tell you."

He glanced my way, then shook his head. "No, take me to my car."

I did. At least I took him to the marina where his car should have been, and getting there wasn't easy. I swear every crazy driver in the United States had come to South Haven just to torment me. Besides Michigan license plates, I saw an abundance from Indiana and Illinois, and a scattering from as far northeast as Maine and as far southwest as Texas. I sighed in relief when I turned onto the driveway for the marina. Wade, on the other hand, tensed.

"Where's my car?" he demanded, leaning forward in his seat and staring at the spot where he usually parked his Jeep.

"Would you have parked somewhere else?" I scanned the parking area, looking for a tan Jeep. Nothing.

"I always park here." He motioned for me to pull into his assigned spot. "I remember clearly parking here Friday night. As that deputy said, I had several things I'd brought from home that I loaded on the boat." Wade looked around. "And Brewster parked there." He pointed at a nearby visitor spot. It was empty.

"His car's gone, too?"

"Damn." Wade closed his eyes. "They took them."

"Who took them?" I didn't understand. It was eerie enough

not to see *The Freedom* tied up in his slip.

"The Sheriff's Department," Wade said and opened his car door.

I saw Ben Gordon on the back of the trawler in the slip next to Wade's. Ben's a retired auto parts worker whose salt-and-pepper beard and weather-lined, tan face make him look a little like Hemmingway. He waved, climbed out of his boat, and met us on the dock. "You and your boy okay?" he asked Wade.

"Yeah, we're both fine." Wade pointed at the spot where I was now parked. "When did they take my car?"

"Couple hours ago. Thought we were being raided. Sheriffs' cars came wheelin' in, then two tow trucks with trailers. Loaded up your Jeep and the Toyota your ex arrived in, and off they went."

Wade said nothing, but I knew he was upset. "I'm going to let Baraka out," I said and walked back to my car.

I've learned it's better to leave Wade alone if something's bothering him. Besides, Baraka did need a potty break. I led him over to a nearby grassy spot. I was close enough that I heard Wade ask Ben, "What's the word? They find any bodies?"

"No word yet. Coast Guard went out at the crack of dawn."

"We saw their boat," I said, walking back toward the two of them, Baraka by my side. "Sheriff's boat was there, too, along with just about every other boat in South Haven. Don't these people have to work on Mondays?"

Ben chuckled. "Probably one of those flu bugs going around." He pointed at a dinghy coming up the river. "I think that's Larry's. He said he wanted to know what was going on."

Larry Locham was a schoolteacher who had a boat tied up at the marina. He often took his dinghy down the Black River to the lake. He said with the cost of gas, it was the cheapest way to travel if he wasn't going far.

We all waited for Larry to tie up and join us. Baraka was the first to greet him. Tail wagging, my dog practically dragged me over to the middle-aged redhead. And, of course, Baraka had to sniff the man's crotch.

I pulled back on the leash and mumbled an apology. I do need to stop that behavior. It's becoming embarrassing.

"What a mess," Larry said and gave Baraka a pat on the head.

"They find any bodies?" Wade asked, his voice tense.

"More like body parts. I had my radio with me." Larry held up his handheld marine radio. "Took me a while to find the channel they'd jumped to, and they used code words, but it was pretty obvious what they were talking about."

He nodded to Wade. "They brought up two body bags, but the way the divers handled them, you could tell there wasn't a body in them, not like you and I have. Just parts."

Body parts. My stomach roiled as I pictured Linda and her husband in pieces. I handed Baraka's leash to Wade and headed for the club house, hoping I'd get to a bathroom before I lost my breakfast.

"She's pregnant," I heard Wade say as I hurried away.

The way he said it, he could have been telling them I had AIDS, and the way they looked at me a while later, when I came back, made me feel even more like someone with a deadly disease. Only Ben said, "Hope you start feeling better soon. My wife was sick all nine months."

That didn't make me feel better, but I managed a smile. "Thanks, Ben. So what did I miss?"

"Nothing," Wade said and handed Baraka back to me.

The way he looked, worry lines creasing his forehead, I was pretty sure it was more than nothing. Larry filled me in. "They brought up some canisters. Guy in a dinghy next to me said that's how they gather evidence underwater, they scoop up everything, including the water, just in case something important is in the sand or floating around the object they're after."

"But you don't know what they found?" If the evidence was in a canister, I didn't see how Larry could tell.

"Over the radio I heard them say they'd found something interesting. Very interesting. And then the other guy on the radio said, 'We got him.' "

CHAPTER TWELVE

Wade told me to go on home, that he planned on staying at the marina for a while, that he wanted to talk to a few people, see what he could learn. I asked him how he planned on getting home since he didn't have a car.

"There's a place on M-43 that rents cars," Larry said and looked at Wade. "You got a driver's license and credit card?"

Wade patted his back pocket. "It's wet, but I've still got my wallet."

"Good enough." Larry faced me. "I can drive him over to get a car when he's ready."

"So see, I'm well taken care of." Wade took my free hand in his and gave it a gentle squeeze. "No need for you to hang around, especially since I also want to run over to Paw Paw and see what's up with my car. I'll call when I get home."

I didn't really want to leave—I wanted to stick around and see if anyone knew what the divers had found—but I had work waiting for me back at the house, so I knew Wade was right. Both Larry and Ben had cars parked in the marina lot. Either one could drive Wade wherever he wanted to go. No need for me to stay. He could tell me what he learned when he called.

He walked with me to my car and waited as I loaded Baraka onto the back seat. "Thanks for bringing me over," he said and gave me a quick kiss.

Reluctantly I drove away, heading back toward Zenith. Traffic wasn't as bad going away from Lake Michigan, and soon I started humming the melody from "Good Vibrations," which was odd. First of all, I don't really like the Beach Boys' songs, and second, the vibrations I'd been getting this morning weren't good. Wade was avoiding talking about the baby, and whatever the divers had found in the wreckage of his boat couldn't be good if law enforcement was saying, "Got him."

My cell phone rang as I neared Kalamazoo. I considered letting it go to voice mail, then worried it might be Wade asking me to come back to South Haven. I pulled over to the side of the road and grabbed my phone. It wasn't Wade but his sister. "Ginny?" I said. "What's up?"

"Is Wade with you?" she asked.

"No, he's in South Haven."

"Darn." She paused, then went on. "P.J., I need a favor. I'm on my way to Linda's house. Well, the house she moved into after she married Michael. Jason wanted some of his own clothes and some computer game he likes to play. All day yesterday there was yellow crime scene tape across the door, but when I called this morning, they said the house has been released, and we can go inside."

I could hear Jason's voice in the background, listing other items he wanted, but I still didn't understand the problem. "So?"

"So I just received a call from a client. A very important client. He wants me to meet with him in an hour, and this isn't a meeting where I can drag a six-year-old along. Any chance you could come get Jason?"

I shook my head no as I thought of the work I needed to do for my own clients, but Ginny is a self-employed interior decorator, and pleasing "important" clients is important for her business, so I told her yes, and that I'd meet her at Linda's house if she'd give me the address.

As it turned out, I wasn't far from the house; nevertheless,

Ginny's car was already parked in the driveway when I pulled up in front of the white two-story McMansion. Lush green lawns, stately pines, and maple trees lined both sides of the street while well-trimmed bushes and colorful flower beds graced the front of Brewster's house. Considering how important money was to Wade's ex-wife, and the fact that Michael Brewster was a successful financial advisor at one of the nation's larger brokerage houses, I wasn't totally surprised by the size of his home or the elegance of the neighborhood. This was what Linda had wanted.

The "For Sale by Owner" sign on the front lawn was tilted to the side, probably from the wind we'd had yesterday. I wondered how much they'd been asking and if anyone had made an offer. The fact that they'd planned on leaving for California in just days made me think maybe they had sold the place.

So many plans. Dreams. All ended in a split second.

That tears started welling in my eyes surprised me. I wasn't a person who cried a lot, not normally. But it did bother me that Saturday morning Linda thought she had everything she'd ever wanted, and now she was dead.

I also wondered how we were going to tell Jason.

I grabbed a tissue from the console and wiped away my tears. The best thing would be to say nothing right now. Not to Ginny or Jason.

Baraka sat up when I turned off the engine, and I rolled down the windows so ample air would circulate through the car. I was about to get out when a black Cadillac Escalade pulled up beside and slightly ahead of my car. Just far enough ahead so the Cadillac's backseat window was in line with my driver's-side window. The Cadillac's windows were tinted so I couldn't see in, but almost immediately the back window went down and I had a clear view of the man inside.

"Well, wadaya know, it's you," he said. "The lady from the hospital."

I recognized him as well—the bald head, broad shoulders, and classy-looking black silk shirt. "And you're the man from the hospital," I parroted back.

"I thought you said you didn't know Brewster."

"I don't." I heard a low, throaty growl behind me and glanced in my side-view mirror. I could see Baraka was on his feet, his head out the side window, and the hairs on his neck standing up.

The guy from the hospital also looked Baraka's way. "Maybe you'd better roll that back window up."

I didn't like the threat I heard in his words, and I had no intention of rolling that window up. "Maybe you'd better just stay in your car."

The guy gave a half-smile, his gaze still on Baraka, and then he looked beyond my car to Michael Brewster's house. "He in there?"

"If you mean Michael Brewster, no. Last I heard, he was in a body bag."

I shouldn't have been so blunt. I had no idea if this guy was a friend of Brewster's or not, but he made me nervous, and I wanted him gone.

"Damn, I told them not to kill him."

If I'd heard the guy right, I knew why he made me nervous. "Who'd you tell?"

I don't think he would have told me, but a car coming up the street behind us ended our conversation. Baldy said something to his driver, and the back window slid up. As quickly as it had appeared, the Escalade drove off.

The Cadillac turn the corner as a white SUV passed my car and pulled into the driveway next door. The neighbor's garage door went up, and the car pulled inside. I waited a second, and then I stepped out of my car. "Stay," I told Baraka, who still stood, waiting to be let out.

With a doggy sigh he sat down on the seat. The way he was panting, even with the windows rolled down, I knew I wouldn't be able to leave him in the car for long. What I needed to do was gather up Jason and head home.

I was heading for Michael's and Linda's front door when I heard a woman call, "Have you heard anything about them?"

I stopped just behind Ginny's car and looked over at the house next door. A slender brunette wearing a short-sleeved flowered blouse, blue crop pants, and blue sandals had exited the garage carrying a paper grocery bag. I guessed her age somewhere between late forties and early fifties, mostly because I could see some gray in her shoulder-length brown hair and some wrinkles near her mouth and eyes. But, of course, I'm not that great at telling ages. And I guess I'm not alone. Most people think I look younger than my age, which now that I'm nearing twenty-nine, is beginning to please me.

"Do they know for sure if he's dead?" she asked as she came toward me.

I gave a quick glance toward Brewster's house, hoping Jason wasn't anywhere around where he could hear her, and I kept my voice low. "It looks like it."

"I'm Carol," she said, stopping in front of me. "Carol Dotson. Are you with the sheriff's department?"

"No, I'm P.J. Benson," I said, surprised that she'd think a deputy would be dressed in shorts and sandals. "I'm a friend of Jason's dad. Linda's ex-husband," I added, in case she didn't know about Wade.

"Oh yeah, it was his boat that exploded, wasn't it?" Carol pointed toward Brewster's house. "There were sheriff's deputies here all day yesterday. Had the house sealed off. Even brought in a bomb-sniffing dog."

Maris Soule

She paused to chuckle. "That was a kick. The dog evidently indicated the presence of explosives. You should have seen those deputies running all over the place, they—"

I interrupted her. "They found explosives?"

"Oh . . . No." She shook her head, still smiling. "Well, sort of. They did find some bottle rockets. You know, the kind that make that really loud bang. Anyway, after they talked to a few of us—" Carol indicated the houses up and down the street, including hers. "And we told them how often Michael used to set those damn things off, even after the Fourth of July, those deputies seemed to calm down. About the only thing I saw them take out of the house was a box, and they weren't acting like it was dangerous or anything. In fact, I heard one deputy tell another there was nothing in the house."

At that, she looked back at me. "So have they figured out what caused the explosion?"

"Not that I've heard." Which was true. All I knew was they'd found something in the wreckage that would prove someone guilty.

Carol glanced back at Brewster's house. "Is Linda's ex in there now?"

"No. His sister and Jason are inside, getting some of Jason's things."

"Really?" She looked back at me. "How'd they get in? I gave the key I had to the deputies yesterday, and they didn't give it back."

"I don't know how they got in."

"Maybe they got the key from the deputies," Carol suggested. "Linda's parents were here yesterday, and they were very upset that the sheriff's department wouldn't let them go inside. I didn't like their daughter all that much, but I felt sorry for them. Here they came down Saturday afternoon to help their daughter pack, and what do they discover . . . that she's prob-

80

ably dead. I know what it's like to lose a daughter. The pain and the . . ."

Her voice trailed off, and for a moment I thought she was going to cry, but then she shook her head and shrugged. "Anyway, I told them once the sheriff's department released the house, I was sure they'd be able to get in, that they should contact the sheriff's department. It really is a shame they have to go through this. The legal stuff alone is a mess."

It could be, I realized. "Do you know if Michael and Linda had wills?"

"Haven't got the slightest. About the only time we talked to either of them was to complain about those bottle rockets." Carol shook her head. "She was a stuck-up bitch. The kid was nice though. He is okay, isn't he? From what they said on the TV it sounded like he was okay. How's he taking all this?"

"He doesn't know his mother's dead, so don't say anything. Okay?"

"Sure. No problem. Her mother must know though. The grandmother, that is. Yesterday she was all tears, blaming the ex." Carol paused and frowned slightly as she looked at me. "Your boyfriend didn't do it, did he? The way Linda talked about him, I wouldn't blame him."

"No, Wade absolutely did not do it."

Carol shrugged. "Well, I can understand how the old lady feels. Two years ago, when my daughter took her life, I wanted to blame someone."

"Oh my, I'm so sorry about your daughter," I said, not sure how else to respond.

Carol looked at me and sighed. "Yeah. She was a good kid. You have any kids?"

"No . . . not yet." I wasn't ready to tell her that would change in a few months.

"If you ever do—have kids, that is—make them the most

important thing in your life. Don't ever think they're old enough that they don't need you." She nodded toward Brewster's house. "The boy's coming outside."

Almost immediately I heard, "P.J., can we go swimming?"

Jason was by my side before I saw Ginny come out of the house carrying two grocery bags stuffed full and what looked like a laptop. She paused to lock the front door, then started for the tilted "For Sale by Owner" sign.

"Can we, please?" Jason begged.

"We'll see," I responded, picturing the pile of work on my desk as I watched Ginny put the grocery bags down and shove something into the base of the sign before straightening it.

"Hey, is Baraka in the car?"

Jason dashed for my car and I barely had time to yell, "Don't let him out," before he had his hand on the door handle.

"I'll put these in your trunk," Ginny called to me, also heading for my car.

I knew Ginny wouldn't be meeting a client dressed as she was in jeans and a tank top, which meant she was in a hurry to get home and change. With Jason ready to open the car door and let Baraka out, and Ginny needing to get into the trunk, I also headed for my car, but I did remember to say, "Nice to have met you, Mrs. Dotson," before I was too far away from her.

"Carol," I heard her call back to me. "Call me Carol."

I popped open the trunk so Ginny could dump the bags of clothes and place the laptop in there. The moment she had it closed, she went to Jason. "Be good for P.J.," she said and gave him a quick hug.

"Thanks," she said to me, and also gave me a quick hug. "I don't have a booster seat for him. Just have him sit in the back, and you should be all right."

I supposed the booster seats that Michigan drivers are supposed to use with children less than four feet nine inches were in the two cars now in Paw Paw being investigated by the Van Buren Sheriff's Department.

"Looks like you'll be sharing the back seat with Baraka," I said as Jason and I watched Ginny back out of the driveway and drive off.

"That's okay," Jason said. "So, can we go swimming?"

"Maybe." Two weekends ago, Wade and I had taken Jason swimming at a nearby lake. I supposed I could take him there for an hour or so. As Carol Dotson had said, children should be the important ones, not work. After Wade arrived, he could entertain Jason, and I could tackle that pile of work.

"Stay!" I ordered Baraka, holding my hand up in front of my dog's face as I opened the back door of my car.

Baraka stood where he was, waiting for my okay to leave the car, but before I could get him to sit down so Jason could climb in next to him, Jason took off running. "Grandma, Grandpa!" I heard him yell as he headed for the Buick pulling up behind mine.

I knew then the vibrations today definitely weren't good ones.

CHAPTER THIRTEEN

Linda's mother was out of the car before I had a chance to react. She wrapped her arms around Jason and hugged him close, but her eyes were on me, the look on her face triumphant. I knew what she was thinking. She had Jason, and she wasn't going to let him go home with me. Not if she could help it.

My stomach churned, bile rising in my throat, and all I could think was *Not now. I don't have time to be sick.*

I swallowed hard and forced myself to smile. "Mrs. Healy, how are you?"

"How am I?" she snapped, releasing her hold on Jason and straightening to her full height. "How do you think I am? That man you're sleeping with killed my daughter."

I winced and looked at Jason. He'd stepped back from his grandmother's side, and I could tell from the way he was frowning that he wasn't quite sure he understood what she'd said.

"Jason, get in the car."

Linda's father had gotten out of the Buick and come around to the front. His deep, commanding voice demanded obedience, but Jason simply looked at him, his mouth slightly open.

"Now!" the man ordered, pointing toward his car.

The anger in his tone frightened me, and it must have triggered a protective instinct in my dog. Baraka had stayed in the car even when I stepped away, but now he was out, dashing toward Jason and his grandparents.

Mrs. Healy screamed, Jason jumped back, and Mr. Healy

84

yelled, "What the . . . ?"

"Baraka, no!" I shouted, not quite sure what my dog was going to do.

He ran between Jason and the Healys, sprinted onto the neighbor's lawn, spun around, and ran back between Jason and his grandparents.

"Baraka!" I yelled and made a lunge for him as he passed me.

This time he ran up the driveway, and I noticed Carol Dotson was still outside her garage, watching us. Baraka stopped, looked at her, then turned and trotted over to the For Sale sign in the middle of the Brewsters' front yard.

"Baraka, no!" I yelled as he lifted his leg and peed on the base of the sign, exactly where I'd seen Ginny place what I guessed to be a spare key to the house.

"I'll get him," Jason yelled and started for the sign.

"Jason, get back here," his grandfather demanded.

Baraka took off again, trotting away from Jason, tail wagging.

Jason ran after the dog. I ran after Jason. The Healys yelled. Carol Dotson laughed.

I would have also laughed if I hadn't been worried about catching Baraka and also getting Jason away from his grandparents. As it was, Baraka led Jason back to my car. I caught up with the two of them just as Baraka jumped onto the back seat. "Get in," I said softly the moment I came up behind Jason. "Get in with Baraka."

I'm not sure why Jason obeyed me, but he scrambled onto the back seat, and I quickly closed the car door behind him. Without pausing, I dashed around to the driver's side. I think it all happened so quickly his grandparents didn't understand what was going on, not until I started the engine.

"Come back here!" Mr. Healy yelled, coming up beside my car.

I hit the lock button at the same time as he reached for the door handle. My heart racing, I shifted into drive and pulled away from the curve. I could see Healy in the rearview mirror shaking his fist at me, his wife coming up beside him.

My sense of exhilaration diminished as I drove away from the older couple. All they wanted was to be with their grandson, and I'd just taken him from them. In a way I was a kidnapper. They, at least, had a blood relationship to Jason. I had no biological ties at all to the boy.

I took US-131 to I-94, skirting downtown Kalamazoo. Every mile of the way, I checked the rearview mirror expecting to see the flashing lights of a police car. It wasn't what I saw but what I heard that made me pull off the freeway onto Sprinkle Road. Jason was crying.

As soon as I could, I turned into a parking area, stopped the car, and undid my seat belt. Half turning in my seat, I looked back at Wade's son. "What's the matter, Jason?"

"Mama," he said and looked at me with those big blue eyes that are so like his father's. "Grandma said some man killed Mama."

Internally I groaned. I didn't want to deal with this. Wade should be the one talking to Jason. He was the boy's father. He knew how much a six-year-old would understand about death. I didn't. He knew if they'd talked about heaven, about angels, or anything like that.

I should have let Jason go with his grandparents, should have let them explain . . .

That thought stopped me. Did I really want Frank and Jean Healy explaining what had happened to their daughter?

Oh, they would talk to Jason all right. They would tell their grandson that his father was a murderer, that Wade had killed his mother. They wanted custody of their grandson, which meant they wouldn't hesitate to turn Jason against his father.

Getting to the truth wasn't as important to them as getting their daughter's son.

"Is Mama dead, P.J.?" Jason asked.

I considered lying, but decided that wouldn't be fair; nevertheless, I wasn't quite ready to declare the truth. So I hedged. "The authorities think so."

Jason looked down and shook his head. "No she's not," he said, but I could hear the emotion in his voice. "No she's not," he repeated and looked up at me, tears glistening in his eyes. "She's not."

"They don't think she got off the boat," I said as gently as I could.

"She swam away. She doesn't remember who she is." The look in Jason's eyes dared me to say otherwise.

"Someone would have found her by now."

"I want to go home." He looked out the side window. "I want to go to *my* home, Mama's home, not *his* home."

I assumed by "his home" Jason meant Michael Brewster's house. Which was fine, I didn't want to go back there. But I'd only been to the house where Linda and Jason lived before she married Brewster once, and that had been when Wade was driving. "I'm not sure I can find it. Besides, your mother sold that house, didn't she? Someone else is probably living there now."

"I don't care," Jason looked back at me, tears pooling in his eyes. "She's there. I know she is."

Okay, so I'm a sucker, but when Jason spouted off the address, I decided why not? The street wasn't that far away from where we were now, and it would be easier to prove his mother wasn't there than to argue with him. Once Jason realized she wasn't there, I reasoned, we could go to my place. Right?

Wrong.

First of all, I was wrong about the house being sold. The sign in front said "Sale Pending." The moment I saw it, I remembered

Wade had said Linda was supposed to sign the paperwork today. The sale of the house was one of the reasons she and Michael hadn't already left for California.

I'd barely pulled up in front of the house and Jason was out of my car. He ran to the front door, rang the doorbell, and pounded on the door, calling for his mother. I parked and got out of my car, but I didn't follow him. When no one came to the door, he ran around the house, calling for her. It broke my heart to hear the hope in his voice turn to desperation.

He came back to the front door and again began pounding on it, screaming "Mama" and "Linda." I saw a woman in the house next door come to her window and look out, and I decided it was time to intervene. "She's not here," I called to Jason as I walked up behind him. "She's gone, Jason."

"No!" he screamed and pounded on the door with both fists. "No!"

I knelt and put my arms around him, wanting to comfort him. He twisted, turning so he faced me. "She'll come. I know she'll come."

"She's dead," I said and immediately wished I hadn't used that word. Jason closed his eyes, his mouth contorted in pain. "I'm sorry," I tried, knowing my apology wasn't what he wanted.

"No!"

His denial tore at my heart, but I knew continuing to deny the truth wasn't going to help him. Before he could react, I scooped him up and carried him, arms flaying and legs kicking, back to my car. Baraka, thank goodness, made no effort to jump out when I opened the back door. I plopped Jason down on the seat, flipped the child guard lever on the door, and closed boy and dog in.

Jason's screaming brought the woman next door out her front door, but I ignored her as I hurried to get behind the wheel before Jason scrambled over to the front. My tires squealed as I pulled away from the curb and sped down the street.

"I want my mama," Jason cried from the back seat.

"I know you do," I said, my eyes on the traffic as I made a right turn. "But she's not there. She's gone, Jason."

"No she's not," he yelled. "Stop it!"

I thought he wanted me to stop saying his mother was dead, but when I heard the slap of his hand and Baraka yelped, I realized Jason had wanted Baraka to stop. Probably to stop licking him. Baraka licked when he was upset, and I was sure Jason was upsetting him.

"Do not hit my dog," I yelled back. "And put your seat belt on."

"No!" Jason screamed.

I decided arguing with an emotionally distraught six-year-old wasn't going to get us anywhere. I only hoped his yelling couldn't be heard outside of my car and that I didn't get in an accident.

Jason's screaming finally turned to sobs, then whimpers. I tried to think of some way to console him, but I was afraid if I stopped and offered to hold him, he'd either start screaming again or run off.

I took the back roads to my house, and when my cell phone rang, I pulled over to the side to answer. I was surprised to hear Wade's voice. "Hi, I hear you have my son with you," he said. "How's it going?"

I glanced at the back seat. Jason was curled up with his feet against the car door and his head resting on Baraka's hindquarters. "Okay, right now," I said softly. "He's asleep."

"I'm in Paw Paw," Wade said. "Looks like they're going to keep my car for a while. Right now I'm waiting for the lead detective. He wants me to look at some things they pulled up from the boat. I'm not sure how long it will be before I can pick him up, but if you need me, give me a call, and I'll try to get away from here."

I didn't like the idea that the sheriff's department was questioning Wade again, or that he'd used the words "try to get away." Would they hold him? Could they? "What number should I call?" I asked, thinking I might just give him a call after I was home, whether I needed him or not.

"Same number as I've always had."

"They found your phone?"

"No, I bought a new one. They just transferred the old number to the new phone. They even transferred my contact numbers."

"They can do that?"

"Yes, P.J., these smartphones really are smart."

I could hear him chuckling, and I was about to tell him what I thought about his *smart* remark when he added, "That information is kept in one of those cloud things. I don't understand how it works, but all my contact numbers and information are on this new phone."

One of these days I need to get a better phone, but for now my old "flip" works just fine. "How about pictures?" I asked. "Does your new phone have the pictures you've taken?"

"No, I lost all of those."

"Darn. That picture you took of Jason lowering the anchor would prove you weren't using your phone to detonate a bomb."

"No reason I couldn't take a picture and then detonate a bomb."

"Dammit, Wade, we've got to prove you're innocent."

"*We* don't have to prove anything. I do not want you playing detective, P.J."

"I've never *played* detective." It was my turn to stress a word. "I can't help it if people die and get me involved."

"Well, you're not involved in this mess."

"But you are. Do you really think I can just sit back and let them accuse you of murdering your—" I cut myself off before I said ex-wife. Jason looked asleep, but he might be faking. "He knows she's dead," I said barely above a whisper. "Your ex-mother-in-law told him."

"And I suppose she accused me."

"She did. I told him you didn't do it, but he was pretty upset. He made me take him to your old place. He was sure she'd be there."

"You took him to that house?"

I heard the accusation in his tone. "I know, stupid. Anyway, the house is still empty. I—" A groan from the back seat made me look. Jason was moving his legs and arms, and Baraka had raised his head, his large, brown eyes looking at me for assurance.

"Look, I've got to go," I said and put the car back in gear. "I'm almost home. Come get your son as soon as you can. He needs his father."

CHAPTER FOURTEEN

Jason woke as soon as I parked in my driveway. He climbed out of the car slowly, not saying a word, blinked his eyes, and looked around, as if reorienting himself. Baraka hopped out on my command and went straight for the gate. I decided the best thing to do was act as if this was simply a visit. "You coming?" I called to Jason as I opened the gate and let Baraka into the front yard.

For a moment I thought he might refuse, then he slowly started toward me. I waited until he'd walked by me before I closed the gate and started for my front door. "Hungry?" I asked as I went up the steps to the porch.

He shook his head.

"Well, I am." I headed for my kitchen. "A peanut butter and jelly sandwich sounds good to me."

Jason followed me into the kitchen, still not saying a word. I pulled two slices of bread from the loaf of bread on the counter and took a jar of peanut butter down from the cupboard. I was heading for the refrigerator for the strawberry jam when I heard a very quiet, "I guess I'm hungry."

"Good," I said and also grabbed the gallon of milk from the top shelf.

I let Jason help me, and we ate our sandwiches and drank our glasses of milk sitting on the front porch steps. Baraka started digging a hole near the far corner of the house. As soon as Jason finished his sandwich and milk, he hopped down the steps and ran over to where Baraka continued to dig. "I think he's after a mouse," Jason yelled back at me.

"That or a mole," I called to him. My front lawn was a maze of mole tunnels. "I think he can smell them under the ground."

"I'm going to help him." Jason came running back and grabbed the hand trowel I kept on the porch.

As far as I could tell, his temper tantrum was over, his mother's death temporarily forgotten—or ignored for the moment. So was his request to go swimming. The mole hunt had begun.

I was watching the two of them when my stomach gave a familiar warning. "Damn," I mumbled and hurried inside.

I'd hoped my one bout of morning sickness while at the marina was it for the day, but it seemed I was wrong, and I wished I'd skipped the PB and J and stuck to soda crackers.

I don't know how long I was on my knees, leaning over the toilet, but when I heard the screen door open and seconds later Jason pushed the bathroom door open, I knew I'd been away long enough for him to turn into a dirt ball. "I kinda got dirty," he said, standing in the doorway. "Are you sick?"

"I'm fine," I lied and laughed. "You kind of did get dirty. Where did you find mud?"

"I tried to wash the mouse out of his hole, but it didn't work."

Next time, I told myself, *don't leave a hose connected to a faucet when there's a six-year-old around.*

I pushed myself to my feet and flushed the toilet. "Okay. No problem. Why don't you take off those dirty clothes, and I'll get you some clean ones from the ones your aunt put in my car."

"Can you bring in the computer, too?" Jason called after me.

I was sitting on a chair in the dining room when Jason came out of the bathroom. His hair was still wet from the shower and there was a trace of mud just below his left ear, but otherwise he was definitely cleaner. He'd put on the clean shorts and the T-shirt I'd tossed into the room, but he held his flip-flops in his hand. "I washed these too, but they're wet."

He started for the porch, but I stopped him. "No, if you put them out there to dry, Baraka will eat them." Standing, I took the shoes from him and placed them on the window sill. "The sun will dry them here."

Jason watched me. Once his flip-flops were in place, he asked, "Are you feeling okay?"

"I'm fine. Just some foods don't agree with me right now."

"Mama makes me lie down when I throw up."

The moment he mentioned his mother, I saw the tightening of his facial muscles and knew he'd remembered. Quickly I tried to divert his attention. "I brought in the laptop. Is it yours?"

"No, it's Daddy Michael's, but he lets me play games on it."

"What kind of games? Can you show me?"

Jason went over to where I'd placed the laptop computer on my dining room table. After scooting up on a chair, he opened the lid and clicked the computer on. "You need to plug it in." He pointed at the electric cord I'd brought in with the laptop. "Otherwise the battery runs down."

By the time I had everything connected, Jason was absorbed in playing a game. I watched for a minute as he moved and clicked the mouse, then I grabbed a soda to help settle my stomach. Baraka whined on the other side of the screen door, but he was as dirty as Jason had been, and I didn't feel up to giving him a bath. "Suffer," I scolded, knowing most of the dirt would be gone once the mud dried and he rolled a few times. That's the advantage of owning a shorthaired dog. An hour from now, once the mud was dry, I could give him a good brushing, and we'd both be happy.

Jason seemed to have forgotten his earlier desire to go swimming and my stomach felt better, so I went to my office and started working on a financial report for one of the businesses that had recently hired me. I know some people dread balancing their checkbooks and working with numbers, but I love it. I always have. Even when I was young, I used to balance my mother's checkbook for her, which wasn't always easy, especially when she was off her meds and either forgot to list checks she'd written or had written the same amount in more than once.

I'm not sure how long I was in my office, but when I came out, Jason was no longer sitting at my dining room table. "Jason?" I called, hoping he was just around the corner in the kitchen, or maybe in the bathroom.

The only response I received was a whining from Baraka.

My dog sat on the porch, looking in through the screen door. The fact that most of the mud on his coat was gone emphasized the reality that it had been a while since I'd last looked at him . . . last talked to Jason.

I'd completely forgotten I was in charge of a six-year-old, one who only a few hours earlier had been throwing a temper tantrum because I wouldn't let him stay at his old house. Would he have tried to go back there on his own?

I stared at the road that went by my place. Although traffic was sparse, cars drove by way too fast, which was one reason why I'd had a fence built around my place. If Jason was on that road, would a car see him in time? And if someone stopped, would that be good or bad?

I pushed open the screen door and stepped out on the porch, my heart racing and my stomach once again churning, but in a different way this time. The gate was still closed. Would a little boy think to close a gate behind him?

I hurried down the steps and crossed over to the fence where I could see a distance up and down the road. No little boy came in view, but I had no idea how long he'd been gone or how far he might have traveled . . . or if someone had picked him up.

"Damn, damn, damn." What kind of a mother was I going to be if I could completely forget a child?

I headed back into the house. I would call Wade, tell him what had happened, and then I would get in my car and go looking for the boy. It was the only thing I could think of doing.

I nearly ran into Jason in my dining room.

"Where have you been?" I yelled at him.

"Upstairs." He frowned. "I found a treasure map."

Upstairs. In the house. Perfectly safe.

I took a deep breath, willing myself to relax. "You didn't answer when I called."

He walked over to the table. "I didn't hear you. See my map."

I glanced at the paper he'd placed on the table. My heart was still beating wildly, my stomach still churning. At first I thought I might have to make another run for the bathroom, but then I took another look at Jason's "map" and my thoughts switched off of my stomach. I stepped closer. "Where did you find this?"

"Under the bed. It was in a box. Do you think it shows where there's hidden gold?"

I stared at the hand-drawn representation of the house we were standing in, the woodshed behind it, and the chicken coop to the backside. A trail led into an area that was labeled "woods," a dotted line going around several circles that I took to represent trees, and then an X or maybe it was a cross.

"I don't think it's gold," I said, unable to look away from the drawing.

"I think it is." Jason grabbed the map and headed for the back door. "And I'm going to find it."

For a moment I stood where I was, my mind racing back to a conversation I'd had with my neighbor, Nora Wright. Two months ago she'd said, "He told me he put a marker on the spot where he buried him."

Could the map Jason found be one my father had drawn?

Was that X where a five-month-old fetus—my half-brother—was buried?

"Wait!" I yelled and started after Jason.

CHAPTER FIFTEEN

The moment I stepped out of the house, I heard the crows caw-
ing. They were clearly announcing that someone had entered
the woods, and they were right. Jason had already gone through
the gate by the chicken coop, and, of course, left it open . . .
which meant Baraka was with him. I wasn't sure if that was
good or bad.

What bothered me most was how quickly the two had gotten
ahead of me. Was I getting so old I couldn't keep up with a six-
year-old? By the time I reached the gate, I saw my dog and Jason leave the path and head into the wooded area to their left.

"Jason! Baraka!" I called after them, picking up my pace.

Baraka came back onto the path and started for me, but I
didn't see Jason.

"Jason, wait for me!" I yelled, hoping I could slow the boy
long enough to catch up.

"Jason, come back here!" a deeper, more commanding voice
ordered.

I stopped where I was and looked back toward my house.
Wade was at the gate, coming my way.

Baraka bumped into my leg, expecting a treat, then saw Wade
and trotted toward him. I stood where I was, a giddy, excited
feeling filling my stomach. I didn't mind this giddiness, and I
don't know why this man always sets my pulse racing, but it's
been that way from the first day we met.

Watching him near, I could feel my shoulders relax and a

sense of calm come over me. Daddy was here. I was no longer solely responsible for Jason's well-being.

"Jason!" Wade yelled again, a warning in his tone.

I turned back toward the trail and smiled as Jason slowly came out from behind a tree, then ran toward us—toward Wade—the paper map he'd found still held firmly in his left hand. "I found a map," he said as he came to halt in front of Wade. "A treasure map. I'm going to find a chest of gold."

"A treasure map?" Wade crouched down so he was eye level with his son. "That's wonderful. Where did you find it?"

"Up there." Jason pointed to the second-story window that belonged to the bedroom my father slept in as a boy and young man. "It was in a box under the bed."

"Under the bed?" Wade repeated. "Upstairs in P.J.'s house?"

"Yeah, and look, there's the house, and here's that little building—" He pointed at the map, indicating each building, and then at the old chicken coop. "And here's the trail." He indicated the ground below our feet. "And in there—" This time he pointed back where he'd been and into the woods. "That's where the treasure is."

Jason glanced up at me, his look questioning, as if expecting me to argue with him. Then he looked at Wade, who'd risen to his feet. "Come on," Jason said. "We gotta go find it."

I'm sure Jason would have taken off—headed back the way he'd come—if Wade hadn't stopped him. "Whoa, Jason, no treasure hunting today. I'm not going in those woods dressed the way I am."

"But, Daddy."

"Besides, if you found that map in P.J.'s house, it belongs to her, not you."

Jason looked at me and glared. "But I found it."

"And I'm sure P.J. is glad you did, but now you need to give the map to her."

"I don't want to."

I tried not to laugh. Kids are so honest. An adult would have come up with legal reasons why he shouldn't have to turn the map over to me, or something like "Finders keepers, losers weepers." But a kid says it like it is. He didn't want to give up what he'd found.

"There's too much junk in the way," I said, using an adult excuse myself to get the map back rather than telling the truth. I mean, how could I tell a six-year-old that I thought that X might indicate where my father had buried Nora's miscarried baby?

"I could climb over the junk," Jason said. "I'm not old like you."

Ouch. That was a bit too much honesty. Besides, I didn't think twenty-eight going on twenty-nine was *that* old.

"I'll make you a promise," I said. "If there is a treasure buried there, I'll share it with you."

"Really?" He looked skeptical.

"Really." I wasn't worried about losing any great fortune. From what I knew about my father, he never had a lot of money when he lived here, which was one reason he joined the Marines out of high school and then re-upped when I was a child. "If I find any sort of treasure, I'll let you see it."

"So will you give her the map?" Wade asked, gently pushing Jason toward me.

"I guess," he said and handed the paper to me.

I gave it another glance, and then motioned back toward my house. "Let's go inside before the mosquitoes find us." One was already buzzing near my ear. "I need some lemonade. How 'bout you two guys?"

★ ★ ★ ★ ★

"We saw Grandma," Jason said as the three of us and Baraka entered my house using the kitchen door. "She wanted me to go with her, but I didn't want to, so I pretended to chase Baraka so I could get in P.J.'s car."

I gave him a thumbs-up, even though he was ahead of me and couldn't see. The kid was smarter than I'd realized.

"Grandma said Mama's dead, but she's wrong, isn't she, Daddy?"

I cringed at Jason's words and saw Wade hesitate before following his son through the kitchen and into the dining room. "We need to talk, Jason," Wade finally said.

"No. She's alive. I know she's alive."

I stood in the kitchen doorway, watching father and son in my dining room. Jason's chin jutted forward, just as Wade's always did when we argued and he was sure he was right. Wade sank down on a dining room chair and motioned for his son to come closer.

Jason didn't move.

"She's alive," the boy repeated and glared over at me. "I wanted to stay at our old house, but P.J. wouldn't let me. I know Mama will come back there. She liked that house better than Daddy Michael's. She told me that."

"Your mother's dead," Wade said quietly. "I'm sorry, but she's not coming back."

"No!" yelled Jason. "She's not dead. Daddy Michael's dead, but not Mama."

"The divers found parts . . . found her body."

"No! No . . . No . . ."

With each denial, Jason's voice lost some of its stridence and came closer to a sob; and with each no he took a step closer to Wade, until his father pulled him into his arms and let him cry.

I felt tears welling in my eyes as I watched Wade carry Jason into the living room, where he sat on the old couch with the sagging springs. Wade spoke softly to his son, and I knew my presence wasn't needed, so I stayed in the kitchen and washed the dishes in the sink, wiped down the stove and counters, and rearranged some canned goods on the shelves.

I was so busy deciding if the creamed soups should be in front of the tomato bisque, I didn't hear Wade approach. I almost yelped when he touched my shoulder. Quickly he said, "Shh, Jason's asleep."

We went out on the front porch and sat on the steps. Baraka went out with us and proceeded to check every corner of the front yard, as if he hadn't done so only a short time earlier. I waited for Wade to speak first.

"They found parts, not bodies," he finally said with a sigh. "They must have been in the cabin when the bomb went off."

"It was a bomb, for sure?"

"They didn't show me what they found down there, but they kept asking me where I bought the C4 and what kind of a detonator I used."

"They've got to be crazy," I said. "Why would you blow up your boat?"

"According to them, I killed my wife so I could gain custody of my son, and could cash in on Linda's life insurance policy," Wade said. "Seems she never changed the beneficiary from when we were married."

"How did the sheriff's department find out about the life insurance policy?"

"Linda's folks told them. They've been more than willing to tell Sergeant Milano all the reasons why I would want to kill my ex-wife. As far as the Van Buren Sheriff's Department is concerned, a life insurance policy worth over a hundred thousand, along with comments I've made about not wanting Linda to take Jason to California, gives me a strong motive."

"But you didn't do it."

"Thank you," he whispered into my curls, then kissed the top of my head. "Thank you for believing in me."

"Of course I believe in you," I said. "I know you wouldn't do such a thing."

Again Wade kissed me, this time on the lips, then he leaned back and watched a butterfly hover near the pansies I'd planted by the steps. I was surprised when he spoke again.

"As Milano said yesterday, my house is being considered a crime scene. I hope you'll let us spend another night here."

"Any time." That he thought he had to ask bothered me. "They searched Michael Brewster's house, too, and held it all day Sunday and part of this morning. Maybe they've released yours by now. Not that I don't want the two of you staying here, I just . . ."

Wade shook his head. "No, my house is still off limits. I just came from there. When I showed up at the station, Sergeant Milano asked if I'd be willing to be present while a bomb-sniffing dog went through my place. I think he was hoping I'd be afraid the dog would find something and I'd confess right then and there."

"I take it the dog didn't find anything." Otherwise, Wade wouldn't now be with me.

"Oh, he found something. When that dog sat down in front of my closet, I nearly had a heart attack." Wade gave a stifled laugh. "I'd forgotten I had a pair of slacks in there that I'd worn when we investigated that bombing in Comstock last month. Evidently they still held the scent of the explosive. Milano didn't look convinced when he bagged the slacks, but I'm pretty sure there are pictures related to that crime scene that will show me wearing those slacks."

"Did the dog find any other evidence of explosives?"

"None there, which pissed Milano. I don't know about my

Jeep. They were taking the dog to Paw Paw next, to go through my car and Brewster's. The dog might alert on my car."

"Why do you think that?"

"Because I bought some fertilizer the other day for my lawn and the bag had a hole in it. I cleaned up most of it, but I'm sure there's some caught in the ridges of the mat. Fertilizer is used to make bombs." He glanced at me and then out toward the road. "It's not going to matter what I tell them. I'm too good a suspect. They're going to hound me until they find something."

I heard his fear. I don't think Wade's ever been in this position. As a sheriff's deputy, he's always been the one looking for evidence, not afraid the police might find some. I grew up with a mother who was always being questioned by the police, taken away to be hospitalized for psych evaluations, and labeled as crazy. I knew what it was like to be afraid of accusations, true or not.

"You know, you're not the only one with a motive," I said, remembering the man in the black Escalade. "There's someone else who might have planted a bomb, or had it planted."

Wade frowned. "Like who?"

"That man who came to see you in the hospital. Or, rather, came to see Brewster."

"I don't know who you're talking about."

Maybe he didn't. I had no idea how much Wade remembered from when he was in the hospital. "There's a man. He's short—not much taller than me—broad shouldered, and bald. White. Probably in his mid-forties, early fifties. I saw him coming out of your hospital room Saturday. He told me Brewster owed him money. I saw him again today, when I was over at Brewster's house. He was in a black Cadillac Escalade. When I told him Brewster was in a body bag, this guy said, 'I told them not to kill him.' "

"You get this guy's name?"

"No." I hadn't even thought to ask.

"Get a license plate number?"

"Part of it. 2 1 B L something, something, something. I got distracted by another car coming up behind me and going by."

Wade frowned. "Could it have been 21 B L K J K? 21 Blackjack?"

"Maybe. I'm not sure."

"Well, if so, that shouldn't be too difficult to trace." Wade sighed and leaned forward, resting his elbows on his knees and his head on his hands. "I'm tired. Tired of answering questions, of feeling out of control, and of trying to remember what happened Saturday."

"Why don't you go in and lie down for a while."

"Maybe I will," he said and looked up. "Or maybe I won't."

I followed Wade's gaze and understood. Coming down the road was a blue Buick. Frank and Jean Healy's blue Buick.

CHAPTER SIXTEEN

I waited to see what Wade would do. I told myself these were his former in-laws—his son's grandparents—no need for me to be involved, but his sigh when the Buick pulled into my driveway melted my resolve. The poor man was tired and in pain. If I could lend a bit of support, I would.

We walked over to the gate together. Wade stood directly behind the latch, becoming a human wall between these invaders and his son. I positioned myself to the side, and hoped this didn't become a physical confrontation.

Baraka came loping over, tail wagging. My dog was the only one who looked happy. Mr. and Mrs. Healy certainly didn't. Frank Healy exited the Buick first, straightening to his full height, shoulders back, and a scowl on his face. Jean came around from the other side of the car and stayed slightly behind her husband. Her expression was as harsh as her husband's, but her eyes were red-rimmed and her shoulders slumped.

Frank Healy spoke even before he reached the gate, his tone of voice and body language an implied challenge. "We've come for our grandson."

Wade didn't move. "Jason stays here."

"You have no right—"

"I have every right. He's my son."

"You killed his mother."

Wade started to say something, but stopped himself when Jean Healy moaned, "My daughter. My beautiful daughter," and started sobbing.

Frank Healy looked at his wife, his expression at first cross, and then softening as he slid an arm around her shoulders and gave her a squeeze. "Now, now, Jean, you've got to get a hold of yourself, if only for Jason."

The hatred was back in his eyes when he looked at Wade. "See what you've done to my wife? You're going to pay for this, Kingsley. I'm going to make sure you get the death penalty."

Frank Healy's anger scared me. Even though I didn't think Michigan had the death penalty, unless Wade could prove his innocence, Wade could end up in jail for the rest of his life.

But how to prove Wade's innocence?

"You can't keep Jason away from us," Healy insisted. "He needs us. Needs the security we can offer."

"Handing him over to the two of you isn't going to help him," Wade said. "He's confused. Angry."

"Of course he's angry. You killed his mother."

"I did not kill Linda." Wade practically shouted the words, then winced. In a softer, more controlled tone, he added, "I don't know who killed her."

"Liar!" Healy yelled, poking a finger toward Wade.

I heard Baraka growl, a deep, throaty growl. My easygoing, happy-go-lucky pup recognized the threat Healy posed. Cautiously I placed a hand on his back.

"Stop it. Both of you," I demanded, keeping my voice under control. There was a fence between us, but I didn't want Baraka lunging for Healy's hand. "Yelling at each other isn't helping anything. Jason's inside the house asleep. He's already upset. He doesn't need to wake up and find you two fighting."

Healy ignored me.

"I'll get a court order," he shouted. "Then we'll see who has custody of Jason."

Wade's response was as loud. "Just you try."

"And you're never getting that life insurance money. I'll see to that."

"Is that what you're so worried about?" Wade shook his head, winced, and closed his eyes. He sounded tired, the energy out of his words when he said, "I don't want any damn money."

"Oh yeah. And how are you going to raise my grandson on that measly salary you make? Michael Brewster was going places. He could have given Jason everything he wanted. But no, your jealousy and your greed killed both our daughter and Michael. You blew up your own boat. You are nothing more than a—"

The way the veins in Healy's forehead were pulsating, along with his flushed face, I was afraid the man might have a stroke or a heart attack right here in my front yard . . . and I didn't need any more dead bodies. "That's enough," I ordered.

Healy sputtered, his glare transferring to me, and I'm not sure what delightful things he might have said about me, but Jason's grandmother stepped in at that moment. "She's right, Frank," Jean Healy said, placing a hand on her husband's arm. "Yelling at each other isn't getting us anywhere." She looked at me, an accusatory gleam in her eyes. "You shouldn't have taken our grandson away from us earlier today."

I didn't want to tell her Jason was the one who didn't want to go with them, so I simply gave a small nod.

"My husband's right. Jason needs us."

This time I shook my head. "Right now he needs his father, and if you're smart, you won't alienate Wade. He did not kill your daughter, and when the real killer is found and you realize that, you're going to need Wade's permission to see your grandson."

"We know who the real killer is," Frank Healy growled, looking directly at Wade.

"Hush," Jean Healy ordered, giving her husband a quick

glance before looking back at me. "Miss—"

"Benson," I supplied, though I'm sure Jason must have mentioned my name to them at some time or other over the summer. "P.J. Benson."

"Miss Benson, what did you take out of that house today?"

"I took nothing."

"But I saw Wade's sister put something in the trunk of your car."

"Oh, those things. Those were Jason's clothes and toys."

"My daughter had a valuable piece of jewelry."

The way Mrs. Healy looked at me I knew she suspected I now had that piece of jewelry. "You're saying it's missing?"

"I don't know. We haven't been able to get into the house."

I smiled. The Healys obviously hadn't seen Ginny place the key at the base of the For Sale sign. "I didn't go inside," I said, "and I'm sure Ginny didn't take any jewelry."

"And you expect us to believe that?" Frank Healy said.

Wade glared at him. "She does not lie."

I was glad to hear Wade say that. More than once—especially when we first met and I kept insisting someone was getting into my house even though the doors and windows were locked—he'd more or less called me a liar.

Okay, so he'd thought at that time that I was crazy . . . like my mother. It still hurt.

"Tell you what," Wade said. "Tomorrow morning. Ten o'clock. I'll meet you at Brewster's house and you can see for yourself. The only things my sister took were what Jason needed."

"Will you bring Jason with you?" Jean asked, looking hopeful.

"We'll see."

That was all Wade promised, but I guess it must have been enough. The Healys left after that. Wade and I remained standing by the gate until we saw the Buick disappear in the distance, then he looked at me. "I sure hope Ginny didn't take anything out of that house except Jason's clothes and toys."

"She also got Michael Brewster's laptop," I said. "Jason was playing games on it this afternoon."

Wade frowned. "The Van Buren Sheriff's Department didn't take his laptop when they searched the house?"

"I guess not."

"Hmm. I'll have to take a look at it, see what's on it."

CHAPTER SEVENTEEN

Wade didn't go on Brewster's laptop. Baraka went running into the house ahead of us and woke Jason, and Wade asked his son if he wanted to play catch—which I think he did to keep Jason's mind off his mother—and somehow the afternoon and evening slipped by without either father or son thinking about the laptop.

Tuesday morning a yelp from Baraka woke me. Not sure what was wrong, I slid out of bed and dashed to the living room. It took me a minute to figure out what was going on. Jason was crouched over the shredded remains of a picture book, Baraka was lying in his crate, head on his paws, and Wade was sitting on the couch, looking as exhausted as I felt.

"Bad dog," Jason screamed and threw part of the shredded book at Baraka.

"Stop it!" I yelled as the book bounced off the edge of the crate and Wade's son reached for a shoe, which I figured would be thrown next.

Baraka cowered lower in his crate, his expression declaring his guilt as much as fear. "Outside," I yelled at my dog and pointed toward the front door.

"He's a bad dog," Jason shouted. "Bad. Bad. Bad."

"That's enough, Jason," Wade ordered.

I hurried past the boy and opened the front door. "Out Baraka," I commanded, feeling tears form in my eyes.

Baraka slunk toward the door and out.

"He ate my book," Jason sobbed.

"Do you have to yell?" Wade asked.

I looked at the two of them, and I knew I had to get away before I either started screaming or crying. The moment I entered the bathroom, the tears commenced.

I'm not sure how much time passed before I heard a knock on the bathroom door. It was Wade. "You okay?"

I wasn't quite sure how to answer. I'd just had over eight hours of sleep, and I felt exhausted. I rarely cry, but right now I couldn't stop crying.

When I didn't say anything, Wade cautiously opened the door. He found me sitting on the edge of the bathtub, using a strip of toilet paper to blow my nose.

"I talked to Jason about throwing things at your dog, and I tossed what was left of his book. I think Baraka must have swallowed some of it."

"Oh great," I moaned, wondering if Baraka would be throwing that up or if I'd have to take him to the vet.

More tears stung my eyes.

Wade sat down beside me and slipped an arm around my shoulders. "It's okay," he said softly and hugged me close.

No it wasn't.

I knew why I was crying, and it wasn't because my dog had eaten Jason's book, or even that Jason had thrown things at him. I was crying because I was pregnant, and I didn't want to be pregnant. I didn't want this pregnancy to turn me into my mother. My crazy mother, who *saw* things, who once thought aliens had landed in our backyard, who couldn't keep a job, and who couldn't even be trusted to live on her own.

I looked at Wade and sobered. The poor guy had enough to worry about without having to deal with a hysterical woman.

A potentially crazy woman.

"Where's Jason?" I asked, realizing I didn't hear the boy in the other room.

"I sent him outside to apologize to Baraka."

"I think Baraka needs to apologize to Jason."

"I explained that dogs, especially young dogs, chew things because they're getting new teeth and chewing helps take the pain away. I also told him he shouldn't have left his books on the floor, that Baraka probably thought they were meant for him."

"I should have put Baraka in his crate last night." He'd been good for so long, I'd gotten lax about doing that.

"We were all tired." Wade kissed the side of my face. "You still look tired."

"You slept on the couch." The idea that he hadn't come to bed with me brought more tears. "I'm so sorry."

"About what? We're the ones who have invaded your house. Jason and I should be apologizing," he said, avoiding the subject of the couch.

"I'm sorry about being pregnant."

I guess I hoped he'd say not to worry about it, that everything would be all right, but he didn't. Wade said nothing, simply sat next to me on the edge of that bathtub, took in a deep breath, and slowly let it out.

And then the phone rang.

His cell phone, not mine.

Wade hurried into the living room where he'd left his new phone on the table near the couch. I stayed in the bathroom, but I could hear his side of the conversation. His "Again?" held a hint of anger, and I understood why when he added, "How many times do I have to tell you I did not plant a bomb?"

I wiped away my tears and blew my nose. Here I was feeling sorry for myself when Wade was the one who had problems. A major problem.

He was sliding his cell phone back in its case when I came out of the bathroom. He forced a smile, glanced out the window to where Jason was playing with Baraka, and then looked back at me. "Any chance you could watch Jason for a little while longer?"

"How much longer?" I asked, not because I was unwilling to keep Jason with me, but because I'd glanced at the clock and had a feeling we had another problem.

"I don't know." Wade shook his head. "They have more questions and want me to look at something." He sighed. "I don't like the way this is going."

"You told Linda's parents you'd meet them at Brewster's house at ten," I reminded him. "It's already eight-thirty."

"Crap." He rolled his eyes, then gave me a pleading look, and I knew what I'd be doing that morning.

I was a little worried about taking Jason with me. I wasn't sure how he would react or if Linda's parents would try to take him from me. We'd escaped once; I doubted we could pull that off twice. I did leave Baraka back at the house, locked in his crate. My dog wasn't happy about that, but I didn't want him shredding any more books or anything else that Jason might have left on the floor.

The Healys' Buick was parked in front of Michael Brewster's house, and the moment I pulled into the driveway, they got out. As soon as Jean Healy saw Jason, she called him to her. I tensed, not sure what was going to happen next, but all the woman did was hug her grandson and start kissing his face. Jason endured the onslaught for a few seconds and then pulled away and ran over to the For Sale sign.

I headed for the front door, but out of the corner of my eye I saw Jason pull the key from its hiding place and heard Frank Healy mumble, "Well, I'll be damned."

As I waited for Jason to bring me the key, his grandfather

came up behind me. "What's the matter, Kingsley couldn't face us again."

"He was called in to work." I hoped I sounded matter-of-factly with my half-truth.

Healy scoffed.

"Hi, Grandpa," Jason said and handed me the key. "P.J.'s dog ate my one of my books. He's losing his teeth just like I am." Jason opened his mouth wide and poked a finger inside. "I got another loose one."

"You're getting so grown up," Jean Healy said, coming up behind Jason and tousling his hair.

I grinned and hurried to open the front door. I know Jason doesn't like his hair mussed, and his expression at the moment told me Jean Healy wasn't winning any points with all of her kisses and hair rubbing.

"I haven't been in here," I said as I removed the key and the door swung open. "Jason will have to tell you where everything is. He—"

My mouth dropped open. I knew Wade's ex was planning on leaving for California this week, so I wasn't surprised to see boxes on the floor. What did surprise me was that every box within my view lay on its side, flaps open, with most of its contents strewn out on the tile and carpeting. In addition to the opened boxes, I could see cushions had been pulled off the sofa in the living room, the coffee table was on its side, boxes of movie DVDs lay on the carpet in front of an empty TV stand, and the walls and windows had words written on them.

"Wow, what a mess," Jason said, looking inside.

I grabbed his arm to stop him from going in, and he looked up at me, and then back into the house. "What's that say?" he asked, pointing at the closest wall.

I didn't want to say the word aloud, so I fudged. "It's not a good word."

"What are you two waiting for?" Frank Healy pushed his way past me and Jason. The moment he stepped inside, he stopped. "What in the . . . ?"

"Baa . . ." Jason said, still looking at the word on the wall. "Bass . . . ?"

Frank Healy wrinkled his nose. "And what is that smell?"

"Bast . . ." Jason continued.

I've seen how Wade, when he reads to Jason, has the boy sound out words. It wouldn't be long before the boy figured this one out, so I decided I might as well tell him. "Bastard. The word is bastard. It's an insult. Not a nice word."

Frank Healy looked back at me. "What happened here?"

"What's going on?" Jean Healy demanded from behind me, the same time Jason asked, "Why'd someone write that on the wall?"

My answer was easy. "I don't know."

"My God, what did you do to this place?" Jean Healy asked, maneuvering herself past me. Once inside, she stopped and looked around—at the writing on the walls and sliding glass door, at the overturned coffee table, and at the boxes, their contents strewn about.

"We need to call the police," I said, the shock beginning to wear off.

"You better believe we're going to call the police," Frank Healy said and started toward the stairway and rooms to the right. "Jason, show me your mother's room."

"Wait. No. Don't go any farther," I pleaded, tightening my hold on Jason's arm. "We shouldn't be inside at all. We might destroy evidence."

Jason's grandfather did stop, but only to glare at me. "Is there something you're afraid I'll find . . . or not find?"

Before I could answer, Jason broke away from my hold and ran into the living room, stopping in front of the empty TV stand. "Who took the TV?" he cried, and began digging through the boxes on the floor. "My Xbox is gone. And my games."

"Jason, show me your mother's room," Frank Healy ordered from where he stood. "Jean, come on."

"It's upstairs," Jason said, looking first at me and then at his grandfather.

"You can't go up there," I protested, but the three of them ignored me. Frank Healy started up the stairs, and Jason hurried to catch up with his grandfather. Jean Healy followed the two, and I, alone, stood in the doorway.

In my head, a jumble of thoughts warred for attention. I was sure the house hadn't looked this bad when Wade's sister and Jason were here. Ginny would have said something. Jason would have said something. That meant someone had ransacked the place after we left. But who? Why?

I should call the police. No, I should call Wade.

I reached for my cell phone and realized I hadn't brought it with me. Last I remembered it was sitting on my night stand, charging.

Maybe that was just as well. If Wade was still at the Van Buren Sheriff's Department, he wouldn't be able to come, and it wouldn't be good for the Kalamazoo police to show up while the Healys and Jason were upstairs.

I could hear footsteps from somewhere above. I assumed the Healys were looking for the piece of jewelry they'd mentioned last night. Would someone else have known Linda owned something valuable? Was that why the house had been broken into?

That explanation didn't make sense. If all you were looking for was some jewelry, why spray-paint a sliding glass patio door and wall? Why make such a mess?

Jason said his Xbox was missing, as well as games and the TV. I wondered what else might have been taken or painted on.

Curiosity got the best of me. I didn't go very far into the house, just a few steps beyond the threshold, but standing at the edge of the tiled entryway, I could easily see most of the living room, dining area, and kitchen. A low counter separated the living room from the kitchen, giving me a clear view of empty cupboards and drawers, the sink, and the side-by-side refrigerator/freezer. Both of its doors were wide open, packages of meat and vegetables strewn across the counter, along with an empty milk jug and opened plastic containers. Catsup and mustard had been squeezed to form a smiley-face on a door that I guessed led to the garage, the red and yellow colors mingling where they'd run a little.

Near the sink flies circulated above what looked like an unwrapped roast and a whole chicken. The sight, along with the smell, made my stomach turn, and I hoped my simple breakfast of soda crackers and ginger ale stayed down.

A thump above my head made me look up. What were they doing up there? Didn't they realize they were disturbing a crime scene? I knew from watching shows on TV that was a no-no, and Wade, more than once, had told me how lawyers could ruin a case if evidence was tampered with.

"Hey!" I yelled, hoping they'd hear me. "You need to come down and call the police."

No one said anything and no one came downstairs.

I wasn't sure what to do next. Stay where I was? Wait outside? I finally decided to make note of what I saw so I could tell Wade later.

Across from me, the sliding door looked slightly ajar, and the letters that had been painted on the glass didn't form any word I recognized but reminded me of letters I'd seen on the sides of freight train cars. They could be a gang symbol. And the sliding door could be how the vandal or vandals entered the house.

The missing TV, Xbox, and video games indicated robbery as

a motive. But what about the word "bastard" painted on the wall? That seemed to make the destruction personal. Did the vandals/robbers know the Brewsters? Did they know Michael and Linda were dead? Their names had been on the news often enough since Saturday, but I'd never heard an address given.

In addition to the food on the counter, by the couch I could see an empty bag of chips and several empty cans of pop and beer. The number of opened cans made me sure more than one person had ransacked the place. I found it interesting that not only the refrigerator and freezer had been opened and emptied, cupboards and drawers also had been cleaned out, some drawers even removed from their tracks.

The vandals were looking for something.

Drugs?

Did Michael Brewster use drugs or deal in them?

Of course, maybe the sheriff's department had emptied the boxes, cupboards, and drawers when they held the house as a crime scene. Wade could ask about that.

On the end of the island counter, close to where I stood, was a telephone/answering machine combination, a light blinking on the answering machine. That the phone was still there surprised me. I thought those things were always removed from a crime scene, especially if there were messages. And why didn't the ones who broke in take it?

I answered my last question myself. If it was a gang that broke into the house, they probably all had cell phones. Why bother stealing something as outdated as a land line?

Next to the phone was a pair of red Mylar balloons, most of their helium gone. They sagged over the edge of the counter, almost as if they were trying to reach the large greeting card on the floor below them. I considered going over and picking up the card. A few steps more shouldn't matter. But then, through a window over the kitchen sink, I noticed there was someone in the neighbor's backyard. Although he had his back to me, I was pretty sure it was a man.

I turned toward the front door, figuring I'd go over and ask the guy if he knew anything about someone breaking into Brewster's house, but before I'd taken two steps, Jean Healy came storming down the stairs, wagging a finger at me. "What did you do with it?" she demanded.

"With what?"

Jason followed her down the stairs, Frank Healy behind him.

"With the necklace I gave her," Jean Healy said. "It was an heirloom. Worth thousands of dollars. Tens of thousands."

"I don't know anything about a necklace," I said. "But look around. Whoever broke into this house and took the TV and Jason's Xbox must have also taken the necklace."

"Likely story," Frank Healy growled and walked by me toward the island counter. "Now I know why Kingsley was so willing to meet us here this morning. Setting this meeting up for today gave you time to come over last night, steal the necklace, and make this mess. Well, you're not going to get away with it."

I saw him reach for the telephone. "You shouldn't use—" I started, once again thinking of the evidence Healy might be destroying.

He didn't listen. "I'm calling nine-one-one," he said, looking at me as if he expected me to object.

Jason stood in the living room, looking as if he might start crying. "Yesterday, when me and Aunt Ginny was here, I wanted to take my Xbox, but she said we had to hurry and that I could get it later. But now it's gone. Who took it?" He looked at me as if I could answer. "Who took the TV?"

"I don't know," I said. "Was anything else of yours missing upstairs?" I hoped Jean Healy understood that whatever had happened had occurred sometime between when she and her husband saw us at Brewster's house and now.

"Grandma thinks so." Eyes glistening with unshed tears, he looked up at his grandmother. "Right?"

"Right," she answered, her gaze locked on me.

I could hear Frank Healy talking to a dispatcher, giving the address and stating there'd been a robbery. As soon as he hung up, he punched the button on the answering machine.

"You have three messages," a scratchy, mechanical-sounding voice announced, giving me another reason why a gang wouldn't be interested in something so old. "First message received at . . ."

The first message would have come in on Monday, right after Ginny and Jason left the house. The caller didn't identify himself and the high level of static on the machine made the message difficult to understand. What I heard was: "Deposit made . . . waiting results."

The time on the second message was later Monday, and I could tell the caller was upset. All he said was, "I'm waiting, Brewster."

With the third message, the static was really bad, often overpowering the man's voice. What I did hear was, "What . . . pulling, Brew . . . ? If you think . . . money without . . . rhythm . . . another thing coming. I've . . . hold on . . . deposit. No algo . . . no money. Under . . . ? . . . Don't care who . . . out to kill you. I—"

The message ended with a beep, cutting off anything else the caller might have said.

"That sounds like someone threatened to kill Brewster," I said, remembering what the bald-headed man in the Escalade had said. "And now he's dead."

Frank Healy merely looked at me. "The police are coming."

Sure enough, I heard a siren in the distance, the sound coming closer. I also noticed Jean Healy had positioned herself between me and the front door, and Frank Healy was now moving over so his body blocked my view of the slider.

To keep me from escaping?

It sure seemed that way.

CHAPTER EIGHTEEN

I was surprised when two uniformed officers from the Kalamazoo County Sheriff's Department, not the Kalamazoo Department of Public Safety, came through the open front door, then I realized we were in Oshtemo township, not Kalamazoo city or township. It would be the sheriff's department—the same one Wade worked for—that would be called. The deputy who seemed to be in charge was a tall female with reddish-brown hair and freckles. Her partner was a shorter, younger-looking male with skin the color of dark chocolate. Both deputies had a hand poised over their holsters and a suspicious look on their faces.

"She took my daughter's diamond and sapphire necklace," Jean Healy stated, pointing at me. "Arrest her."

I shook my head and hoped the two deputies wouldn't jump to conclusions. The female looked at me and frowned. "You look familiar. Have we met before?"

"Maybe," I said, but I honestly didn't remember her. "I'm P.J. Benson. I'm friends with Deputy Wade Kingsley."

"Ah, Kingsley. That's it." She smiled. "I'm Deputy Sawyer, and this is Deputy Lewis." Deputy Sawyer turned her attention back to Jean Healy. "You say a necklace was stolen?"

"Yes. My daughter's. And now . . . Now . . ." She started crying, and Frank Healy took over.

"You'll have to excuse my wife," he said. "Our daughter is dead. This woman's so-called friend, Kingsley, killed her."

He glared at me as he went to his wife's side and led her to a chair that was still in one piece. He could glare all he wanted. I was more concerned with how Deputy Sawyer and Deputy Lewis were going to react to Healy calling Wade a murderer.

Sawyer merely gave a nod and glanced at Lewis. Neither said anything, and once Healy had his wife seated, he went on with his version of what happened Saturday. At one point I started to contradict Healy's distorted facts, but Deputy Sawyer stopped me with a raised hand and the slight shake of her head.

After that I wasn't as worried about what Sawyer or Lewis might think of Wade as I was about Jason's reaction. On the drive over, I'd talked to the boy about his mother and the explosion. I was concerned that we'd have a repeat of his behavior the day before, but Jason was calmer. He told me his dad didn't cause the explosion, that he couldn't have because they were busy lowering the anchor. He also told me his mother was in heaven watching over him. I think Wade told him that, and I remembered how my mother told me something similar when we were informed that my father was dead.

From what I could gather now, even though Frank Healy's voice dominated the room, was that Jason was telling his grandmother pretty much the same thing he'd told me . . . that his mother was in heaven. Jean Healy dabbed at her eyes and tried to smile. I felt sorry for her. The woman had lost her daughter, her only child. How would I feel in her place? Even though I'd just discovered I was pregnant, I already felt protective of the child growing within me.

"She knew exactly where the key to this house was," Frank Healy finished, once again pointing at me. "She's sleeping with my daughter's ex-husband. That gives her motive and opportunity."

"What motive?" I asked, angered by his accusation and confused by his reasoning.

"What motive?" he repeated, his voice rising. "Why, robbery. Vengeance. Just look at this place."

"I did not do this," I argued, facing Sawyer. "I didn't even know the man who owned this house. Why would I write something like that on the wall?" I pointed at the word, and then at the letters on the sliding glass door. "Or that?"

"Oh, such innocence," Jean Healy snarled, rising from her chair and glaring at me. "Don't let her fool you, Officer. Maybe she had no reason to put that on the wall, but *he* did."

She emphasized the word "he" and I assumed she meant Wade. I started to say something in his defense, but Jean Healy wasn't finished with her diatribe.

"Yesterday," she argued, "when we were at her place, we told her our daughter had a valuable piece of jewelry. Did she suggest coming over here right away to look for it? No. They told us to wait until today. They had plenty of time after we left to drive over here and do this."

"We did not come back here," I insisted, my own voice rising. "This is the first time I've even been *in* this house. And why would we paint words on the walls? Dump and break things?"

"To make it look like a robbery," Frank Healy growled, moving back to stand by his wife. "Kingsley would do that just to throw us off." He pointed at Sawyer. "Make you think vandals ransacked the place. And maybe *she* wasn't here, but that doesn't mean our ex-son-in-law wasn't. He could have come here last night."

"When was Deputy Kingsley in this house?" Deputy Sawyer asked, looking at me.

"I don't know," I said, "but not last night. Not since the accident, I'm sure of that."

"Accident!" Frank Healy sputtered. "That was no damn accident."

Much as I hated to agree with the man, I was beginning to

believe he was right. Especially after listening to the messages on the answering machine and remembering the comment made by the man in the black Escalade. "There are some messages on the answering machine," I said. "You should listen to them."

Deputy Sawyer looked at the phone and answering machine on the counter. "I was here Sunday, with the Van Buren Sheriff's Department's deputies," she said. "They checked the machine. The two most recent messages I heard were from Saturday morning, one wishing Mr. Brewster a safe trip, the other an unidentified man asking Brewster to call."

"The calls I heard," I said, "came Monday night and this morning, after you and the others were here."

She nodded. "I will check it out."

"They took my Xbox," Jason said, standing over where the TV once sat. "If Daddy took it, he would have given it to me."

Sawyer looked at the boy and nodded. "I remember seeing one when I was here. My son has one, too." Her gaze came back to us. "Okay, what did the four of you touch before we arrived?"

I answered first. "In these rooms just the phone, answering machine, and the chair Mrs. Healy was just in. I don't know about upstairs. I didn't go up there with them."

Sawyer pointed across the room. "Was that sliding door open when you arrived?"

"Yes," I said. "Exactly as it is now."

"Upstairs," Frank Healy said, taking over, "I looked in every room. Clothes, shoes, books . . . everything's been pulled out of the packing boxes up there, the walls have been spray-painted, and I won't go into what they did in the bathrooms."

"They were all yucky," Jason said, screwing up his nose. "Mama's gonna be really upset."

His grandmother looked down at him, and I saw a flicker of sadness cross her face before she looked back at Deputy Sawyer.

"I think they did it to cover up the fact that they took our daughter's necklace. I looked everywhere where Linda might have kept it. It's gone."

"So's Daddy Michael's big computer," Jason said, "But I found—"

Jason didn't have a chance to say what he found before his grandfather interrupted, but I saw what the boy had in his hand. A small thumb drive. No one else seemed to notice as Frank Healy grumbled, "What's it matter what we touched or took? Linda was our daughter. We have a right to be here. She's the one you need to arrest." He pointed at me. "Her and our daughter's ex-husband."

"I'll decide who needs to be arrested," Deputy Sawyer said, her expression daring him to argue. "And I think you'd better give me that, son," she said, pointing at Jason.

I realized then that she had seen the flash drive.

"But it might have some good games on it." Jason closed his fist and put his hand behind his back.

"I'll give it back," Deputy Sawyer promised. "Just as soon as I'm sure there's nothing important on it." She held out her hand. "Okay?"

Jason didn't move, and then he sighed and handed her the flash drive. "You promise?"

"I promise," she said and handed the flash drive to Deputy Lewis. "Now, everyone outside," she ordered and motioned toward the front door.

Jason and Jean Healy exited the house together, Jason's small hand encompassed in his grandmother's larger one. I followed them, and as I went out, I heard Deputy Sawyer call in and ask for a crime scene unit. Once she finished, she ushered Frank Healy out, leaving Deputy Lewis just inside the doorway.

The temperature had risen at least ten degrees during the short time we'd been in the house, the humidity on the verge of being oppressive. The dog days of August were upon us, and I wished I'd brought some bottled water. I had the feeling we were going to be here a long time.

Carol Dotson, the neighbor I'd met the day before, was standing next to the man I'd seen earlier through the kitchen window. Her husband, I presumed. He was now watering the flowers planted alongside their house, and the sight of that water made me realize that rather than wanting a drink, I needed to go to the bathroom . . . badly.

Carol waved when she saw me and shouted, "What's up?"

"The house was broken into last night," I called back. "These are Linda's parents." I motioned toward Jason's grandparents. "Mr. and Mrs. Healy, this is—"

"Oh we know who she is," Frank Healy grumbled and turned his back on us. Jean Healy gave a small nod and also turned away, taking Jason with her and walking closer to their car.

Their rudeness surprised me, but if the Healys' behavior bothered Carol, she didn't show it. She smiled and pointed to the man standing next to her. "This is my husband, Alan."

He turned slightly toward me, and I realized, for the first time, that he was missing his right hand, a hook where his palm and fingers should have been. Before I even thought to ask, Carol explained, walking toward me as she did. "It was an IED," she said in a normal tone of voice as she neared. "Over in Afghanistan. He's a Marine."

"My father was a Marine," I said automatically.

Although I didn't think I'd said it that loudly, Alan responded. "Once a Marine, always a Marine."

I shook my head. "In his case it's a was. He's dead."

"Still—" Carol said.

I knew she was trying to impress on me that alive or dead, once someone was in the Marine Corp he or she was considered a Marine; however, my father's past wasn't important at the moment. I had a more urgent problem. "Any chance I can use your bathroom?"

Carol hesitated and glanced over at her husband, then shrugged and smiled. "Of course."

CHAPTER NINETEEN

I told Deputy Sawyer where I was going. For a moment I thought she might object, but then she gave the okay. All she said was, "Stick around. I'm going to want to talk to each of you privately."

I also told Jason where I was going. I didn't want him worrying that I'd left him. But he didn't seem to care. He'd found one of his toy dump trucks in the dirt by the front steps—probably one Linda planned on leaving since it was badly rusted. Jason glanced up at me, nodded, and dumped another scoop of gravel into the truck's bed.

Carol led me inside through a door in the garage that opened to a short hallway. Immediately to my left was a small laundry area and just beyond that and across from the kitchen was a bathroom. I thanked her and entered the room, relieved that I only had to pee. A couple times in Brewster's house the smell and mess had made me feel like throwing up, but I'd managed to control the urge.

While washing my hands, I noticed three decorative glass bottles on the corner of the counter by the mirror. Although all three were close in height—give or take a couple inches—no two were alike. The tallest one had the widest neck and swirls of red and blue throughout the glass echoed the color scheme of the bathroom. That bottle was filled with dried rose petals. Next to it was a pale blue bottle, its slender neck twisted into a knot. As far as I could tell, it was empty.

It was the third bottle that fascinated me. I had to pick it up to make sure I was seeing what I thought I saw. Although the third bottle was shaped like a regular green wine bottle, this one had a bottle within itself, and the bottle on the inside was filled with what looked like marbles.

I came out of the bathroom holding that bottle. "Where did you get this?" I asked when I found Carol in the kitchen, pouring a dark-red liquid into the sink out of a similar green-tinted wine bottle.

"That?" She set the empty wine bottle down and faced me. "I made it."

"You made it?" I looked at the bottle again. "I've read about ships in bottles, how the ship is collapsed and slipped through the neck of the bottle and then—with the use of strings—pulled into shape, but how did you do this? You couldn't simply pull a string and have a bottle take shape, especially a bottle filled with marbles."

Carol grinned. "Look real carefully at the outside bottle. Run your finger over the surface."

I did as instructed, and I felt what she wanted me to feel; still, I was surprised. "You glued two half bottles together. Wow." The blending of the two sides was so smooth it was barely discernible.

"And the other bottles in the bathroom . . ." I asked. "You made those, too?"

"Yep." She motioned toward several more uniquely shaped and colored bottles on her kitchen counter. "I've been taking classes for two years now."

"Wow," I repeated. "I'd love to learn how to do this."

I carefully returned the bottle within the bottle to the bathroom. Back in her kitchen, I took time to look at the other bottles on her counter. No two were the same. Some had twisted necks, one had a handle that was part of the bottle, and one had a wide mouth and could be used as a vase. "You've made all of these?"

"Yep. My shrink suggested I take up a hobby, so I thought I'd try glass blowing. They give classes in Kalamazoo. I've been trying to get Alan to take a class, but he'd rather work in the vineyard."

She lowered her voice. "He hasn't completely mastered his mechanical hand, and he's broken three of the bottles I've made, which frustrates him . . . and me." She held up the bottle she'd just emptied. "So he probably should stick to the wine making."

"So you make your own wine, too?"

"We started last year." She snorted. "Ironically, Michael got Alan interested in trying it. Michael has made homemade wine for years. He used to give us a bottle at Christmas."

I remembered something Wade had said. "Brewster had a couple bottles of homemade wine with him when he got on the boat Saturday."

"Really?" Carol looked at the bottle in her hand and smiled. "Well, I hope his was better than ours. We've got to get new corks. That or label ours as vinegar."

"You said your husband likes to work in a vineyard." That had me confused. Their backyard certainly couldn't be considered a vineyard. "Where's that?"

"Over near Paw Paw. We bought ten acres. It's not a lot, but it gives Alan someplace quiet to go. Working with the grapes has helped with his PTSD." Again she lowered her voice. "All this commotion—the sheriff's cars, that dog Sunday, and now what's going on today—isn't good for him. What happened over there, anyway?"

"Someone broke into the house between when I met you yesterday and this morning. It's a mess. You didn't see anything? Hear anything?"

She shook her head and set the empty bottle back on the

counter. "We were gone most of yesterday afternoon and into the night. As I said, all this commotion has been bothering Alan. He had another episode, and I had to take him over to Battle Creek to the VA hospital, which, of course, means hurry up and wait. We didn't get back here until quite late. You say the house was broken into. Was anything stolen?"

"A TV, an Xbox, and some video games for sure. And Mrs. Healy can't find her daughter's diamond and sapphire necklace. She's sure I took it." I laughed. "As if I'd have any place to wear a necklace like that."

"You could always sell it. Put it on Craigslist or eBay."

I hoped she didn't think I had taken the necklace.

Before I could protest, she added, "Another place, two blocks over, was broken into last week. From what I've heard, they think it might be a gang of teenagers who did that."

"There were some letters painted on the sliding glass door that looked like gang signs and the word 'bastard' was on one wall."

"Fitting," she said. "He was one."

"You mean Brewster?" That surprised me. "Why do you say that?"

"Because he . . ."

She didn't go on, and I waited, surprised by the tension I saw in her face. Slowly her jaw softened and she smiled.

"Sorry," she said. "Personally, I think the guy is—was—a bastard, but my shrink says I need to let go of the past. And I think he's right. All is good now. Afghanistan is behind us, and Michael may have called Alan a wimp, said post-traumatic stress disorder was just an excuse not to work, and laughed when I told him how making these bottles was helping me cope, but we are alive and he's dead. All is good."

She looked me in the eyes. "Right?"

"Right," I said, not sure what I was agreeing to. That Michael

Brewster was dead and that was good? Or that Michael Brewster could no longer insult Carol and her husband? Whichever, I decided it was time for me to leave.

"Thanks again for letting me use your bathroom," I said. "I love the bottles you've made. Would you be willing to sell one?" I pointed at the wide-mouthed one on her counter. "Maybe that one?"

"That one has a flaw, but I could make you one like it. Or you should give it a try yourself. The West Michigan Glass Art Center is right downtown. They offer lots of classes."

"I might do that some time."

As she walked with me out of her house, she asked what color I would want my wine-bottle vase and what size. We also decided on a price, and I gave her my phone number. The moment we stepped out of her air conditioning, I felt as if I'd walked into a steam room. "Rain's coming," Carol said, glancing up at the sky.

"I hope it cools things down." I could already feel a prickling of perspiration along my hairline.

"It will," she said with an assurance that surprised me. I glanced her way and she grinned. "At least I hope it will. Looks like you've attracted a crowd."

I quickly saw what she meant. A crime scene van had arrived while Carol and I were inside, and a number of neighbors had come out of their houses and gathered near Brewster's yard. Even a few cars had stopped and parked along the side of the street.

I looked for one car and one man in particular and wondered if Carol had ever seen either around. "I think Brewster owed someone money," I said. "Maybe from gambling. Have you seen a black Cadillac or a short, bald-headed man with wide shoulders around here?"

She shook her head. "I haven't seen anyone like that, but the kid—Jason—he told me Michael liked to play cards on the computer. I thought he meant solitaire, but maybe Michael was gambling online."

"We have Brewster's laptop," I said, remembering the one Jason had picked up yesterday. "Jason's been playing some sort of game on it."

"He's a nice kid. I was glad to hear he wasn't hurt." Her gaze switched to Deputy Sawyer. "Have they figured out what caused that boat to explode?"

"I don't think so, and speaking of Jason," I said, looking around for the boy. "I need to find him. I don't trust his grandparents, and Wade would never forgive me if I let them take his son."

CHAPTER TWENTY

I couldn't see Jason, but the Healy's Buick was still parked in front of Brewster's house, so I wasn't overly worried. And once I could see past the sheriff's car parked on Brewster's driveway, I spotted Jean and Frank Healy. They were standing on the lawn by the For Sale sign talking to Deputies Sawyer and Lewis. Jason sat by his grandmother's feet, pulling up tufts of grass. I was about to join them when a man standing next to a silver BMW sports car called me over.

He looked to be in his early to mid-thirties and was wearing khaki slacks, a blue-and-white striped, short-sleeved dress shirt open at the collar, and black loafers. Something about his appearance—mostly his concerned expression—captured my curiosity, and I detoured his way.

As I neared, I noticed a shimmer of sweat on his forehead and caught a whiff of his cologne or after-shave. The cloying sweet scent didn't set well with my stomach, and I stopped a few feet back.

"You the neighbor?" he asked.

"No. She's back there." I pointed at Carol's house.

He nodded and then looked back toward Brewster's house, where yellow police tape now blocked the entrance. "Well, do you know why they're here?"

"The place was robbed last night."

"Robbed?" He swallowed hard, his eyes widening. "What was taken?"

His reaction had me curious. "Did you know Brewster?"

"Know him?" He blinked and let out a breath. "I'm sorry, I should have introduced myself. I'm Steve Richardson. I work . . . worked with Mike. And you're . . . ?"

"P.J. Benson," I said, quickly adding, "Just the initials."

"P.J.," he repeated and extended his right hand. "Did you know Mike?"

"No." I noticed his palm was sweaty, but I wasn't sure if that could be blamed on the heat or on his nervous behavior. Even as we shook hands, his gaze flitted back to Brewster's house. I finally asked, "Is there a problem, Mr. Richardson?"

"No. Yes." He looked down at the ground and then back up and gave one more sigh. "Last Friday Mike took something of mine. I need to get into his house and see if it's there."

"What did he take?" I figured I might have seen it while I was in the house and could at least let him know if it was there.

"A, ah . . ." He hesitated before adding, "Just something important."

His behavior added to my curiosity. "What kind of 'something important'?"

Richardson totally ignored my question, his eyes widening again as he looked back at the house. "What are they taking out? What did they find?"

I also looked that direction. A woman was walking toward the crime scene van carrying two paper bags. "I don't know. Evidence, I suppose."

"Will they take his computer? His flash drives?"

"From what I've heard, the Van Buren Sheriff's Department has his computer," I said. "I've got his laptop, and Deputy Sawyer . . ." I motioned her way. "Has a flash drive Jason found today."

"You have Mike's laptop?" Richardson gave me a strange look. "He gave it to you? When?"

"No, Mr. Brewster didn't give it to me." I tried to think of the best way to explain. "Monday, Brewster's stepson—Jason—brought a laptop to my place. He's been playing games on it."

Explaining the situation made me realize one thing. "I need to tell Deputy Sawyer I have it. If she wanted the flash drive, she'll probably want the laptop, too."

"Did you find anything on it?" Richardson asked. "Anything besides games? Any . . ." He hesitated, as if groping for the right word. Finally, he said, "Any files named *Bonanza*?"

"I haven't looked at what's on it," I admitted. "I just know Jason has some games he plays."

"And you said the deputy has Mike's flash drive?"

"Yes. Jason gave it to her." I pointed at Deputy Sawyer. "Why don't you come with me and talk to her? Tell her what you're looking for. I'm sure she'll—"

"No . . . No, that's all right." He held a hand up in a "stop" position and stepped back, closer to the BMW. "Later. Maybe later."

I would have asked him why he was acting so edgy, but just then I heard Jason yelling my name. The moment I looked for Jason, I didn't care why Richardson was nervous or what he was looking for. I had a bigger problem. Jean Healy was heading for the Buick . . . and she had Jason with her.

"Hey!" I yelled. "Where are you taking him?"

Jason's grandmother ignored my question. Holding her grandson's hand, she kept moving toward her car. "Frank!" she called to her husband. "It's time for us to go."

"Oh no you don't," I said and raced to position myself between the Buick and Jason and his grandmother. "He is not going with you."

"He's my grandson," Jean Healy said firmly, but she did stop where she was.

"And his father asked me to watch him today until he could get here."

"His father is a murderer," Frank Healy growled as he marched by his wife, heading straight for me.

"No he is not." I was afraid the man was going to run right into me if I didn't do something fast. Hitting him was not an alternative. I don't hit people, especially elderly people, and Healy was a large man, who probably wouldn't even notice if I punched him. I also wasn't going to step aside and let the two put Jason in their car. "Deputy Sawyer!" I shouted. "Don't let them take this boy."

"Mr. Healy," Deputy Sawyer responded, stepping toward the four of us.

Healy ignored her, shoved me aside, and reached for the back door handle.

I struggled to keep my balance and not end up on the lawn or in the gutter. I did see Deputy Sawyer put her hand on the weapon at her side, and there was no ignoring the threat in her voice when she yelled, "Mr. Healy, do not open that door."

Hand still on the handle, he looked back at her. "This is my grandson."

"He does not have custody," I said, once again ready to take on Healy. "Wade is Jason's father."

"And he killed my daughter," Jean Healy said, her voice cracking as she pulled Jason even closer to her side.

"No he didn't," Jason shouted, wiggling out of his grandmother's grasp and moving away from both of his grandparents, the Buick, and me. "My daddy said he didn't. Ask Mama. She's in heaven. She's watching me, and she knows everything we say." He looked my way. "Right, P.J.?"

"I'm sure you're right," I agreed and waited to see what would happen next.

"Where is Sergeant Kingsley?" Deputy Sawyer asked, looking

at me for an answer.

"He's at the Van Buren County Sheriff's office."

"No he's not!" Jason shouted and pointed down the street past me.

I looked the direction he indicated, at first confused by Jason's assertion. A white sedan was heading our way, not Wade's tan Jeep. Then I remembered his Jeep had been impounded, and Wade was now driving a rental. Jason had recognized it, even as it slowly moved toward us, pausing here and there to allow the people standing in the street to move out of the way. After going around the crime scene van and the Healys' Buick, it pulled in directly behind my Chevy.

"Daddy!" Jason yelled and ran toward the car.

"Looks like he's here," I said, looking at Deputy Sawyer, but aware of the Healys. Once again, they'd lost their chance to take Jason.

Wade lifted his son up with a hug and carried him over to my side. I wanted to smirk at Jean Healy; however, a part of me did empathize with how she must feel, so I didn't. Instead, I said to Wade, "Your timing was perfect."

"What's going on?" His gaze moved swiftly from Deputies Sawyer and Lewis to the yellow crime scene tape across the open door of Michael Brewster's home, and then to Linda's parents, before coming back to me.

I answered. "The house was broken into sometime after your sister and Jason were in it yesterday."

"They took the TV and my Xbox," Jason added, pointing at the house. "And all my games."

"Linda's necklace is missing," Frank Healy stated, his tone accusing.

"That necklace has been in my family for two generations," Jean Healy added, moving over to stand beside her husband. "You have no right to it."

"You're talking about her diamond and sapphire necklace?" Wade again looked at the house. "You're sure it's not in a safe in there?"

"If there's a safe, we didn't find one." Frank Healy looked at his wife. "Did we?"

"We looked everywhere," she said, speaking to Deputy Sawyer.

"Maybe Linda kept the necklace in a bank box," Wade suggested.

Jean Healy shook her head. "No, Linda told me she wanted people to see the necklace, that it would be a crime to hide it."

Frank Healy snorted, and I knew what he was thinking . . . the crime was *not* hiding it. "Was she wearing it Saturday?" I asked.

Wade answered immediately. "No, I would have remembered that. She used to flaunt the value of that necklace. Used it as an example of what I couldn't afford to give her. When we got divorced, I told her never to wear that damn thing around me."

"What about her purse?" I asked. "Would she have brought the necklace on the boat in her purse?"

Again Wade answered before either of the Healys had a chance to say anything. "She left her purse in Brewster's car, didn't take it on the boat. And as you know, the Van Buren Sheriff's Department now has Brewster's car and everything in it, including Linda's purse."

He set Jason back down and walked over to the two deputies. "How are you doing, Lisa? I haven't seen you since you started working over on this side of the county." To Deputy Lewis he nodded and extended a hand. "And I don't believe we've been formally introduced. I'm Deputy Sergeant Wade Kingsley."

As Lewis nodded and shook Wade's hand, I felt Jason bump against my side. When I looked down, he grinned and reached for my hand. I knew the gesture must gall his grandmother, but it pleased me. In the four months I've known Wade, I haven't had much contact with Jason, but I've always enjoyed the time we have had together, and I hoped he felt the same way.

"I heard you were on suspension, Sergeant," Deputy Sawyer said, giving Wade a quizzical look. "Has the sheriff lifted that?"

Wade shook his head. "No. I'm afraid I'm still a 'person of interest.' "

"Then I probably shouldn't tell you anything," Sawyer said, but she smiled and began briefing Wade on what they'd found when they arrived in response to the nine-one-one call Frank Healy made. Deputy Lewis added a comment now and then, and both Frank and Jean Healy forcefully reiterated their accusations that either I or Wade or Wade's sister must have taken their daughter's necklace. They even suggested we might have taken the TV to make it look like someone else had robbed the place.

"The only items I have from here," I said just as loudly and firmly, "are some of Jason's clothes, a few toys, and a laptop." Not that I thought Linda's parents would believe me.

Jason pulled on my arm and motioned for me to lean down. "You won't have to keep my things for long," he whispered near my ear. "If I'm really, really good, Mama will come back."

"Oh, I don't think so, honey," I said, afraid it would be worse to give him false hope.

"Yes, she will." His little chin jutted out. "I know she will. I just have to be very, very good."

I had no idea where he'd gotten that idea. I was sure Wade hadn't told him being good would bring Linda back. "Where did you hear that?"

"Grandma." Jason looked over at Jean Healy. "She said I had to be really, really good. If I was, I'd make Mama happy, and everything would be all right."

Not exactly the same as saying being good would bring his

mother back, but I recognized how Jason's reasoning fit the normal stages of grief. Yesterday he'd been in total denial, then very angry. Now he'd come up with a bargain that would bring his mother back. How did you explain death to a child? I, myself, found it difficult to understand how one moment someone could be alive and the next gone, forever.

"What are you telling my grandson?"

Jean Healy's angry shout startled me, and I stared at her for a second before mumbling, "Nothing."

"We're not the bad guys," she insisted. "We just want what's best for him."

Her best, not mine, I supposed. Her use of the term "bad guys" did remind me of one thing. "Wade, there's a message on the answering machine," I said, straightening and raising my voice so Wade and the two deputies could hear me. "Several messages, in fact. I think Brewster was supposed to deliver something for a lot of money, but he didn't deliver it, and by the third message, the caller was getting really angry."

"Any idea what he was to deliver?" Wade asked.

"Something about an allegory . . . or something like that. That man—" I turned so I was facing where I'd last seen Brewster's coworker.

He was gone and so was the silver BMW.

"There was a man here." I looked back at Wade and the deputies. "He said his name was Steve Richardson, that he worked with Michael Brewster, and that Brewster had taken something from him. Maybe it was whatever Brewster was supposed to deliver."

"But he didn't say what it was?" Wade responded.

"No. But listen to those messages. It sure sounds like Brewster was doing something pretty . . . strange. Maybe even illegal."

CHAPTER TWENTY-ONE

Deputy Sawyer couldn't go back into the house and check that answering machine until after the crime scene investigators told her it was okay, so while we waited, she took me aside and questioned me regarding my whereabouts from the day the Healys' daughter went out on Wade's boat until today. Jason was also questioned, then Wade. I'm sure Officer Sawyer was looking for any discrepancies in our stories—or explanations that sounded scripted. Since I knew I was innocent, I wasn't worried, but maybe I should have been. Frank and Jean Healy certainly didn't believe anything I said.

While Deputy Sawyer questioned us, Deputy Lewis questioned the Dotsons and then several of the other neighbors. From what I could gather, no one had seen any unusual activity at the house between Ginny's visit yesterday and our arrival today. When one of the crime scene investigators came out, Deputy Sawyer went over and spoke to him. The two of them went back inside the house together. A few minutes later she came out and called Wade over. Together they went inside.

"What's going on?" Jean Healy asked, frowning as she moved closer to where I was standing. "Did they find the necklace?"

"I think they're listening to that answering machine," I said. "If Linda's husband took something, maybe that's why the boat blew up."

Frank Healy snorted at the idea, and Jean Healy turned away from me and walked back to his side.

"I'm hungry," Jason said, looking up at me. "I want a hamburger."

A hamburger sounded good to me, too, but I knew we couldn't leave, not yet. "Wait until your dad comes back out. Then we can see about getting something to eat. Okay?"

Jason faced the house. "When's he gonna come out? I don't want to be here anymore."

"I don't either," I mumbled, tired of all the questions, of the heat, and of the Healys' accusations.

"I'm thirsty."

"Do you want a drink from the hose?" I could see one attached to a faucet near the front door.

"No." Jason sank down on the grass near my feet. "I wanna go home. I want my mama."

"Oh, you poor baby," Jean Healy said, swooping back and reaching down for him. "You poor, poor, baby."

"No." He batted her arms away, slapping her in the process. "I am not a baby."

"Jason!" I scolded. I could understand how his mother's death had his emotions in a turmoil, but I also felt sorry for his grandmother. She was only trying to comfort him.

"And you're not my mama," he yelled, scrambling to his feet and running away from both of us.

"Jason!" Wade called, coming out of the house.

Jason stopped his forward motion, stared at his father for a moment, and then ran to him.

I watched Wade scoop his son up in his arms. Jason said something, his words muffled, and Wade responded, his voice low, the words for the boy alone. I stayed where I was, Jean Healy nearby. She rubbed the spot on her arm that Jason had hit. "I hope," she said softly, her voice shaky, "for his sake that he didn't kill her."

"I'm sure he didn't," I said.

Jean Healy looked at me as if she'd forgotten I was there, scowled, and walked back to her husband's side.

"Jason and I are going out for a hamburger," Wade said, coming toward me, Jason still in his arms. "Then we're going to my house. They've released it, and I have a feeling it's going to be a mess. I'll give you a call this afternoon. Okay?"

Okay? What could I say? *No, you have to come back to my place.* Or maybe, *Why can't I come with you?*

More than needing to clean his house, I knew he needed some time with his son. But darn it, I also needed some time with Wade. I needed to be told being pregnant was all right, that it wasn't my fault, that he loved me, and we would get married and have this baby . . . and that I wouldn't go crazy.

"I have a headache," he said.

"Again? Still?" I wasn't sure if it was an excuse or something I should be worried about. After all, less than three days ago he'd been in the hospital with a concussion. "Do you feel dizzy? Nauseous?"

"No. I'm okay. Probably just tension." He leaned close and kissed me on my forehead. "I'll call."

It sounded like a brush-off. I swallowed hard against the lump in my throat.

Since I was already in Kalamazoo, I decided to go see my mom and grandmother. Mom was sitting on the front porch, smoking. In the last two months, she'd put on some weight. I'd mentioned it to Grandma who told me she thought it was a side effect of the pills Mom had been taking for her schizophrenia. Since the pills seemed to be helping my mother cope with reality and keep a job, I figured a little weight gain wasn't a bad thing. It was nice to have a mother I could actually talk to.

Today she had a faraway look in her eyes, and when I said hi, she startled. "Oh, Priscilla Jayne, what are you doing here?"

I hate it when she calls me by my birth name, it always reminds me of the teasing I went through in school. Kids can be so mean. It took them no time at all to change Priscilla to Prissy. "Missy Prissy is having a hissy." Once I was old enough, I legally changed my name to P.J., but Mom has never accepted that . . . or she simply doesn't remember.

"I was in town and thought I'd stop by," I said, not wanting to go into detail about the boat explosion or the apparent robbery at Brewster's house. "You're not working today?"

"I called in sick. Couldn't sleep last night." She took a drag on her cigarette and let the smoke out slowly, all the while looking at me almost as if she couldn't figure out who I was.

"Grandma here?" I asked, thinking I needed to see what she thought about Mom's behavior.

My mother nodded and then smiled. "I understand you're a little pregnant."

So Grandma told her. I didn't bother to mention that one was never "a little" pregnant. I simply nodded back.

Mom looked away, facing the street and the house across the way. "Your father's dead, isn't he?"

Her question took me by surprise. I thought we'd cleared this up back in April. Nevertheless, I answered the question. "He's dead."

"I dreamed about him last night. He said he was sorry for getting me pregnant." Her gaze came back to my face. "Do you see things?"

I saw a woman I loved, even when she was accusing me of stealing her things, or yelling at me, or cowering in a corner. There were times when I was growing up that I'd been afraid of her, and other times when I'd wanted to hug her close and protect her. What really frightened me was I saw what I might become.

"I don't think so," I said, knowing she was asking if I saw

things that weren't really there.

"Does he want the baby?"

"I'm not sure."

"If you go crazy, he'll leave you."

I knew Mom was thinking of my father. He joined the Marines so he could escape my mother. He disappeared from our lives.

Would Wade do that?

"I hope not," I said aloud.

Mom stubbed out her cigarette. "Ben said he no longer wants to see me."

"Oh, Mom, I'm sorry." I scooted closer and slid an arm around her shoulders. She'd been seeing a man named Ben for over two months. I thought they were getting along fine. "What happened?"

"I don't know." She pushed my arm away and picked up the pack of cigarettes beside her on the step. Her gaze on the pack, she tapped out another cigarette. "Why did he blow up his boat?"

It took me a moment to realize she'd jumped back to Wade. Flip-flopping from one topic to another was a symptom of schizophrenia. So was her chain smoking.

"He didn't blow up his boat."

"Paper said they're investigating it as a crime." She lit the cigarette, took a puff, and then asked, "If he didn't do it, who did?"

I shook my head. "I wish I knew."

"Who had a motive?"

Good question, I thought. A logical question. "There was a message on Brewster's answering machine that made it sound like he was in trouble. I think he owed money to someone. Lots of money."

"You know who this someone is?"

I said no, but then immediately thought of the bald-headed man I'd met in the hospital and again outside of Brewster's house. I corrected my response. "Maybe. There is a guy that I've met twice. Both times he was looking for Brewster. He even said something that sounded like some of his men might have killed Brewster."

"So there's your killer."

I wished it were that easy. "There's another possibility. Brewster was supposed to send something to someone. The message on the answering machine wasn't real clear, but I think it might be something he took from where he used to work. A guy I met today was looking for whatever it was, and he wouldn't talk to the deputies about it. Maybe he's the one who caused the explosion."

"And the plot thickens." Mom blew out a smoke ring.

"You can also add that someone broke into Brewster's house last night. They took the TV, an Xbox, some video games, and maybe a valuable necklace." I wasn't sure how that connected to anything, but my mother might see a connection.

"I think Ben likes someone else," Mom said.

"Ben? Oh, Ben." So much for connections. She'd switched topics again. "That's too bad." I wasn't sure what else to say.

"He thinks you should have this baby."

"Ben does?"

Mom looked at me as if I were daft. "No. Your father."

"Oh." I rose to my feet. "I think I'll go find Grandma." I needed to talk to someone who made sense.

I thought the smell of stale coffee and cigarettes would trigger my nausea, but I made it to the kitchen without any ill effects. Grandma was fixing sandwiches. She looked up and smiled as I entered the room. "I thought I heard your voice," she said. "Want a sandwich?"

"No, thanks." Although I was hungry, as long as my stomach

was staying calm, I wasn't going to chance upsetting it by eating one of Grandma's sandwiches. Her philosophy is if a little mayonnaise is good, a lot is better, and that's after buttering the bread. I don't see how she stays so thin. "Is Mom all right?"

Grandma put down the knife she was using to cut the sandwiches in half. "So you noticed."

"She's talking about Dad again, said he wants me to have the baby."

"He probably would. How are you feeling?"

"Better than I was yesterday. The lemon trick and soda crackers seem to be helping."

"Have you made an appointment with a doctor?"

"Not yet. I haven't had time." I could have lamented about all my time being taken up watching Jason and worrying about Wade, but I didn't want to talk about myself. "Is Mom still taking her medicine?"

"I'm not sure." Grandma sighed. "Damn that Ben. Evidently he made some comment about her weight gain last week, and then Sunday, while they were at the Rib Fest, he must have said something more. She came home in a huff, said she's sure he's seeing someone else, and that he could go to hell. I watched her take a pill this morning, but then she went into the bathroom right away, and I heard the toilet flush. My bet is she spit the pill out." She shook her head. "I don't know what to do, P.J. I'm not going to be around forever to watch over her."

"I'll take care of her," I said, though I wasn't sure how. "You've done more than enough."

"No, I know you don't like the smoking or living in the city, and you're going to have enough to take care of once your baby arrives. And we don't know if . . ."

She trailed off, but I knew what that "if" was. If I also became a schizophrenic, I wouldn't be able to take care of Mom. I might not even be able to take care of myself, much less a baby.

The thought caused a tightness in my chest.

"I'm taking your mother to see a social worker this afternoon," Grandma continued before I had a chance to say anything. "I'm hoping we can get your mom into a group home where her behavior and medications will be monitored, but she'll still have her freedom."

"Have you told Mom about this?" I had a feeling she wasn't going to like the idea.

"Not yet. We'll see how things go this afternoon." Grandma looked back at the sandwiches on the counter. "You're sure you don't want anything?"

"No, I need to get back home. I left Baraka in his crate. He chewed up one of Jason's books this morning."

"How's the boy doing?" Grandma asked. "How's he taking his mother's death?"

"I feel sorry for him." I really did. "He thinks if he's good his mother will come back." I remembered one other thing. "Oh, and he found a map yesterday. He was up in Dad's old room, and he found a drawing of what looks like the woods behind the house. There's an X on one spot. Jason thinks there's buried treasurer there. I think it might be where Dad buried Nora's baby."

I knew Grandma would understand the importance of this map. She was with me when Nora told us about the baby. Not knowing where my dad buried the fetus was driving Nora crazy.

"You haven't checked it out?"

"Jason was headed that way when Wade showed up. Since that time, I haven't had a chance to look." I shrugged. "And you know it's not going to be easy to find that location. Once off the main path—"

"Walking is almost impossible," she finished for me. "So are the three of you going to look this afternoon?"

I scoffed. "Wade's taken Jason home with him, and I have no

idea when I'll see him again."

"You told him about the baby?"

The way Grandma asked the question, I knew she understood my concern. "I told him, and I'm not sure how he feels about it. Right now he's afraid he's going to be accused of murdering his ex and her husband, and I'm afraid he might be right."

"They're sure it wasn't an accident?"

"They're certainly not treating it as one."

"Could someone with a grudge against Wade have caused the explosion?"

"I suppose so." Wade didn't say much about the arrests he'd made, but I was sure some of those people weren't happy about being put in jail. But were they upset enough to try to kill Wade? "Actually, I'm starting to think Michael Brewster was the target. He wasn't the good guy we thought he was."

The way Grandma's eyebrows lifted, I knew I had to explain, so I repeated my list of suspects. Mom came into the house just as I finished naming those men who might want Michael Brewster dead. "You never know a person's true character," she said as she headed for the coffee pot. "Sometimes the one who looks the least guilty is the one who did it."

I had to agree with her. Last June I was nearly killed by a person I never would have suspected. In this case, however, I had no idea who might look the least guilty. For me, it would be Wade, but I know he would never kill Linda. Even though he didn't want her taking Jason away, he wouldn't resort to murder.

Would he?

I shook my head at the thought.

Who else might seem innocent? Her parents?

Again I shook my head.

No, it had to be someone Michael Brewster knew. Someone he'd cheated or robbed. Someone who hated him and wanted him dead.

"It had to be Ben," Mom said. "Ben did it. My sandwich ready?"

"Ready," Grandma said and gave me a wink before placing one of the sandwiches on a paper plate for Mom.

I smiled and nodded. As far as I knew, Mom's ex-boyfriend didn't even know Michael Brewster, much less have a reason to kill him.

CHAPTER TWENTY-TWO

I planned on spending the afternoon working. I do have clients who depend on me to do their payrolls, and a hair salon that just opened in Zenith asked me to look over their financial plan. I also needed to call our family doctor for an appointment, and I wanted to take that map Jason found and see if I could locate the spot where my father had placed an X. That was, if my father had made the map.

As soon as I arrived home, I let Baraka out of his crate and sent him outside to pee. I knew I should eat something, but I no longer felt hungry, and it seemed so nice not to be throwing up, that I didn't want to chance food upsetting my stomach again. While Baraka did his business, I sat down on the couch . . .

And that was the last I remembered until I woke with a start at the sound of Baraka barking.

For a moment I didn't know where I was or what day it was. In a daze, I stood and looked out the window. Baraka was on the front porch, facing the east edge of the house. The hairs on his back and neck were raised, his body rigid.

I stumbled toward the front door, banging into the edge of my dining room table in the process. A sharp pain in my left hip made me pause and grimace. One more bruise to add to my body. In the last few months I'd acquired many bruises, some from roughhousing with my energetic Ridgeback, others from getting involved with people who considered physical force the best way to get what they wanted.

Again Baraka barked, the panicky pitch expressing fear rather than aggression. Unsure what to expect, I slowly pushed open the screen door and looked the direction he was facing. Something landed on my face, and I squealed and quickly brushed it off. Behind me a robotic voice said, "Come play. Come play."

I felt something crawling on my arm, and looked down to see a brownish-black bug about a half-inch in length crawling toward my shoulder. Reddish-orange lines outlined its wings. Its red eyes glowed.

I brushed it off and stepped back into the house, letting the screen door slam closed.

Another bug flew by my face.

Landed in my hair.

Panicking, I wildly brushed my hands back and forth over my curls. Retreated. Bumped into the table again.

"Come play. Come play," the voice behind me repeated.

I screamed.

Bugs were everywhere. Flying by my face. Landing on the walls. On the table. Crawling up the outside of the screen door, heading toward the space at the top where the door and frame didn't exactly meet. Dozens of them, their brownish-black undersides striped with red lines, six spindly legs and two long antennae extending out from their oval bodies.

I grabbed a salt shaker and began slamming it down on the bugs on the table, then wished I hadn't as a pungent smell made my stomach turn.

"P.J.?" I heard a man call.

Startled, I spun back toward the door. I recognized that voice. It belonged to my neighbor.

But I saw no one.

Had I imagined it?

Cautiously I stepped closer to the screen door. "Howard?"

Baraka stopped barking and went bounding off the porch. I still didn't see anyone, but when a black and tan coon hound ran into the yard, the two dogs circling each other, sniffing butts, and then romping toward the side of the house and out of sight, I sighed. If Jake was here, Howard was real.

Howard Lowe came into view a second later. "You okay?" he asked as he neared my porch.

"I don't know," I said and pointed at the screen door. "Do you see bugs on this door?"

"I certainly do." He came up the steps, and with his hand he began swishing off the ones on the screen. "Boxelders," he said. "They usually start showing up in August, but normally not until it's a little colder." He flicked the last of the bugs off and opened the door. "Maybe they know something we don't."

As usual Howard was wearing bib overalls and scuffed and worn hunting boots. But today he didn't have a shirt on, and even though he's in his sixties, I could see well-developed chest and arm muscles. That surprised me. I hadn't realized how physically fit he'd kept himself. I also noticed a long white scar that ran under the left strap of his overalls. Whether that came from his years in Special Forces or after he returned state side, I didn't know, but it looked nasty.

"I was pretty sure they were real," I lied. "I was able to squish the ones that landed on the table, and I could feel the one crawling on my arm, but . . . ?" I paused, not sure how to ask my next question. "What about a voice? Do you hear a voice?"

Howard's bushy eyebrows came together. "What sort of voice?"

"Sort of, I don't know, a mechanical voice. Computerized. It keeps saying 'Come play.' "

"Do you hear it now?"

I listened and then shook my head.

"Computerized?" He looked over at my dining room table. "Could it be coming from that?"

The moment I saw what Howard was pointing at, I felt stupid. The laptop Jason had brought back from Michael Brewster's house lay with its lid almost closed. Jason had been sitting there, playing a game on the computer before we left to meet his grandparents at Brewster's house. At the time I hadn't been paying much attention to what he was doing, but now that I wasn't in a panic—didn't think I was going crazy—I did remember hearing something that might have been "Come play."

I went over and lifted the cover, and once again the voice called out, "Come play," and the graphic for a game activated.

"It was his game," I said, relieved and embarrassed at the same time.

"What did you think it was?" Howard asked as he came over and lifted something out of my curls.

I didn't want to tell him I thought I was hearing things, so I pointed at the boxelder bug he'd just removed from my hair. "Do these bite?"

"As a rule, no. They're just pests. They want to get somewhere warm for the winter. Didn't you have them when you lived in Kalamazoo?"

"Maybe. I don't know. Not like this." I pointed at the screen door. Once again it was covered with at least a dozen of the bugs. "Are they going to be like those ladybugs we had last spring?"

"They can be a nuisance." Harold went over and tapped the screen, scattering them, then he cracked open the door and released the one he'd taken from my hair. I laughed, and he turned back toward me, frowning as he pulled the screen door shut. "What's so funny?"

"You're really a softy at heart, aren't you?"

He harrumphed. "So what had you all panicky?"

"Baraka was barking at something."

"Probably me and Jake. I might have been teasing your dog a bit." He adopted a look of innocence. "Just trying to get him so he'd pay more attention to who was around. He sure didn't bark at that fancy car that pulled into your drive a while ago."

"A car pulled in here?" I looked toward my driveway. There was no car there. "When?"

"Maybe ten, fifteen minutes ago. A silver sports car. You didn't see it?"

"I was asleep." I tried to think of anyone I knew who drove a silver sports car.

"Then why did you sound so panicky when I arrived?"

I swallowed and looked down before I answered. "The bugs. The voice."

"Think you were going crazy?"

He'd put into words what I didn't want to admit. I nodded.

"Well, I've always thought you were a little crazy, moving out here, stopping me from hunting those woods of yours, and getting yourself all involved with murders. Any reason why you'd be crazier now?"

I figured I might as well admit it. "I'm pregnant, and it was when my mother got pregnant with me that she started seeing and hearing things."

"Pregnant, huh?" Howard grinned. "I'm assuming it's the sergeant's. He gonna marry you?"

Why did everyone have to ask that question? "I don't know. He's got problems of his own right now."

"They still fingering him for that explosion?"

"I think so. He doesn't tell me a lot, but they keep wanting to talk to him."

Howard hesitated a moment before he said, "Want me to see what I can find out?"

I wasn't quite sure what he meant. "Do you think that group

you belong to—the CROWS—would know something?" I didn't believe the boat explosion had anything to do with wayward biotechnology, but maybe I was wrong.

"No, they wouldn't know anything, but I do have other connections." He winked. "And if you sort of said it was okay for me to hunt those woods of yours, I might do a little asking around."

I understood what he was saying. And for a moment I considered giving him permission to hunt in those woods— anything to help Wade—but then I reconsidered and shook my head.

"Oh well." He grunted. "It was worth a try. Why don't you tell me what you know so far."

CHAPTER TWENTY-THREE

As I told Howard about the two men I'd met who seemed upset with Brewster, I remembered that Steve, Brewster's coworker, did drive a silver BMW sports car. Had he come to my house? If so, why? And how did he discover where I lived?

"Besides those two men," I added, "There were some messages on Brewster's answering machine. The caller evidently didn't know Brewster was dead, and it sure sounded like Brewster was involved in something illegal."

Howard said he'd see what he could learn.

I also showed him the map Jason had found in my father's old room, and I made a copy for him. As often as Howard's in my woods—which he swears is only because Jake slips his collar and heads that direction—he might find the spot marked by the X faster than I would.

As Howard was about to leave, he tapped my screen door, sending dozens of those boxelder bugs flying. "You have an empty spray bottle?" he asked, looking back at me. "The kind you can find in dollar stores or markets?"

"No." I'd never had a need for one.

"Buy one," he said. "Put about a quarter cup of dish soap in it and fill the rest with water. Then spray that mixture on your screen, around the door and your windows. That'll keep the bugs away."

"Dish soap?"

He shrugged. "Don't know why it works, but it does."

He left then, taking his dog with him. I let Baraka back in the house. One thing I noticed when I stepped outside was the wind had picked up and the temperature had dropped at least ten degrees. Maybe those boxelder bugs clinging to my screen door and the side of my house knew something after all. I knew I needed to plug the gap between the door and the door frame or I was going to be inundated with bugs.

Duct tape took care of that problem.

A glance at the clock told me if I was going to call the doctor's office, I'd better do it soon. Nevertheless, I hesitated. I hadn't thrown up once since yesterday afternoon, and my stomach felt fine. Maybe that pregnancy test was wrong. Maybe I'd simply had the stomach flu.

"And maybe you're a dreamer," I mumbled and headed for my cordless phone. Not feeling sick to my stomach didn't eliminate the missed period or how tired I felt even after nearly sleeping the afternoon away.

The receptionist who answered my call put me on hold and I almost hung up, but then my doctor's nurse picked up, and I stumbled through an explanation of what I feared. They wouldn't be able to get me in until next week, but I said that was fine. I think I was hoping this would all go away, that I'd soon wake up and discover the last few days had been a dream: no boat blowing up, no positive reading on a pregnancy test, and no wondering if I'd end up as crazy as my mom.

Well, actually, dream or not, I always worry about ending up as crazy as my mom.

Baraka came over and stared at me with those big, brown eyes of his. He didn't bark and he didn't whine, but he was clearly letting me know it was his dinner time. Only after I'd fed him did I remember I'd had almost nothing to eat all day. Problem was, nothing sounded good.

I finally decided on soup and a cottage cheese and sliced

banana salad.

After two days of having Jason and Wade around, my house seemed unusually quiet. Lonely. Wade hadn't called. I'm sure I would have heard the phone if he had, but just to be certain, I checked both my cordless and my cell phone. Nothing. No indication of a missed call and no messages.

I carried my bowl of soup into the dining room first, then headed back to the kitchen for my plate of cottage cheese and sliced banana. Once again I bumped the edge of the table and heard a voice. "Come play, come play."

As soon as I was seated at the table, food in front of me, I pulled the laptop over so I could look at the screen as I ate. An animated, cartoon figure of a boy filled the center of the monitor, but as soon as the laptop was moved—or bumped—the figure activated, waving an arm as if motioning the viewer to follow, and the computerized voice begged the viewer to "Come play."

I clicked the mouse and a new screen appeared, this one giving me a choice of several games. I clicked on a couple, just to see what they were like. Both were far more complicated than I'd expected a six-year-old to be playing, but both also showed scores for a JWK, which I assumed were Jason's initials.

I tried playing one of the games as I sipped my soup and ate my salad. I'd like to blame my low score on the fact that I wasn't really concentrating on the game; nevertheless, it was a bit embarrassing to get a score lower than a six-year-old's. I clicked out of the game and out of the program. I'd had enough of that tinny voice begging me to play.

Once out of the game program, I saw the icons for other programs on the laptop. Jason might have been into games, but Michael Brewster was into gaming. Online gaming. Which wasn't a complete surprise considering the fact I'd already learned he owed someone money. Seemed he liked sports betting and playing poker. I didn't know his login passwords for any of the sites, so I couldn't see how he fared on any of them, but I had a feeling the Van Buren Sheriff's Department might be interested.

Then again, it might be the Kalamazoo Sheriff's Department who should get the laptop.

I had told Deputy Sawyer I had a laptop from Brewster's house. She hadn't said anything, but maybe she didn't realize Michael Brewster also used it. Which he obviously did. And not just for games. In addition to the gambling sites, there was an icon for the brokerage firm Brewster had worked for up until last Friday.

Like the gambling sites, the brokerage site was password protected.

I wasn't about to guess at the password . . . or have my computer guru buddy, Ken Paget, figure it out. In June I'd asked Ken to find out what was on a cell phone and that had nearly gotten him killed. He'd forgiven me somewhat—but I knew he wouldn't be happy if I called on him again, especially since I already knew something Brewster had done had pissed his co-worker.

What was his name?

Steve. Steve Richards? Richman? Neither name sounded right, and I wished I'd written it down right after he told me. That always helped me remember. I did remember Steve What's-his-name was looking for a file named "Bonanza." I didn't see that on the list of files, but it could have been under another file name. Maybe in the brokerage company's program.

Would Steve kill to get the missing file back? I considered the idea, and then discarded it. After all, how would he know Brewster would be on Wade's boat Saturday? And even if he did, how would he get a bomb on the boat?

I had no answers, but the fact that Steve What's-his-name

might have driven into my driveway only a short time ago made me nervous. And maybe I was just using the laptop as an excuse to call Wade, since he hadn't called me, but I decided he should know about these programs. He would also know which sheriff's department should have the laptop.

Wade answered on the fifth ring, and I could hear the television in the background, a canned laughter track competing with Jason's loud screams of "No!"

"What?" Wade yelled into the phone, probably out of frustration as well as a need to overpower the noise.

"Things not going well?" I asked, in a way pleased since it was his choice to take Jason home and leave me on my own.

"I'm trying to get him to take a bath."

"Is it that important? He took a shower yesterday, before you got here." Not that I knew much about parenting, but I couldn't see getting into a yelling match over a bath.

"He may have taken a shower yesterday, but today he was playing with the neighbor's dog, which must have rolled in something that died. Jason stinks," Wade said, almost on a sigh. "But maybe you're right. He's tired. So am I."

"Does your head still hurt?"

"Some. Yes. But no, I don't need to go to the doctor's."

"Okay, okay." I knew better than to argue with him. I don't know what it is about men and going to the doctor. Grandpa Carter was the same way. Stubborn. Always sure whatever was wrong with him would go away on its own.

The Alzheimer's never did.

I dropped the subject of his head. "Just hug Jason and tell him you love him."

"But he stinks," Wade repeated, but this time with a chuckle in his voice. "You're right, it's not that important. Not tonight."

"Okay, no bath," he shouted away from the phone. "But turn that TV down."

The yelling stopped immediately, and a second later the noise from the television decreased. Once it did, Wade asked, "How are you feeling?"

"Okay. Tired. I slept almost all afternoon."

"It's been a rough few days for all of us. I've never seen Jason so irritable. We just went through a temper tantrum because he wanted me to drive out to your place and get that laptop he left there."

"I'm sure he's still trying to come to terms with the loss of his mother. That's going to take a while. And I called because of that laptop. When I went to turn it off, I noticed some online gaming programs and an icon for that brokerage firm Brewster used to work for. Have you seen those programs?"

"No, I'd never even seen the laptop before yesterday. What did you find?"

"Nothing. Everything requires a password. But I thought, since Brewster seems to have owed money, and since Steve, his coworker, said Brewster had taken something of his . . . Well, you know, maybe Brewster stole some money from Steve, or an account. You hear about things like that all the time."

"P.J., did you try to break into those programs?"

I could hear the accusation in his voice. He's such a by-the-book guy. "No, I learned my lesson last June." *Evidence should be investigated by law enforcement, not civilians.* That was Wade's stand. "I just thought you'd want to know about them."

"You need to get it to the Van Buren Sheriff's Department. I don't know why they didn't take it when they searched Brewster's house Sunday."

"I don't know why, either, but you're the one who should take it to them." I was sure it would look better if he turned over the evidence.

For a moment Wade didn't say anything, and then I heard him sigh. "Not tonight. I'll come over in the morning and get the laptop. Okay?"

"Sure. Whatever works for you."

I had hoped he would come tonight. I could understand that he and Jason were tired, but so was I, and he didn't seem to care how I felt. Tears were forming in my eyes and knew I had to get off the phone. "Okay, that's all I wanted to say," I mumbled and hit the disconnect button.

Wade didn't call back, which was good because I couldn't stop the tears. I slumped down on the nearest dining room chair, more exhausted than I'd ever been. If this was what it was like to be pregnant, I didn't like it.

Baraka came over and sat directly in front of me. I absently rubbed his head and neck, and he licked my cheeks. Normally I don't let him lick my face—after all, I've seen the other places that tongue has gone—but tonight the act was comforting.

When the tears finally stopped, I carried my empty soup bowl and salad plate into the kitchen, but I didn't have the energy to wash dishes. For a while I watched TV, but after I dozed off a couple times, I turned it off and headed for my bedroom. I don't even remember brushing my teeth or putting on my nightgown, but I guess I did because I was wearing it when Baraka's barking woke me.

It was dark out, and for a moment I simply sat up in bed and listened. Baraka often barks in his sleep, moves his legs, and whines. I'm sure he's chasing something in his dreams. But this was different. His bark was higher pitched, sounded panicky . . . frightened.

I cautiously got out of bed and worked my way to my dining room and front door. Baraka had stopped barking, but he stood facing the door, looking toward the roadway. I glanced that direction and saw the taillights of a car halfway to the corner. It was too dark out to tell what kind of car or color, and I knew it could simply be a coincidence, but it made me nervous.

I did turn on the outside light and looked over what I could see of my front yard, almost hoping I would spy an opossum or skunk. I saw nothing, and by then Baraka had turned away from the door and was looking up at me, tail wagging. "So what spooked you?" I asked, wishing he could talk.

I would swear he sighed before trotting into the kitchen.

As far as I could tell, whatever had disturbed him was gone. I looked out at my yard again. That's when I realized the gate was open.

CHAPTER TWENTY-FOUR

"I think someone tried to break into my house last night," I told Wade the moment he and Jason arrived. "Baraka woke me with his barking, and when I came out here to see what he was barking at, I saw a car heading away from here, and the gate to the yard was open."

"What kind of car?"

"I don't know, it was too dark to see and the car was already halfway to the corner. Do you think someone tried to steal Brewster's laptop?"

"Who would know you had it here?"

"I don't know, but yesterday, when I was at Brewster's house, I told those deputies I had the laptop, and I mentioned it to Carol Dotson, Brewster's next-door neighbor. And—" I paused for emphasis, "I also mentioned it to the guy who worked with Brewster. Steve Richman or Richards, or something like that. He was driving a silver BMW." Again I paused. "Yesterday Howard said he saw a sports car pull into my yard. A silver sports car. I think the guy was casing my place, that he came back last night, and . . ."

"And what?"

"And what?" I repeated, surprised he'd had to ask. "To steal the laptop, that's what."

"But he didn't, right?" Jason said, looking around for the laptop. "Where is it?"

"It's in my bedroom," I said and looked at Wade. "It seemed

safer to have it nearby."

Jason started for my bedroom, but Wade stopped him. "I'm afraid you can't play on it today. We've got to give the laptop to the sheriff's department."

"I'll never finish my game," Jason grumbled and stomped off into my living room.

"He's being a brat," Wade said, shaking his head. "I'm not sure what to do with him."

"Give him a little more time. He's still grieving. He may even feel guilty because he's alive and his mother isn't."

Wade sighed. "I guess you're right. I know I've been feeling edgy—irritable—lately."

You're telling me? I wanted to say, but didn't, and from the other room we heard, "Yuck."

Both Wade and I looked in that direction and saw Jason bend over something on the floor. "What is it?" we both asked.

"A bug." He wrinkled his nose as he picked it up. "One of those boxy bugs." He came toward us. "It landed on my head. Here."

He thrust the dead bug toward me.

"Give me a minute," I begged and hurried into the kitchen to get a paper towel.

By the time I returned, towel in hand, Wade had taken the dead bug and tossed it in the wastebasket in the corner.

"Let's say Brewster's coworker did try to steal the laptop last night," Wade said, continuing the conversation we'd had earlier. "How did he know where you lived?"

"I don't know. But have you ever tried looking up someone on the computer? If you know their name, it's not that hard to find out where they live." And she had told Brewster's coworker her name. "When I talked to him yesterday, he acted very upset. He said Brewster had taken something from him, something from where Brewster worked, and he wanted it back."

"Daddy Michael said they gave it to him," Jason said, sounding confused. "He said they were sorry to see him leave. Mama told you that," he said, looking at Wade. "Remember?"

Wade frowned. "I'm not sure I know what you mean, Jason."

"The basket. The one Mama brought on the boat. She said it was a present 'cause Daddy Michael was going to a new job. You told them not to open the wine until we were on the lake, that the coast people didn't like people drinking on boats."

"That's right." Wade paused, and I could tell he was remembering more from that morning. "I definitely need to call the Van Buren Sheriff's Department," he said, a new enthusiasm entering his voice. "I thought they meant *my* wine bottles . . . the ones I brought onboard last month."

I wasn't following his train of thought. "What's so important about the wine bottles?"

He pulled out his cell phone and punched in some numbers. "They found shards of glass, the kind used with wine bottles. They're pretty sure—" His attention switched from me to the phone. "Yes. Sergeant Kingsley here. From the Kalamazoo County Sheriff's Department. I need to speak to Sergeant Milano."

Wade once again paused, and I assumed he was waiting to be connected to Milano. But then Wade frowned, his shoulders tensing. His next words explained the change in his mood.

"He's coming here? To Ms. Benson's place?"

It was my turn to frown, and I mouthed, "Why?"

Wade gave a slight shake of his head, his brow furrowed. "No, I understand," he said and ended the call.

For a moment he said nothing, but the way he exhaled a breath, I knew he wasn't happy. Finally, with a sigh, he looked at me. "If you have any marijuana or anything you don't want found, you'd better stash it now."

"Marijuana?" It upset me that he even suggested I might

have some. Wade knew I didn't smoke, much less smoke dope. "What's going on?"

"Milano has a search warrant. He'll probably be here any minute."

"Here? Why would he want to search here?"

"Well, the desk clerk wasn't about to tell me, but my guess is, since they didn't find any signs of explosives at my place besides those trousers, they want to check your place."

"That's crazy."

"Do you have any?"

"Explosives? No."

"Ammonia? Fertilizer? Dynamite? C4 caps?"

"I have cleaning ammonia." Though I hated using it because of the smell. "As for fertilizer, if there is any, it would be some my grandfather had in the woodshed. I don't know about that, but I'm sure there's no dynamite or anything like that."

Wade walked over to the screen door and looked out. "I've executed a lot of search warrants over the years. Those people always claimed they had nothing to hide, but I never believed them. Seems strange now to be in that position."

"Yeah, as I recall, you didn't believe me last April." Back then Wade was the deputy at my door, informing me he had a search warrant. I knew I hadn't killed anyone, but he wasn't convinced, especially when one of the deputies found a gun in the wood-shed.

Wade came back and slid his arms around me, hugging me close. "I'm sorry. Sorry about that. Sorry about now. You shouldn't be involved in this."

I felt him blow a kiss into the curls on top of my head, and I rested my head against his chest. The thump of his heart and the warmth of his body were reassuring, but I couldn't stop the fear creeping through me. What would we do if we couldn't prove Wade was innocent? What would happen to Jason? To me?

"Are you two going to get all mushy-faced?" Jason asked from nearby.

Wade's chuckle vibrated against my cheek, and he gave me an affectionate squeeze before he stepped away. "We'll try to keep it under control," he said, his attention now focused on his son.

"In a little while those deputies you met last time you were here will be here again. They're going to want to look around P.J.'s place, so we're going to have to stay out of their way. Do you have any ideas about what you want to do while they're here?"

Jason brightened and hurried toward my office. "We can go look for buried treasure," he said, ducking through the open slider and popping back out a second later holding the map he'd found on Monday.

How he'd already discovered that I left that drawing in my office after making a copy for Howard, I didn't know, but Jason eagerly brought it to us. I looked at Wade, unsure what his response would be.

"I don't think so," he said, giving me a quick glance. "I think those deputies are going to want us to stay around here."

"That's okay, I can look by myself."

Wade shook his head. "No, that's not a good idea. There's too much junk in those woods. You could get hurt."

"No, I wouldn't." Jason reached over and gave Baraka a pat on the head. "I'll take Brak with me."

"No," Wade repeated, firmer this time.

"You never let me do nothin'." Jason glared at his dad.

I'm not sure what Wade might have said or done next. Two sheriff's cars pulled into my driveway at that moment, one from the Van Buren County Sheriff's Department, the other from the Kalamazoo County Sheriff's Department. Both Wade and I turned and watched four deputies—three men and one woman—get out of the cars. I recognize Milano and Blair, from the times I'd met them at the hospital and here. I also recognized Deputy Dario Gespardo from Wade's department. The female deputy was one I hadn't met before.

I braced myself. From the looks on the deputies' faces, I had a feeling this wasn't going to be a friendly search.

Chapter Twenty-Five

Wade and I stepped out on my front porch. The four deputies acknowledged Wade, but Deputy Milano spoke to me. He explained that the Kalamazoo County deputies were with him because my farmhouse is in Zenith Township, Kalamazoo County, but since Wade's boat blew up on the part of Lake Michigan that's under the jurisdiction of Van Buren County, they were the ones who had initiated the search warrant. I asked to see the paper.

Wade looked over my shoulder as I read through the warrant. In spite of the legalese, I gathered these four people had the right to look through my house and all of my outbuildings for any material that could be used to produce a bomb. I started to make a smart remark about how they hadn't included the woods and farmland I'd inherited along with the house, but Wade pinched my arm before I got three words out, and I remembered it was better to say absolutely nothing.

So I shut up.

Wade told Jason to stay outside and play with Baraka while the deputies were in the house. Still sulking, Jason obeyed. I asked if I could get a light jacket before they started, and Deputy Milano said fine, but he sent Deputy Semler, the female officer, with me.

"Excuse the mess," I said as she followed me into my bedroom. "I'll never win a prize for neatness, and now that I'm working from my house, I've really become lax about hanging things up."

The room was a mess, but Semler said nothing.

"Can you believe how quickly the weather changed?" I asked and opened the armoire that used to be my grandparents'. "One minute you're roasting, the next you're freezing."

Hearing nothing from my companion, I glanced over my shoulder to make sure she was still there. She was, a slight frown wrinkling her brow. I had a feeling, considering how neatly pressed her uniform appeared, that Deputy Semler's closet didn't look like mine . . . nor her bedroom.

"Cold weather's bringing in those boxelder bugs," I said as I dug through the pile of jackets and sweatshirts lying on the bottom of the cabinet. Finally, I found and grabbed my light-weight blue jacket. Straightening, I faced her. "In your search, feel free to kill them."

Her frown became a scowl, and I smiled as I walked past her and out of the room. Maybe she wouldn't talk to me, but I'd gotten some reaction.

"Now what?" I asked when I joined Wade outside.

"Now we say nothing as they search your house," he grumbled and walked over to the picnic table under the maple tree in my front yard.

"Did you tell Milano about Michael Brewster's laptop?" While in my bedroom, I'd noticed the laptop on my dresser, but I hadn't thought to say anything to Deputy Semler.

"I told him," Wade said. "He wasn't pleased to hear it wasn't picked up Sunday when they went through Brewster's house . . . or that you'd had it since Monday, and we hadn't told him."

"So now he thinks we were hiding evidence?"

Wade shrugged but didn't make a comment, and for the next hour the only time he said anything was when Jason came over and asked if he could play in the old chicken coop. Although the deputies had gone through the building and hadn't found anything, I hadn't finished scraping the laying boxes or swept up the floor, and there was a chance Jason playing in there might stir up the Hantavirus. I shook my head. Wade's response was more abrupt. "No. Stay away from the buildings."

Once again in a huff, Jason—with Baraka by his side—dashed off, disappearing around the side of the house. Wade gave a heavy sigh. I knew he wasn't happy. I understood how he felt. I was tempted to say, "See, this is how I felt when you came here in April, all huffy and sure I'd hidden a gun."

But that wouldn't have been fair. He didn't know me back then. Back in April he was simply acting on an anonymous tip. Also I really couldn't take any pleasure in the fact that the shoe was now on the other foot, to use an old cliché. This situation was too serious. These deputies were looking for something to tie him to the murder of his ex-wife and her new husband.

I was sure they weren't going to find anything at my place to perpetuate that idea.

That's how foolish I can be sometimes.

One hour after they arrived, another van pulled into my driveway. I watched a uniformed officer get out and open the back door. Only then did I see the dog on the back seat, a large black-and-tan German shepherd. "Bomb-sniffing dog," Wade said under his breath.

I immediately rose from the picnic table. "I need to get Baraka. I don't know what he'll do."

Wade came with me, and we found Jason and Baraka back near the stone pile where Jason liked to look for arrowheads. So far Baraka wasn't aware there was another dog in the area, which was good, but I knew it wouldn't take long before he did catch the dog's scent. I needed a leash and collar since I don't leave a collar on him when he's in the house or yard—there are too many spots where he could get hung up—but with the house off limits, I couldn't get either. We ended up using Wade's belt as a makeshift leash/collar, and the four of us returned to the picnic table.

Actually Wade and I sat there, Baraka by my side. As soon as Jason saw the German shepherd go into the house, he ran up on the front porch and watched what was going on through the window. Occasionally he broke away from his vigil to swipe boxelder bugs off the screen door and siding, which reminded me I needed to buy a spray bottle and try Howard's soap mixture.

Jason was the one who told us they'd taken the dog out of the house to the woodshed. We caught that information as he ran by us and around to the back of the house. Baraka tried to follow him, but I stopped him with a sit-and-stay command.

I had a feeling something was up—something not good—when I heard one of the deputies call out, and the other three headed for my woodshed. Wade and I got up from the picnic table, and with Baraka by my side, went around to the back of the house and joined Jason. "They found something," he said, his childish voice laced with excitement. "The dog found something."

I looked at Wade. His gaze was locked on the woodshed, and I could feel his tension. "I don't know what they could have found," I said.

Wade glanced down at me, his mouth a tight line, then looked back at the shed, not saying a word. Milano's buddy Blair scurried back to their cruiser, grabbed a bunch of empty paper bags out of the back, and returned to the woodshed. The dog handler and his dog came out of the shed, shook hands with Sergeant Milano, and walked to his car.

"I haven't been in there since it warmed up and I stopped making wood fires," I whispered. "I've been concentrating on cleaning the chicken coop."

The van with the dog handler and dog backed out of my yard the same time Deputy Blair and Deputy Gespardo came out of the shed, each carrying two bags that they took to the Van Buren cruiser. "Can he be loose now?" Jason asked, coming over to pat Baraka.

"I guess so." I removed the belt from around Baraka's neck. I was more concerned with what the deputies were doing. Sergeant Milano had come out of the shed, along with Deputy Semler and another deputy. The two deputies headed straight for the back door to my house while Milano came toward us. "Where do you have the primer?" he asked as he approached, the question seemingly directed at both Wade and me.

"Primer?" I repeated, trying to remember what I had seen in the woodshed. "I don't know. I haven't done any painting."

"He doesn't mean that kind of primer," Wade said, looking at Milano. "What did you find?"

"Why don't you tell me what we found?"

"I have no idea, and neither does she."

Milano grunted his disbelief. "You should have hidden those fireworks better."

"Fireworks? What kind of fireworks?" I hadn't bought any this year. Not even a sparkler.

"Fire crackers. Rockets." Milano smiled. "Oh, they're old, but I'm sure you were able to get enough gunpowder to create a bomb. You do drink wine, don't you, Ms. Benson?"

"Yes. I mean, I used to." I glanced at Wade. "What's he getting at?"

"They think the explosive was in a wine bottle," he explained before speaking to Milano. "I tried calling you this morning, Sergeant. My son reminded me that Brewster and my ex brought a picnic basket onboard Saturday, and that they had wine with them. Two bottles, to be exact. Bottles they'd received as a farewell gift from the company where Brewster used to work. The company he very well may have stole something from."

Wade emphasized that last sentence, and Milano frowned. "And just what is it that Michael Brewster supposedly stole?"

"I don't know." Wade glanced at me, and then back at Milano. "But yesterday, while she was at Michael Brewster's house with my son and former in-laws, Ms. Benson heard three messages on Brewster's answering machine. I did, too, and so did another deputy from my department."

"Wait a minute, now." Milano's frown deepened. "I checked that answering machine Sunday. The most recent messages were left Saturday." Sergeant Milano looked toward the Van Buren cruiser where Officer Blair was lighting a cigarette. "Mr. Brewster's answering machine shouldn't have even been there. It was supposed to be taken in as evidence."

"Well, it *was* there yesterday," Wade said, his tone neither accusing nor mocking. "And the three calls I listened to came in *after* the house had been released by your department . . . and *after* my sister was there on Monday."

I didn't think "when" was as important as "what," so I spoke up. "There was a lot of static, but what I gathered was Brewster was supposed to deliver something in exchange for a large sum of money, and the caller was really upset because Brewster hadn't sent it."

"You have any idea what this something was?" Milano asked.

"No, but not long after I heard those messages, a man who said he worked with Brewster told me Brewster had stolen something of his. His name was Steve. Steve Richard-something-or-other."

"Did he say what Brewster took?"

"No, and when I told him he should talk to Deputy Sawyer, he basically took off."

Milano looked at Wade. "What were you and Deputy Sawyer doing at the house?"

"I was there to pick up my son." Wade looked puzzled. "Haven't you received a report about the break-in at Brewster's house?"

Milano shook his head. "You're saying Brewster's house was broken into after we went through it Sunday?"

"Sometime either Monday evening or early Tuesday," Wade said. "My ex-in-laws are sure a necklace was stolen."

"My men did not steal a necklace, we—"

Wade stopped him. "They're not accusing you. I'm the one they're sure took it."

"And did you?"

That Milano would even ask made me angry. "No, he didn't!" I practically shouted before Wade had a chance to say anything. I would have said more, except just then I saw Deputy Semler and the other deputy come out of my house. The other deputy was carrying Brewster's laptop; Deputy Semler was carrying my computer tower.

"Wait! What are you doing?" I yelled at the woman. "That's not Brewster's. That's mine!"

The two ignored me, came down the steps, and headed for the Van Buren cruiser. I started for the cruiser, but Deputy Milano caught my arm. "We're taking them for evidence," he said.

"But the tower is mine, not Brewster's." I tried shaking Milano's hand off my arm. "I have all my accounts on there. My business."

"I'm sure you do," he said, just the hint of a smile indicating he thought he'd find more.

I looked at Wade and then back at Milano. "*We* didn't kill anyone."

Milano's expression didn't change. "Maybe you only meant

to injure them. Maybe scare them. It doesn't matter. They're dead."

"You're not going to find anything on her computer," Wade said.

I watched Deputy Semler put my computer tower into the back seat of the cruiser. I wanted to run over and stop her from closing the door, but I knew it was no use. Instead, I yelled at her. "Make sure that doesn't get damaged. Put something around it, or strap it in."

I glared at Milano. "If I lose one bit of data, I . . . I . . ."

I wanted to threaten him, to warn him that he couldn't simply march into my house and take my livelihood. I wanted to sound strong and forceful. Instead, I started crying, the tears flowing down my cheeks and choking off my words. And to make matters worse, it started raining. Not a gentle drizzle, but a total downpour.

"Don't think of going anywhere," Sergeant Milano warned, backing away from us, and then turning to dash for his cruiser. "We'll be in touch," he yelled over a rumble of thunder.

Wade grabbed my arm and pulled me toward the house. In seconds the rain had drenched us. I stumbled behind him, my gaze locked on the two cruisers as they backed out of my driveway onto the road. I couldn't believe what had just happened. They'd taken my computer, treated me like a suspect.

"What's going to happen?" I asked Wade as we entered the kitchen, water pooling on the linoleum.

He didn't answer me. Instead, he called out, "Jason!"

Jason didn't respond, and Baraka didn't come bounding into the kitchen.

"Damn," Wade swore. "You'd think that kid would know enough to come in out of the rain."

A flash of lightning lit up the darkened sky, its ear-deafening crack almost immediate. I couldn't tell for certain, but it sounded like it had hit in the woods behind my house.

I looked at Wade and saw the panic in his eyes. He turned around and stepped back out onto the concrete landing. "Jason!" he yelled, this time into the backyard.

Again no response, and no dog in sight.

CHAPTER TWENTY-SIX

"I'll check upstairs," I told Wade. "You look in the chicken coop."

I hurried up the stairs that more-or-less divide my house into two halves. "Jason!" I shouted once I reached the top of the stairs.

No response.

I stood still for a moment, catching my breath and listening for any sound that might indicate Jason was nearby. Again I called out his name. Again nothing.

I checked my father's old room first. My grandparents had done little to change the room after he moved out, which was one reason I thought the map Jason found could be one my father made. I looked under the bed. Other than dust bunnies, some old magazines that I'd checked them out once—they were *Playboys*—a few papers, and a pair of dirty socks, I saw nothing. No six-year-old boy.

The second bedroom was nearly empty of furniture and had no closet. It took me less than a second to see Jason wasn't in there. The storage area took longer. Simply moving things around stirred up dust, and I had to stop twice for sneezing fits.

I remembered hiding in the storage area as a child. It was one of my favorite places to go when Dad brought me out to the farm. Back then I'd imagined the open areas behind the stacks of boxes were secret rooms. Sometimes I pretended I was a princess locked in a castle, sometimes an orphan living amid cardboard boxes on the street. There were several spots where Jason might hide, but when I checked, each was empty.

Certain that Jason was not upstairs, I went back down to the main level. We'd already noted he wasn't in the kitchen or dining room, and a quick check of my bedroom, my office area, the laundry section, and the bathroom confirmed that Jason wasn't in any of those rooms. The only other place he might be in the house was the Michigan basement, but we've told him more than once never to go down there. I didn't think he would; nevertheless, I opened the door and from the top of the stairs called his name.

The musty smell of dirt, and probably some mold, greeted me, but no little boy's voice.

I called again.

Still no response.

I flipped on the light. As far as I could tell from the dust on the steps, Jason hadn't gone down there. No one had.

I turned off the light and pulled the door closed.

I hoped Wade had had better luck outside.

The moment I stepped through the kitchen door onto the concrete landing, I encountered rain. Not the totally drenching rain that had come down earlier, but steady enough to immediately wet my hair and face, forcing me to wipe the water out of my eyes. Rumbles of thunder continued to accompany flashes of lightning, though both seemed to be moving to the east. I could hear Wade somewhere in the distance yelling for Jason, and the gate that led to the woods behind my house was wide open. *That little rat,* I thought and headed for the gate. I'd bet, in spite of what we'd said, Jason was looking for his "treasure."

Since Baraka still wasn't anywhere around, I started calling his name. Maybe Jason wouldn't respond, but my dog might come back. Not that he'd lead us to Jason. Baraka wasn't like

Lassie or Rin Tin Tin. I couldn't simply tell him to find someone and expect him to do so. That took special training.

I wished I'd studied that map better. I remembered the dotted line left what I assumed was the trail at about a third of the way into the woods. What I didn't know was how accurate the drawing might be, or if the trees were still standing that Dad had indicated with circles. Add thirty years of junk, and even with the map there was no guarantee anyone could find the spot marked with an X.

I heard Wade call Jason's name again, then say, "Baraka." I could tell Wade wasn't far ahead of me, just around a bend in the trail.

I also called Baraka's name, and a moment later my dog came into view, running toward me, his mouth open so it looked as if he were smiling, his tongue lolling to the side. The rain had soaked his coat, turning the hair a darker shade of red-wheaten, and the instant he stopped in front of me, he shook his body, spraying droplets of water on me.

I didn't care. My clothes were already soaked, my curls plastered to my scalp and the side of my face. I scratched Baraka's neck and praised him for coming to me. Up ahead I heard Wade say my name, and I hurried to catch up with him.

"I think he's in there," he said, pointing away from the trail and into the woods. "That's the way your dog came."

"He's following that map."

"You shouldn't have given it to him."

I glared at Wade. "I didn't. And I'd like it back."

"You're right," he admitted. "I should have taken it from him when I had the chance." Wade looked the direction he thought Jason had gone. "Damn. I hope he doesn't hurt himself. Your grandfather should have been cited for dumping all this junk in here."

I said nothing. I agreed. The junk was a menace. Old tires

collected water whenever it rained, creating a haven for mosquito larvae. Rusty, broken metal machinery parts and rotting boards with nails in them posed a danger of scrapes, cuts, puncture wounds, and tetanus.

"Go back to the house," Wade ordered. "Get some dry clothing on. You don't want to get sick, not in your condition."

"I'm pregnant, not sick," I said and moved past him.

"Still—" He put a hand on my shoulder, stopping me from going any farther.

"Still nothing." I shrugged off his hand and stepped over a rusting metal fence post. "Let's find Jason. Then all three of us can go back to the house and dry off."

Baraka brushed by me and trotted around a wild blackberry bush. Maybe he would help us find Jason after all. I followed his lead.

I'm not sure if we found Jason or he found us. I saw him first. "There," I said, pointing at a spot between two trees.

Head down, Jason stumbled over something on the ground, took two weaving steps, and finally regained his balance. His shorts, T-shirt, legs, and arms were covered with mud. I couldn't tell if he still had on flip-flops. His feet were simply globs of brown.

He held what I guessed was the map in his right hand, the paper soggy and in shreds. He didn't realize we were there until Baraka ran up to him, shoving his head against Jason's side. In the process of pushing Baraka away, Jason looked up, and his face crumbled into a sob.

He ran toward us, stumbled over a rock, and fell to his knees. He cried harder, tears streaking through the spattered mud on his cheeks. Wade rushed to him and lifted his son, smearing mud over his own clothing. "It's okay," he said over and over. "I've got you."

He carried Jason back to the house, murmuring soothing words of comfort. I followed, saying nothing. I could tell there was nothing left of the map Jason held. Rain and mud had wiped out the markings my father had made. When Jason dropped the paper, I left it where it fell.

Only Baraka seemed to be enjoying himself. The rain had turned to a drizzle, the storm moving off to the east. My dog ran ahead of us then back, splashing water as he plunged through puddles.

At the side of my house, Wade set Jason back on his feet near the hose Jason had used two days earlier to try to drown out a mole. "I think we'd better wash off here," Wade said, nodding for me to turn on the water.

Considering the amount of mud on Jason—and now on Wade—I agreed. As the water washed off the mud, I could see that Jason did have flip-flops on his feet, and that he'd skinned both knees. I could also see the boy was shivering.

So was I.

"As soon as you get that mud off, come inside," I ordered and headed for my front door.

If we'd thought using the hose outside would keep my house clean, we'd forgotten about Baraka. As I entered the house, he pushed his way in beside me and into the dining room. Right away he gave a shake, spraying water on everything around him, and then he proceeded into the kitchen, leaving muddy paw prints along the way.

I grabbed a towel from the bathroom and quickly rubbed him dry, cleaning his paws as I worked on each leg. Once my dog was taken care of, I grabbed another towel for my hair and turned a portable heater on in the bathroom.

★ ★ ★ ★ ★

One hour later, we'd all taken showers. Mine wasn't very hot after Jason and Wade took theirs but once I had dry clothes on, I felt better. Just tired. Extremely tired.

Although Wade had a change of clothes at the house, he'd taken Jason's to his place, so while their dirty ones went through a wash cycle in the laundry area, Jason wore one of my sweatshirts. I promised him it wouldn't take long for his clothes to dry, and as Wade doctored Jason's scrapes, I fixed hot chocolate for the three of us.

Jason only drank half of his before he crawled onto Wade's lap and fell asleep. I wished I could also crawl onto his lap, cuddle up, and fall asleep. Instead, I simply sighed and stared off into space, not sure what to say.

Wade spoke first.

"You didn't know about the fireworks?"

I shook my head. "I remember one time my dad and grandfather shot off fireworks on the fourth of July, but that had to be twenty years ago, if not more. I don't know if Grandpa Benson bought more fireworks after that. I haven't had time to go through that building. I do have to work for a living, you know."

Except now I couldn't.

My gaze drifted to the door to my office. "What am I going to do, Wade? They took my computer."

"They'll give it back. Once they see you don't have anything on there about explosives, they'll realize you weren't involved with the boat explosion."

His words didn't calm me. "I looked up explosives," I said. "Sunday, while you were sleeping. I wanted to know what might make a boat explode."

"How about before Sunday? Before Saturday? Did you ever look up explosives before the explosion?"

"Explosions, not explosives." In my mind there was a big difference. "Back in June I looked up gas leak explosions. This is an old house. I was worried about the possibility of a leak here."

Wade shook his head.

"What?" I didn't understand. "Because I look up explosions they're going to blame me?"

"I don't know what they're going to do."

I could tell he was frustrated . . . and worried. "Well, I know I didn't do it. And I'm quite sure you didn't blow up your boat. So who did?"

Wade shook his head, and I realized he really didn't have any ideas. "Okay," I said, deciding we needed to calmly consider the facts. "You said they think the explosive was in a wine bottle. Is that right?"

He nodded. "They found glass shards in the body parts, and the medical examiner found traces of explosive on a couple of those shards."

In the body parts. The image of an ME doing an autopsy on body parts made my stomach turn over.

So much for staying calm.

I don't know if I would have gotten sick. Just as I stood and started for the bathroom, my cell phone rang. I'd left it on the end of the table, and I grabbed it as I hurried toward the bathroom. By the time I had the door closed, I had the phone to my ear and heard my grandmother's voice.

"I need your help, P.J.," she said, a frantic tremor to her voice. "Your mother's taken four hundred dollars I had set aside for a rainy day, and has gone off to that new casino with one of her co-workers. You know how she is when she doesn't take her meds. There's no telling what she might do."

CHAPTER TWENTY-SEVEN

The rain had started again by the time I picked up Grandma Carter. The windshield wipers made a steady swoosh as we headed for Lake Michigan. "It was that meeting yesterday," Grandma grumbled as she glared out the side window. "Why that darn counselor had to keep mentioning how much one of those residential homes costs, I don't know. That's got to be the reason Flo's gone to the casino. That and that coworker she's made friends with, the one who's been telling her stories about how much money she's won at this new casino."

Grandma half-turned in her seat and wagged a finger at me. "Don't you ever take up gambling, P.J. The only ones making money at those casinos are the operators."

"I know," I assured her as we headed northwest, away from Kalamazoo.

"Your Grandpa Carter used to play poker. Sometimes he won a few dollars, but more often he lost."

"Michael Brewster evidently gambled and lost," I said. "He had some poker games on his laptop, and twice this week I've run into a man looking for him. I have the feeling Brewster owed him a lot of money."

"You think someone put a bomb on your boyfriend's boat 'cause Brewster owed money?"

I'd considered that possibility, especially after baldy said something about "going too far." But it didn't make sense. "Why kill someone who owes you money? You're certainly not going to get paid if the guy's dead."

"Teach him a lesson," Grandma said. "Maybe show others you mean business."

"That's a pretty drastic way to do it. On the other hand, maybe he didn't expect the bomb to be that lethal." Sergeant Milano had suggested that possibility. "Maybe it was just supposed to injure or scare Brewster."

"Was it one of those pressure-cooker bombs?" Grandma asked.

"No. At least nothing has been said about a pressure cooker. Wade said they think the bomb was in a wine bottle, and this morning the deputies who came to my place asked if I drank wine. I think they were looking to see if I had any bottles they could match to the glass shards they found in the bodies."

"You had deputies at your place?"

"I've had a very busy day," I said and proceeded to fill Grandma in on all that had happened, starting with Wade and Jason arriving at my place, the Van Buren Sheriff's deputies showing up and taking both Brewster's laptop and my computer, and finishing with Jason taking off and ruining the map I thought my dad had created.

By the time I finished my story, we'd reached the White Water Casino, Michigan's newest and most friendly casino, according to the ads on television. A gigantic marquee stood in front of the parking lot, flashing a display of winners, prizes, and the casino's current promotion. The casino itself was a large, rectangular building, its blue-and-white stucco exterior echoing the colors of Lake Michigan. Centered above the south entrance were four stylized breaking waves, each holding one of the four card suits.

What amazed me most was the parking lot. Here it was, early afternoon on a Wednesday, and not only was the lot in front of the casino full, but the auxiliary lots also had cars. I ignored the valet parking and actually found a spot not too far from the middle of the building. The rain had subsided to a drizzle; nevertheless, Grandma and I scurried to the entrance, only to have to wait as a security guard stopped and checked the IDs of two young women who had arrived ahead of us. Once the guard had okayed them, she motioned us inside. Although I was glad to be out of the rain, it depressed me that she didn't even question my age. Jason was right, I was getting old.

The moment we stepped through the doors, we were assaulted by loud music, clanging bells, mechanical voices, announcements, and crashing sounds. It all blended into a cacophony of noise accompanied by constant movement as players, workers, and security personnel flowed from one section to another. Slot machines of all sizes and shapes displayed enticing video screens and intriguing names—The Sorcerers, King of the Wind, Fort Knox. For a moment I simply stared, fascinated by the whirl of tumblers giving and taking credits as men and women—most around and beyond Social Security age—sat on cushioned seats, pushing buttons and hypnotically watching images twirl in front of them. Thin black cords—almost like umbilical cords—connected players to the casino's "credit" cards inserted in the machine. It was like stepping into a sci-fi movie.

Besides the noise, the air around us was filled with cigarette smoke. Although I grew up living with smokers, I hate the smell, and I wasn't sure how my sensitive stomach might react. I quickly checked where the restrooms were located. I wanted to be prepared if I needed to find one fast.

Once I'd located the signs for those areas, I looked beyond the slot machines, to the center of the casino where half-circle tables offered blackjack and poker. Although my mother loved to play cards, I doubted she'd be able to concentrate long enough to play at one of those games, so I decided Grandma and I should focus on the slot machines.

"We know she won't be in the non-smoking area," I said, ruling out the east end of the building. "So we might as well start here."

Grandma nodded, and I began walking along the edge of the casino, only to stop after a few steps when I realized Grandma wasn't following. A glance back showed me why. She'd paused to light a cigarette. Once that was accomplished, she came up beside me. "I'd forgotten," she said, "that the casinos are exempted from Michigan's no smoking in public places law."

Her sigh told me she was happy. I wasn't.

As we walked along the front inside wall of the casino, glancing down each row we passed, I found myself also checking out the different machines. Most took a penny or a nickel to play, but every so often I'd see one for a dollar or more. Even the penny machines could entice a player to spend more. Play one row. Two. Ten. Double the bet. Raise it more.

Bells dinging. Lights flashing.

One slot machine began chiming as we walked by, and I stopped to see what the woman had won. On the face of the screen, the numbers two hundred sixty were highlighted. "Wow," I said. "That's nice."

The woman playing the machine punched a button and glanced my way, her expression neutral. "That's two dollars and sixty cents," she said and reached for the slip of paper coming out of the machine.

"Oh."

Grandma chuckled, and we walked on.

We found Mom on the north side of the casino, standing next to a middle-aged man with a slight potbelly and long, white hair tied back in a low ponytail. A younger woman, probably in her thirties, stood next to him. Grandma marched up to my mom. "Flora Gardenia, just what do you think you're do-ing?"

My mother looked surprised to see us, but her look of surprise quickly changed to a big smile, and she leaned against the man standing next to her. "Winning, that's what I'm do-ing."

"With my money," Grandma sputtered, glaring at the man. "I thought you two broke up."

"Misunderstanding," he said and slipped an arm around Mom's shoulders before giving her a quick peck on the cheek.

So this was Ben.

Grandma quickly introduced me, and I nodded a greeting his way. Grandma had once described him as odd-looking. I didn't agree. Maybe his eyes were a little close-set, and his nose a little long, but he had a nice smile. However, if he was criticizing my mother for her weight gain, he needed to look in the mirror.

"I want my money back," Grandma demanded and held her hand out to my mother.

"Jeez, all I did was borrow it." Mom simply stared at Grandma's hand for a moment, and then she looked up at Ben. "Honey, could I borrow a couple hundred?"

Grandma rolled her eyes. "I thought you said you were win-ning."

"I am. Sort of." Mom shrugged and again looked at Ben, giv-ing him one of her seductive smiles.

To my surprise, Ben released his hold on Mom's shoulders and pulled out his wallet. He extracted two crisp, one-hundred dollar bills and handed them to Grandma, who harrumphed, thanked him, and stuffed the bills into the pocket of her jeans.

"That's half," Grandma said, again looking at Mom.

"Yeah, yeah." Mom dug into her jean's pocket.

The bills she handed Grandma were crumpled into a wad, and it took Grandma some time to straighten the tens and twenties. Once she'd reached two hundred, she handed the remaining wad back to Mom and said, "Don't you ever take money from me again without asking."

Mom shrugged. "Whatever."

I thought Grandma might explode. My mother sounded more like a teenager than a woman in her fifties. I'm not sure what would have happened next if the other woman—I assumed this was the friend from work—hadn't hit a jackpot at that moment. Bells went off, lights flashed, and both Mom and Ben switched their attention from Grandma to the machine.

Grandma raised a hand for a moment, as if she were going to say something, but then she shook her head and looked at me. "Let's go," she said and walked away from the three of them as others in the casino hurried to see how much Mom's friend had won.

"You're just going to leave her here?" I asked, hurrying to catch up with Grandma.

"Might as well. Either her friend or Ben will get her home. I have my money, and I don't think Ben will let her go too far in debt when it's *his* money." She looked at me. "God, I hope it skips you."

I understood and nodded before I said, "I think if we're leaving, I'd better use the bathroom."

"You feeling okay?"

"Fine," I lied. Seeing Mom had made me sick in a different way. I needed a few minutes to myself.

"If you don't mind," Grandma said, looking over at a bank of penny machines. "I wouldn't mind playing a couple dollars."

So much for Grandma's warning against gambling. "Take your time." I wasn't eager to return home.

I left Grandma as she inserted a dollar bill in one of the machines near the middle of the casino, and I took my time in the bathroom. I don't wear makeup, and with my hair cut short, it doesn't take much more than a few passes with my fingertips to give my curls some bounce and imitate a hairdo, but I washed my hands thoroughly and put on some lipstick, so when I exited the women's bathroom, I felt relaxed and ready to face the world again.

I found Grandma standing near the cashier's area, counting several bills and smiling. "You won?" I asked as I neared.

"Twenty dollars." She nodded toward a section on the east end of the casino. A sign above the entryway indicated it was a restaurant. "How about some lunch . . . on me? Or rather, on the casino."

That sounded good to me. I was actually a little hungry.

We chose a booth toward the back of the restaurant, away from the constant clamor of the casino. A waitress brought us menus and took our drink order—a ginger ale for me and an iced tea for Grandma. I was studying my menu when two men walked by our table and slid into the next booth.

I saw just the back of the man who took the seat directly behind Grandma. He had a bald head, broad shoulders, and was wearing a black shirt. I didn't realize who it was until I heard his voice.

"I hope you know, buying me lunch isn't gonna get you off the hook," I heard him say to the man seated across from him.

Baldy, I thought to myself. From the hospital and Brewster's house. *Was he following me?*

I immediately dismissed that idea.

Our waitress returned with our drinks and asked if we were ready to order. I quickly glanced at the menu and picked a turkey sandwich. Grandma went with a salad. From our booth, the waitress went to Baldy's. I was rather surprised when he ordered coffee. He made me think of a gangster, and I expected him to ask for a Scotch or whiskey. It was the other guy who did that.

"It's sad," Grandma said, looking out toward the casino floor, "seeing all these old people here, probably playing their Social Security checks, hoping to hit a big jackpot."

"Very sad," I agreed, but I wasn't really listening to her. Baldy was talking again.

"I'm not asking you to pay it all," he said. "But I can't let this go on. I made that mistake once, and it's costing me big time."

"It's not healthy," Grandma continued, "spending hours in a place like this. They should be—"

I put a finger to my lips and pointed toward her. She frowned, but stopped talking. I moved my hand so I cupped my ear, and again I pointed toward her. With her right hand she indicated the back of her seat, and I nodded. Using hand motions she asked if I wanted to change seats with her. I thought about it for a moment, then shook my head. I didn't want to chance him realizing I was in the next booth.

The other guy had been talking while all of these hand motions were going on. I'd caught most of what he'd said. Things hadn't been going well for him. Medical bills. Fewer overtime hours. Lady Luck turning against him.

Baldy wasn't saying anything.

Finally, the guy ran out of excuses. I heard the desperation in his voice when he said, "You've got to give me more time."

"Your wife have any expensive jewelry?" Baldy asked. "Diamond rings? Sapphire necklaces? Something you could pawn?"

"You want me to pawn my wife's rings?" the guy asked, sounding shaky.

"It would show me you truly plan on paying your debt. A good-faith gesture."

"But my wife . . . ?"

"Doesn't need to know. Tell her you're taking it in for a cleaning, that you want it appraised. Tell her whatever you want."

I could imagine Baldy smiling as he said that, and I pitied the other guy. I could also imagine Michael Brewster in a similar situation, being pressured by Baldy to pay his gambling debt. Pushed into doing something desperate, like steal from his coworker . . . pawn his wife's necklace.

Maybe take his own life.

I don't know what else I might have overheard. At the same time the waitress brought Baldy's coffee and the other guy's drink, the man stood. "I'm not going to pawn my wife's jewelry. I'll get you your money," he said, a desperate pitch to his voice. "I don't know how, but I'll get it."

He hurried out of the restaurant. Grandma's eyebrows rose and the waitress stood, holding the man's cocktail, looking as though she didn't know what to do. Baldy solved the problem. "Here," he said, handing her some money. "This should cover everything."

He took the drink from her as he got up, took a sip, and then set it down on the table. He saw me when he turned to leave. He hesitated for a second, staring at my face, then smiled, gave a slight nod, and walked on. I let out a breath I hadn't even realized I'd been holding and looked at Grandma. She was watching me.

"What was that all about?" she asked.

I smiled. "I think I know what happened to Linda's necklace."

Chapter Twenty-Eight

"You think Brewster pawned it?" Wade said after I finished my story.

"Yes." Grandma and I had discussed the possibility while we ate lunch. She, too, had heard Baldy mention a sapphire necklace. "He specifically said sapphire necklace. That's quite a coincidence, don't you think? And he said he'd let someone borrow a lot of money and it was costing him big time now. With Brewster dead, he can't get his money back."

Wade frowned. "That's what he said?"

"No, but we know . . . at least, he told me that Brewster owed him a lot of money. I don't think he showed up at the hospital or at Brewster's house to wish him well. He wanted to know if Brewster was alive, if he was going to get the money Brewster owed him."

"And you never got this guy's name?"

"No. but he's not real tall, has broad shoulders, and is bald."

Wade smiled, and I realized that description probably matched a lot of men. "Did you ever check on that license plate number I gave you?"

It was Wade's turn to say no. "I haven't had a chance."

"Well . . ." I left it at that. Besides, I didn't think Baldy's name was that important, but finding Linda's necklace was. "You need to check the pawn shops."

"I can't imagine Linda giving Brewster that necklace to pawn."

"I don't think she knew he'd pawned it. I think he hoped he'd get the money from whatever deal he had going with the guy on the answering machine, pay off Baldy, and get the necklace out of the pawn shop before Linda knew it was gone."

"Damn." Wade frowned and looked away. "How did I miss the gambling? Before Linda married Brewster, I did a background check on the guy. After all, Brewster was going to be a father figure for Jason. Why didn't any of this show up?"

I couldn't answer that question, but I hoped he had the resources to discover one thing. "If he did pawn the necklace, there will be some sort of record of the seller, won't there? I'd like to show her parents, show them they were wrong to accuse us."

"I'll tell Lisa . . . that is, Deputy Sawyer, to check into it, but knowing Frank and Jean, I'm sure they'll still find some way to blame it on me. Anything to make me look like the bad guy and get Jason away from me." He glanced into the living room where Jason was seated on the linoleum floor, playing with some of the toys he'd brought Monday from Brewster's place, Baraka stretched out beside him.

"How's it been going today? Did you find something to fix for lunch?" I asked, realizing I'd left before fixing anything.

"Jason and I had peanut butter and jelly sandwiches. I didn't know what to give your dog, so I put a little of his dry kibble in his dish."

"I don't usually feed him lunch, but thanks." I also usually soaked Baraka's kibble in water or broth—the extra moisture cuts down on the dog farts and lessens the chances he'll bloat— but I figured a little dry wouldn't hurt him.

"How about you?" he asked. "You said your grandmother bought you lunch. You're still feeling all right?" Wade lifted the mug of coffee that he'd been nursing since my arrival back from the casino. "You're not running to the bathroom."

"So far no problem." I was surprised myself that the smell of coffee hadn't triggered any nausea.

"Maybe you're not pregnant after all."

The way he said it—almost as a question—upset me. "That would make you happy, wouldn't it?"

"Yes. No." He looked away and then back at me. "I don't know, P.J. This is not a good time for you to be pregnant."

"Oh, I'm so sorry I forgot to check your calendar for when it would be a good time."

I shoved back my chair and started to stand. Wade caught my hand. "Don't go. I'm sorry. I didn't mean that the way it sounded. I'm just so damned confused and worried, I . . . If only I could remember more of what happened that day."

I settled back onto my chair. "Do you remember more?"

"Not really. Bits and pieces, maybe. I'm not sure what I actually remember, and what I'm hoping happened."

"What are you hoping happened?"

Wade hesitated a moment, and then said, "That Brewster caused the explosion. That he brought a bomb on board."

"You think he was that desperate?"

"I don't know." Wade shrugged. "Maybe there was no job in California, no way to pay off the rest of his gambling debts. Maybe he realized he'd made a mistake marrying Linda. Maybe he was crazy. I just don't know."

"That message on the answering machine indicated he was going to have money to pay those debts," I reminded Wade.

"That was *if* he sent something to the caller. We don't know what that something was or if Brewster actually had it to send. If something went wrong with his plan, then yes, he may have been desperate enough to commit suicide and take all of us with him."

I closed my eyes at that thought. Thank goodness Wade and Jason were on the bow of the boat and thrown off when it exploded. A concussion and a cut were a lot better than ending up in pieces.

"How is your head?" I asked, looking at him again. He'd removed the bandage the doctor had applied, and the cut looked ugly, the ends of stitches sticking up, but it didn't look infected, and his eyes were clear, his pupils the same size and not dilated. "Do you still have a headache?"

"Just a slight one." He scooted his chair closer and reached over to caress my cheek with the backs of his fingers. "I'm sorry, honey. I've been in such a foul mood. If you're pregnant, that's wonderful."

I wasn't sure he meant what he was saying, but I didn't comment. I knew nothing would be wonderful until he was cleared of causing Brewster's and Linda's deaths.

"Oh, and don't worry about those fireworks they found in your woodshed," Wade said, straightening in his chair. "Gespardo called while you were gone. He said those fireworks were so old, there's no way the gunpowder could have been used to make a bomb."

"Did he say anything about my computer?"

"No. Van Buren took that. They'll be the ones who have it analyzed."

"So no idea when I'll get it back." That irritated me the most. Frustrated, I stood. "How am I supposed to run an accounting business without my computer?"

Wade looked up at me. "Don't you have backups of your files?"

"Yes, but no computer. No program to run them on."

"We'll get you a new computer tomorrow." He rose from his chair and slipped his arms around my shoulders, giving me a hug. I know he was trying to make me feel better, and as he gently rubbed his hands over my back, I did feel myself relax a little. Especially when he said, "Things will be better tomorrow."

I sure hoped so.

Chapter Twenty-Nine

Wade didn't spend the night with me, and when my cell phone rang Thursday morning, I knew he wouldn't be going computer shopping with me, either.

"I need to meet with Jean and Frank," he said. "They want Jason to be at Linda's funeral and with them during the visitation."

"Is that a good idea?"

"I don't think so, but they're adamant about it, feel it would give him closure. I told them Jason had a bad night last night, but that didn't seem to faze them. I'm hoping I can change their minds."

"Poor kid." I felt sorry for Jason. He was the innocent in this mess.

"At least the funeral's going to be here in Kalamazoo, not up north."

"When?"

"Saturday. The medical examiner released her body yesterday."

Body? More like body parts, I thought. I wondered how a funeral home prepared a body in that condition. I doubted they'd have an open casket.

"Linda's parents also said they're filing for custody."

"They can't do that, can they?"

"They can if I'm in jail." He sounded despondent.

"You keep saying that, but you haven't been arrested. Maybe

they've realized you didn't do it."

A grunt was his response.

"Well, they didn't find any explosives at your place, did they? And they didn't find anything here but those ancient fireworks. How can they arrest you if they have no evidence?"

"Don't forget, the bomb-sniffing dog alerted on my car," he said.

"And on Brewster's car," I reminded him. Wade had said he didn't know why, but I didn't care. I figured the two alerts cancelled each other out.

Wade kept listing the negatives. "I have motive, and if Jean and Frank are called as witnesses—which I'm sure they would be—they'll have a jury believing I'd do anything to keep Jason with me. Add that damned life insurance policy, and I'm on my way to jail." He gave a sigh of frustration. "Why she didn't take me off as the beneficiary, I don't know. Logic says she *should* have."

I couldn't answer that, so I said nothing, and he went on. "I think they're expecting me to bring Jason with me today, but I don't want him hearing them call me a murderer and blaming Linda's death on me."

"Do you want to bring him here?" It would ruin my plan to go computer shopping, but it didn't seem right not to offer.

"No, Ginny said she'd take him to the Binder Park Zoo. So you have a day to yourself."

Maybe I should have been happy, but I wasn't. I felt slighted. Wade hadn't even asked if I'd want to join Ginny and Jason, or if I'd want to go with him to talk to Jean and Frank Healy. I was the outsider.

"Well, I hope all goes well," I said. "See you."

I ended the call and sank down on the nearest dining room chair. The tears came all too quickly, and Baraka came over and put his head on my lap. I tried to stop crying, but the way

Baraka looked at me with those sweet brown eyes of his brought even more tears. "I'm being silly," I told him, leaning close to rub behind his ears. "It's good for Ginny to spend time with Jason." I kissed the top of Baraka's head. "And Wade doesn't need me with him when he meets with Linda's folks. I'd be in the way. I'd . . ."

I wasn't sure what I'd be, but Baraka licked my cheek and I hugged him and laughed. What a mess I was. Feeling sorry for myself. Crying. Throwing up.

Why I didn't get sick yesterday when I came back to the house and found Wade drinking coffee, I didn't know, but the moment I picked up that carafe this morning and poured out the old coffee, my stomach did a warning flip. I quickly changed my mind about making a fresh pot. Soda crackers and a ginger ale became breakfast.

Once I had my emotions under control, I let Baraka out for his morning investigation of the yard. The weather report indicated a thirty percent chance of rain and a temperature in the mid-seventies. Quite a change from earlier in the week, but I preferred the lower temperature, especially with less humidity. After taking a shower, I put on a pair of denim shorts, a blue short-sleeved top, and sandals. I then called Baraka in. Since that "thirty percent" might hit anywhere in Kalamazoo County, I didn't want my dog out in the rain while I was gone. And since Jason's toys were strewn around the living room floor, I decided the best place for Baraka was in his crate.

To my surprise, he went in willingly.

I planned on writing a check for whatever I purchased, which meant I needed to stop at the bank and transfer some money from my savings account to my checking account. Normally I would have done that online, but without a computer, that wasn't possible. I wasn't really surprised when Sherry, the teller, greeted me with, "I hear the police were at your place yesterday."

"Yep," I said and handed her the slip to make the transfer.

She looked at the paper and clicked some keys on her computer. "You get robbed or something?"

"I think someone tried to break into my place night before last," I said. Not that Baraka barking and me seeing someone drive away had anything to do with the deputies invading my place, but no need to tell her that.

"That's scary." She clicked a few more keys. "I can't imagine anyone breaking into your place with that dog you have."

"I think he scared them away. He woke me barking."

"Good for him. Did the police find anything?"

"Not that I've heard." Which wasn't really a lie since they'd decided the fireworks were too old to be dangerous, and so far I hadn't heard that they'd found anything on my computer.

Sherry shook her head and pressed a key that started her printer. "Even when something's taken, the police don't always find who did it."

Or when boats blow up, I thought. As far as I could tell, the sheriff's department still had no idea who caused the explosion on Wade's boat.

I took the slip confirming the transfer and thanked Sherry. "Have a great day," she called after me as I headed for the door.

I know I was smirking as I walked to my car. I'd managed to get through that transaction without actually saying why the deputies were at my place. One thing I've learned after eight months of living in a small town is how quickly gossip can travel. I didn't want people knowing Wade was still a suspect or that the sheriff's department thought I might be involved. I was pretty sure being a "person of interest" wasn't the best advertisement for a CPA.

Although Kalamazoo was farther from Zenith than Battle Creek, I decided I'd find more places there to look for a computer. More stores, however, didn't guarantee variety. After a while all the stores began to look alike, and all the salesmen sounded alike as they spouted off the virtues of one computer over the next.

I didn't want to spend a lot of money on a new computer. Wade had said I would get mine back once the deputies were through checking what I had on it. That was, of course, if I wasn't arrested for having looked up bombs and explosions.

That thought kept me on edge.

I finally decided a laptop would be the best buy. Assuming I did get my PC back, the laptop could act as a backup and would be convenient to take with me when I visited a client. With that idea in mind, I went ahead and bought the more expensive one.

CHAPTER THIRTY

It was past noon by the time I returned to Zenith. My stomach growled as I stopped at the one and only blinking red light in the middle of town. The rumbling reminded me that soda crackers and soda weren't the most nutritious or lasting breakfast foods. That in turn reminded me that I needed to stop at the grocery store and pick up some staples. Having Jason at the house had nearly depleted my supply of milk, bread, and peanut butter and jelly, and in the last few days, I'd been going through soda crackers and ginger ale like candy.

Instead of heading home, I turned right and drove to Zenith's one and only grocery store.

I'd just parked and gotten out of my car when a man rode into the parking lot on a Harley Davidson. Although he was wearing a helmet that covered most of his face, I was pretty sure I knew who it was. I'd seen those tattooed arms before. And the moment he removed the helmet, exposing his bald head and dark brown goatee, I called out his name.

Ken Paget looked my way, smiled, and shook his head. "Stay away from me, Pajama Girl. You are nothing but trouble."

I might have taken offense, but he was partially right.

"How's the jaw?" I asked, walking toward him. Back in June I'd given Ken a cell phone I'd found. Ken and a friend of his thought they could figure out the password and see why others wanted the phone. What we didn't realize was there were people who would kill to keep that information secret. In a way Ken was lucky to just end up with a broken jaw.

He touched a hand to the side of his face. "Not too bad considering what that bruiser did to me."

"And your friend?"

"Okay, I guess. He's sort of disappeared." Again Ken smiled. "Police aren't too happy about that."

I stopped beside him. "What about you? You're not in jail. Did they drop the drug charges?"

"My lawyer pulled some strings. I'm now helping the Kalamazoo Public Safety Department install a new computer program, and I had to teach a computer class to a group of underprivileged children." He slid an arm around my shoulders and gave me a squeeze. "What about you? Found any cell phones you need to break into? Any murders to solve?"

"No cell phones, but . . ."

"But . . . ?" He edged back a little so he could look at me. "But what?"

"Yesterday the Van Buren Sheriff's Department took my computer because they think I'm involved in a boat explosion."

"You talking about the boat that exploded last weekend?"

I nodded.

"You weren't on the boat, were you?"

"No, but it was my boyfriend's boat."

Ken frowned. "So you're still hanging around with that deputy guy?"

"We're still together." At least I hoped we were.

"Meaning I should stay far, far away from you." He chuckled. "But of course, I won't. How about a beer?" He pointed back toward the center of town. "I just finished a job for the township, and was going to buy something here for lunch, but that bar makes great hamburgers. I'll even buy."

"I, ah . . ." I didn't want a beer, but a hamburger did sound good, and Ken might be able to help me with a question I had.

"Give me a ride on that," I said, pointing at his Harley, "and you're on."

Of course it wasn't much of a ride. The Pour House is less than a half mile from the grocery store, but it was fun to ride into town on a Harley behind a tattooed stranger. As Ken pulled into the Pour House's parking lot, a woman coming out of the beauty salon next door looked our way. For a moment she frowned, and then she waved, and I realized it was Sondra Sommers, my neighbor who, with her husband, owns the dairy farm on the road north of the road I live on. A northwest wind often brings the smell of their barn my way. Not that Sondra can do anything about that.

I waved back.

Sondra knows I've been dating Wade, so I wasn't surprised when her expression changed to puzzlement as she realized I wasn't with Wade. I doubt she'd say anything to Wade, but I have a feeling others will hear about me riding around with a guy who looks like Howie Mandel.

Inside the bar, it took a moment for my eyes to adjust to the dim lighting. Although Michigan's no-smoking law has been in effect for several years, the stale smell of cigarette smoke and spilled beer seems to be a permanent part of the Pour House. A slightly giddy sensation tickled my throat, and I hoped I wouldn't be making a dash for the bathroom.

Both the dining section and the counter were nearly empty, only two tables occupied by lunch customers and one shaggy-haired bearded man at the counter nursing a beer. Ken headed for a table toward the back of the restaurant area, away from where the others were seated and closer—to my relief—to the bathrooms. A woman came out from the kitchen carrying two plates of food, which she delivered to the nearest occupied table. "Be right with you," she called to us on her way back to the kitchen.

Within seconds she returned with menus. "What can I get you to drink?" she asked, looking at me.

"A ginger ale," I said, hoping the soda would calm the giddy sensation that hadn't gone away.

"Ginger ale?" Ken repeated, giving me a quizzical look. "Sure you don't want a beer or something?"

"No, no beer." Besides doctors recommending no alcohol during a pregnancy, just the idea of a beer increased the nausea in my stomach. "And I'd like a hamburger, medium well, no onions, no mayonnaise, no French fries, and no bun."

"You want a dill pickle?" the waitress asked. "Tomato? Lettuce?"

"A dill pickle sounds good . . . and a tomato."

Again Ken's eyebrows rose, but he didn't say anything to me until after he'd ordered a beer, a hamburger with everything on it, and a double order of fries. The waitress said she'd simply give him the fries I wasn't going to have and left to get his beer and my ginger ale. That was when Ken asked, "You on a diet?"

"My stomach's been giving me problems," I said, hoping that would satisfy his curiosity.

"You pregnant?"

"Jeez, why jump to that conclusion?" I didn't think I had a sign on my forehead announcing it to everyone.

He grinned. "So when are you due?"

I gave up. "I don't know. I have a doctor's appointment next week. Can we talk about something else?"

"Sure." He nodded a "thanks" when the waitress brought our drinks and waited until she'd walked back to the kitchen before he asked, "What do you want to talk about?"

"You know a little about stocks, buying and selling them, don't you?" The time I'd been in his shop in Kalamazoo, I'd seen a nine-by-twelve envelope with a brokerage house's return address on it.

"A little," he repeated.

"My knowledge," I confessed, "is limited to schedule Cs and filling out 1099 forms for my clients. What could someone—a stock broker, for example—steal and email to someone else that would be worth a lot of money?"

"Information," Ken said. "Insider information. If the stock broker knew something that would make a stock go up in value in the next few days, something that wouldn't be public information for awhile, he could inform his clients so they could buy the stock at a lower price and then sell it later, after the price went up, for a profit. That's known as insider trading."

I knew about insider trading, but the phone message I'd heard at Brewster's house didn't fit that description. "This would be more than information about a company," I said. "This would be something that could be mailed or sent over the Internet."

Ken leaned back in his chair and stroked his goatee, a slight frown furrowing his brow. "Can you be more specific?"

"I heard a message on an answering machine. It wasn't real clear. Lots of static. I heard the word rhythm. The caller was expecting something with rhythm sent to him, and he was going to pay a lot of money for it."

"But it wasn't sent?"

"Evidently not. The caller, in a later message, was really upset and said he wasn't going to pay if he didn't get whatever it was."

"What's the stock broker say?"

"Nothing. He's dead." I realized I needed to tell Ken the whole story. "He was on Wade's boat when it blew up Saturday. His name was Michael Brewster and he married Wade's ex. From what I've been learning, he wasn't as nice a guy as everyone thought. He gambled and owed money, and I think he stole something—this something he was supposed to send—from one of his coworkers."

Ken leaned forward and took a gulp of his beer before he asked, "Was the person he was sending this 'something' to also a stock broker?"

"I don't know. I imagine the sheriff's department has Brewster's phone records, but no one's told me anything."

"Well . . ." Ken settled back in his chair. "Have you ever heard of algorithmic trading? It's sometimes referred to as automated trading or algo trading."

I stopped him then. "Algo. I heard that word. On the answering machine. The caller said something like, 'No algo, no money.' I didn't know what it meant."

"Algorithmic trading uses a mathematical model that determines the best time to buy or sell a stock. They're designed so the orders are broken up. That is, rather than one very large transaction, millions of smaller transactions are executed every micro second. This way the stock's price isn't dramatically affected. It's called flash trading, and institutional traders use them. If this stock broker created an algorithm that was producing consistent positive results, it could be very valuable."

"I think Brewster's coworker must have created the algorithm. But wouldn't it be the broker's clients who benefited? How does the broker benefit?"

"The broker earns a fee off of every purchase or sale of a stock, and often they create and manage a portfolio for a client. If a broker or a brokerage house can show their clients they can make more money investing with them . . . well, you can see the advantage."

I did. "And if Brewster sells this algorithm to another broker . . . ?"

"Now you have two using the same system." Ken stopped talking as the waitress brought us our hamburgers, mine a plain patty on a plate with a slice of tomato and a dill pickle on the side, his with a bun and everything on it as well as a heap of

French fries.

It wasn't until after the waitress left that he went on. "Worse than selling it to another broker would be if this guy sold it to a software group. Now the algorithm can be purchased by multiple brokers or anyone who buys and sells stock. The creator of the algorithm has lost his advantage."

I held off asking Ken another question until he'd had a few bites of his hamburger and I'd eaten half of mine. The pause gave me time to consider what Ken had told me and think back on what Brewster's coworker had said. Finally, I asked, "Would someone kill to stop this from going public?"

CHAPTER THIRTY-ONE

Ken didn't have an answer to my question, and he asked me questions I couldn't answer. He said, "Assuming this coworker did kill Brewster, how did he know Brewster would be on your boyfriend's boat when the bomb went off? How and when did he get a bomb on the boat? And how did he trigger the bomb?"

All I could say was, "I don't know."

When Ken asked me the name of the brokerage firm Brewster and this other man worked for, I realized I didn't know that either and needed to find out.

I may not have wanted to discuss my pregnancy, but somehow Ken managed to maneuver our conversation back to that topic. I didn't tell him my fear of going crazy, and when he asked if Wade and I would get married, I kept my answer vague. "Until this mess about his boat exploding is cleared up, we're not even going to consider it."

It was nearly two o'clock by the time Ken took me back to the grocery store. We said our goodbyes, and he gave me a peck on the cheek before he put his helmet back on. His face mostly covered, I couldn't tell if he was serious or not when he said, "There's always me, Pajama Girl. Just call."

I did a lot of thinking as I picked up the grocery items I needed, my mind jumping from wondering if Brewster's coworker did plant a bomb and, if so, how, to Ken's parting statement of "Call me." From the first time I called him, back in April asking for help with my computer, Ken had been asking me out. Back then, all I had was his voice, and he sounded young. I'd guessed him to be in his teens. It wasn't until June, when I met him in person, that I realized only his voice was young, that he was actually quite a bit older than me. We never did date, and I thought that me putting him in a position where he ended up with a broken jaw had cooled his ardor.

But maybe not.

On the other hand, I hadn't experienced any romantic feelings, not even when he hugged me. It was nice knowing he found me attractive, but if things didn't work out between Wade and me, I wasn't going to rush into marriage. Not with Ken, not with anyone. I saw nothing wrong with being a single mom. I already had the advantage of working at home. At least I did when I had a computer.

With my new laptop, three sacks of groceries, and an un-bagged gallon of milk in the trunk of my car, I drove out of the village of Zenith, feeling better than I had all day. I would soon be able to get back to work, I'd had a delightful lunch with a friend, and so far I hadn't thrown up once.

That good feeling ended about a mile from my house. My car's engine coughed, then coughed again. The car gave a jerk. A shudder. And then the motor died. I barely managed to steer over to the gravel shoulder.

Damn.

For a moment I stared out the window, and then I turned the key, first to the off position and then to try to again start the motor.

Nothing.

I tried again, then again, and again.

I banged my fist against the steering wheel. "Why?" I shouted. "Why now?"

As far as I could tell, I had plenty of gas. I pushed the lever to pop the hood and stepped out of the car. A truck went whizzing by, heading back to Zenith. I don't think he realized I was in trouble. He didn't stop. I was glad it wasn't as hot as Tuesday; still, beads of sweat formed on my forehead. I checked under the hood, not sure what I was looking for. A loose wire? There were too many wires, but none looked broken or loose. A broken fan belt? Again, I couldn't tell.

Finally, I dropped the hood back in place and glanced down the road. My house wasn't that far. I could walk there. I had perishables that needed to be put in the refrigerator. I couldn't leave them in the car. I had my new laptop.

Two more cars drove by without stopping.

Only one thing to do, I decided. I rearranged the items in the grocery sacks so I had everything that needed refrigeration in one bag. I then grabbed my purse, the gallon of milk, the box with my new laptop, and the sack with the perishables and pushed the car door shut with my hip.

The milk was heavy, the laptop box awkward, and the bag of perishables weighed so much the plastic handles were cutting into my fingers. I wasn't far from my car, perspiration running down my face, when I heard a car's tires on the gravel shoulder behind me and the beep of a horn. "Want a ride?" Howard Lowe asked.

I turned to face his old blue Ford. He didn't get out, simply poked his head out the open window and motioned for me to come to him. Which I did. He leaned over and pushed open the passenger-side door, and a Styrofoam coffee cup rolled out. Food wrappers, tools, and ammunition covered both the front and back seats. I had no idea where to put my things.

"Well, are you gettin' in or not?" he barked, frowning at me.

"Where?" I asked.

He grunted and reached for my items, putting them in the back, on top of his junk. I glanced back at my car, trying to decide if I should go back for the rest of my groceries. Howard cleared his throat, and I got the message. So I pushed most of the empty food containers on the passenger's seat onto the floor, checked for anything that might poke me if I sat on it, and scooted in.

As soon as I had the door closed, Howard steered the car back on the road.

"What happened?"

"I don't know. My car just stopped running."

"You have gas?"

"Yes. Half a tank."

He grunted.

Moments later, we were at my place, which was lucky. Even with the car's windows down, the stench of old food wrappers, coffee cups, and dog hair was getting to me. Much longer and I might have added to the mess in his car. "Thanks," I said and got out.

"Let me take a look at it before you call anyone." Howard handed me the laptop box, milk jug, and grocery sack.

"I have two more sacks of groceries in the trunk," I told him. "Nothing that will spoil, and I can walk back and get them as soon as I put these things away."

"I'll bring them to you."

"Okay. Again, thanks." Sometimes the man surprises me. One minute he's a grizzly bear, the next a teddy bear.

I let Baraka out of his crate as soon as I was in the house and my hands were free. He went straight to the front door, so I put him outside. Boxelder bugs still covered the screen door and windows. I had bought a spray bottle, as Howard had suggested, but it was still in my car, along with the other items that didn't need refrigeration.

Perishables went into my refrigerator and freezer, and then I unpacked my new laptop. Although I hadn't budgeted for this purchase, having a laptop with me was going to make visiting clients so much easier. That was my thought until I attempted to load the accounting program I'd purchased eight months ago, when I first started my own business.

What should have been easy, wasn't. "Why?" I grumbled, staring at the error message on the laptop's screen. "What am I doing wrong?"

I tried reloading the program, tried bypassing the opening screen, tried opening a file I'd saved on a thumb drive. Nothing worked. I even tried calling Ken. He was the computer expert; he should know how to get this damn thing to work.

Except, Ken wasn't answering his phone.

"I need help," I said when directed to leave a message. "I can't get my accounting program to load on this new computer. What do I do?"

After ending that call, I stared at the laptop. I couldn't see any sense in uploading files if I couldn't get the program to work, and I wasn't in the mood to check emails, especially since I had a feeling one of my clients might be emailing me to find out when I'd have his spreadsheet done. I wanted to swear at the Van Buren Sheriff's Department for taking my computer, to yell at the salesman who assured me this laptop would do everything I needed, to throw things . . . to cry.

Or maybe take a nap.

But no, I didn't want to sleep the day away.

I looked around. What I should be doing was housework. My bed was unmade, there were dirty dishes in the sink, and I hadn't dusted or vacuumed for over a week. In a way, I realized, I wasn't unlike my grandfather. Grandpa Benson's woods were filled with junk primarily because he was too lazy to cart the unwanted items to the dump. My house was always a mess because I didn't want to take the time to clean it.

Heredity. Why, I wondered, do we always inherit the bad genes?

I wanted my grandmothers' genes. Both Grandma Benson and Grandma Carter were energetic, loving women. Caring women. Sane women.

Baraka whining at the door pulled me out of my depressing thoughts, and I decided what I needed was a walk. A walk with my dog in the woods.

I didn't bother locking the front door. I wasn't sure how long I'd be gone, and if Howard came back with those last two sacks of groceries, I wanted him to be able to get into the house. I did take my cell phone with me. If Ken got my message and called, I wanted to talk to him.

I noticed a drop in temperature as soon as I passed the chicken coop and entered the woods. I also noticed an easing of the tension in my shoulders and a lift to my spirits as I watched Baraka trot along the trail ahead of me, pausing here and there to sniff at a bush or tree. What did he smell? I wondered. A rabbit? Fox? Deer? Or Howard's dog, Jake?

Tramped-down ferns and bushes with broken limbs indicated the spot where Jason and Baraka had left the trail and gone deeper into the woods yesterday. I wished I had that map he'd found in my father's old room. I tried to remember where Jason had dropped its sodden remains, but I didn't see any signs of the soaked and shredded paper. Howard, I assumed, still had the copy I'd made for him, but I hadn't thought to ask him for it earlier, when he drove me to my house.

"Let's see how far Jason got," I said to Baraka and left the cleared path for the one the boy had made.

Baraka ran ahead of me and then back, making it difficult for me to decipher what was newly crushed underbrush and what had occurred earlier. "Calm down," I ordered, trying to keep him behind me. Again I marveled at the variety of items my grandfather had dumped in these woods. I had a feeling some of the stuff, such as rolls of chicken wire, were being stored, not dumped. A farmer never knew when he might need more chicken wire. But over time that wire had rusted, weakened, and became unusable . . . became junk.

Both a fallen tree and the ring of my cell phone stopped my forward progress. "Ken," I said as soon as I answered. "Thanks for calling back."

I told him my problem. He suggested I go on the Internet to the program's website and see if there might be something I could download. "And if that doesn't work, call me back," he said when I told him where I was.

I didn't run back to the house, but I did walk fast. Baraka raced ahead of me, through the back gate, around the side of the house, and out of sight. I started running when I heard a man yell, then cuss, along with the sound of something crashing.

The moment I came around the side of my house, I saw the silver BMW parked in my driveway. A few steps more and I saw the man I'd met in front of Brewster's house. I also remembered his name. Steve Richardson.

Today Steve-the-stock-broker was wearing a blue sports jacket, tan slacks, brown loafers, a pale blue shirt, and a blue-and-red striped tie. He looked as fashionable as the first time I'd met him, except he was now flat on his butt on my front porch, Baraka standing next to him, my dog's nose in the man's crotch.

Richardson pushed my dog's head away and started to get to his feet, but he stopped when I yelled, "Don't move!"

I wasn't worried if he'd hurt himself. He could have broken every bone in his body as far as I was concerned. What upset me was my brand-new laptop now lay on the concrete steps below him, the lid sprung open and at a weird angle.

"Your dog knocked me down," he protested. "Attacked me."

Baraka was attacking him again, his nose not in Richardson's crotch, but nudging the guy's jacket pocket. Swearing, Richardson tried to shove Baraka's head away, only to have Baraka return to the same area.

"Forget my dog. Is that my laptop?" I asked, even though I was sure it was.

"I, ah . . ." He pushed Baraka away again.

"You, ah, what?" I walked closer to the steps. There was no doubt about it. The laptop was mine. First thing I'd done after taking it out of the box was tape my business card on the lid.

He looked at me and then at my dog. Baraka was edging toward that pocket again.

"Baraka, sit!" I ordered, not wanting Richardson distracted, but liking the idea that he saw Baraka as a threat. "You're Steve, right?" I said. "Steve Richardson?"

"Yes." He kept his gaze on Baraka.

Although Baraka normally obeys my commands, my dog was once again moving forward, sniffing around Richardson's jacket. I finally caught on. "What do you have in your pocket?"

"My pocket?" For a moment Richardson's expression changed to a frown and his hand went to the pocket on the right side of his sports jacket.

"No. Your other pocket," I said, wanting to know what Baraka was after.

"Oh." His frown turned into a smile as he pushed Baraka's head away. "You mean this." He slid his hand into his left pocket and pulled out one of those bones they sell in grocery stores. It was still in its plastic wrapper.

I stepped closer and held out my hand. "Give that to me."

"I didn't think you were here," Richardson said as he handed me the bone.

"So you were going to keep my dog busy with this."

Richardson didn't say anything, but he watched as Baraka left his side and came over to sit beside me.

"Do you realize you just ruined a brand-new laptop?" I could see a crack in the lid, and I had an urge to hit the guy over the head with the dog bone he'd just handed me.

"I didn't know it was new. I thought it was Brewster's."

"Well, it's not. What else did you take?"

"Nothing." Richardson glanced at Baraka, who now sat by my side, staring at the bone I held in my hand.

It seemed to me, Richardson said "nothing" a little too quickly.

He started to stand.

"Stay where you are," I ordered.

He ignored me. "Sorry about the laptop," he said as he straightened to his full height and brushed off the seat of his slacks. "Blame it on the company you keep."

When he glanced toward his car, I knew what he was thinking. "Don't you dare leave," I said, pointing the dog bone at him.

He obviously didn't consider a dog bone a dangerous weapon. Without saying anything, he marched down the steps and headed for the open gate and his car.

"Come back!" I yelled and hurried after him. I grabbed the back of his jacket with my left hand and pulled back, catching him off balance, and swung the dog bone at his head with my right hand.

I heard the bone thunk against his skull and saw him stagger back a step, but I wasn't ready when he swung around and hit me in the face with his fist.

Pain shot from my cheek to my eye to my temple. Stunned, I wobbled on my feet, trying to keep my balance. I barely saw Baraka go streaking by me, heading for Richardson, but I heard the man's yelp of surprise when ninety pounds of muscle hit his side. I also heard Howard Lowe yell, "What the hell is going on!"

CHAPTER THIRTY-TWO

By the time Richardson was on his feet, Howard had a shotgun in his hands, pointed at the man, and Baraka had come back to me. I hugged my dog, and then used him to get to my feet. The right side of my face felt numb, and all I could think was, *Here we go again. Another black eye.*

I'd had one in June, when a brute took me by surprise and grabbed a briefcase an elderly woman had given me. For nearly two weeks I had to explain that black eye. I didn't want to go through that again.

"Your dog attacked me," Richardson grumbled, staring at Baraka.

"No." I wiggled my mouth, hoping all my teeth were still intact. "He knocked you down." And as Richardson was getting up, I'd seen him tap his right pocket, as if checking to make sure nothing had fallen out. That had me curious. "What do you have in your pocket?"

"Nothing."

Once again he'd said it too quickly. I didn't believe him. "Take it out."

Richardson glared at me as he slid a hand into his right pocket.

"Take it out slowly," Howard ordered.

Richardson switched his gaze over to Howard—at the shotgun—shook his head, and slowly pulled his hand out of his pocket. I knew right away what he was holding. "That's my flash drive."

"Not Brewster's?" Richardson looked down at the thumb-size gadget he held.

"No, it's mine." I stepped closer and took the flash drive from him, thankful we'd stopped him before he got away with it. The backup files for all of my clients were on that small device. Without it, and without my computer, I might as well apply for unemployment.

"You're sure it's yours?" Richardson didn't look convinced.

"Yes, I'm sure. And if you're looking for that algorithm, I don't know where Brewster had it."

Richardson's eyes widened. "But if you know about it . . ."

"I know because I overheard a message. And if it makes you feel better," though I didn't know why I cared, "Brewster didn't get it to the person he was going to sell it to."

"He didn't?" Richardson's entire demeanor changed, his features softening and his stance more relaxed. But only for a second, and then he frowned. "If he didn't sell it, what did he do with it?"

"I have no idea."

"Dammit, I've got to have it back."

Richardson took a step toward me, and Baraka quickly put himself between the broker and me, but it was Howard, loudly clearing his throat, that reminded the man there was still a shotgun pointed at him. Richardson stopped his forward motion and Howard spoke up. "What do you want me to do, P.J.? Take him out back in the woods and dispose of him?"

Mr. Suave Broker blanched at that idea, and I had to force myself not to smile. "Let's go inside," I suggested. "I think we'll let the sheriff's department decide what to do with him."

"Please, I'm sure we can work this out. I didn't know . . ." Richardson switched his attention from Howard to me, and then back to Howard.

Howard motioned toward my front porch with the shotgun and Richardson sighed. Shoulders slumped and his head hung low, he walked past me and back to the steps. I followed him, Baraka by my side, while Howard came along behind me. I picked up my broken laptop before going up on the porch and into the house. Oh how I wished I'd purchased that extended warranty plan the store had offered. "You are buying me a new laptop," I told Richardson, not sure how I was going to force him to do that, but determined to try.

"Sure, sure. Whatever." For a moment he stopped just inside the dining room, and then he went ahead and sat on the nearest chair. "God, what a fool I was." He leaned his elbows on the table and cradled his head in his hands. "Mike must have had a flash drive with him that night. Must have put something in my drink that knocked me out."

"Tell me what happened," I said and pulled out a chair opposite him. Howard, I noticed, slipped into the living room and sat on the couch, his shotgun leaning against the arm rest. Baraka went off to see if any food had miraculously appeared in his food dish.

"It was last Friday night," Richardson said, looking up at me. "I don't know if it was a coincidence or something Mike set up, but my wife and kids had won tickets to the evening performance of the circus that was in town. Mike dropped by about a half hour after Jill and the kids left. He had a six pack of beer with him and said he just wanted to get together one more time before he left town."

"Did you two get together often?" I asked.

"Not often, but occasionally, especially before he met Linda." Richardson smiled. "I stood up with him at their wedding." Then he shrugged. "It wasn't a big wedding. Mike didn't have much family here in Michigan. Most of them live in California, which I assumed was why he was moving back there."

"So his coming over didn't surprise you?"

"No." He sighed. "I suppose I should have been suspicious when he started asking me about the algorithm I created, if I kept it on my computer at work or on my home computer. But by that time I'd had two beers. We were reminiscing about the years we'd worked together. It seemed natural that the topic of my algorithm came up."

"You alone created this algorithm? Brewster didn't help you?"

Richardson scoffed and glanced back at Howard. "Did you know Michael Brewster?" he asked.

"Nope."

That was all Howard said, and after a second, Richardson looked back at me. "He wouldn't really shoot me, would he?"

"I'm never quite sure what Mr. Lowe will do," I said, keeping my expression serious. "Tell me more about last Friday night. So you're saying Brewster didn't help you create this algorithm, but he knew about it. How did he know about it?"

"How?" My question seemed to surprise Richardson. "Mike might not be the sharpest broker in town, but he saw my earnings over the last eight months. He knew I had something that was telling me when to buy or sell. He finally guessed it was an algorithm, but he didn't guess I'd created it. He figured it took a committee to come up with all the factors that predict if a stock price is going to go up or down. I suppose I bragged a bit when I told him I, alone, came up with the data."

"And last Friday night he asked you where you kept this algorithm you created?"

Richardson nodded. "I didn't think anything of it at the time, just told him I had a copy on my computer at work and one there, at my house. I wasn't worried about him stealing it. First of all, he was my friend . . . or I thought he was. And I had the files password protected."

"But he figured out the password." I said it as a statement, not a question.

Again, Richardson nodded. "I don't know how, but I'm pretty sure he put something in that third beer while I was in the bathroom. I just vaguely remember after that he kept asking me questions about my family, my pets, and where I went to school. He also kept urging me to drink my beer. He was gone when my wife and kids came home. She said she tried to wake me and finally gave up and left me asleep on the couch. Next morning, I was still in a stupor when I woke and found the note he'd left. I called him as soon as I understood what he'd done, but he just laughed and said, 'Thanks, you've made my life easier.' "

"What did the note say?"

"That I should have followed our brokerage house's guidelines and made my password more difficult."

"Meaning he figured out your password from something you told him?" That sounded too simple.

"I guess so. When I went on my computer, I saw that the file had been copied the night before. I didn't copy it, so it had to be him. Onto a flash drive, I'm sure."

"Did you break into his house Monday night?"

"No." He shook his head. "To be honest, I've been a mess since Friday night. Saturday I had a headache that wouldn't stop. I was throwing up. Felt terrible."

Sounded like my Saturday.

"As I said, as soon as I realized Mike had the algorithm, I called him. It took me a while after that call to get myself over to his house. When I did arrive there, he was gone. A guy came out of the house next door. He said he didn't know where Mike went, but that Mike had his wife and stepson with him, along with a picnic basket. The guy was weird," Steve muttered, then stopped talking and cradled his head in his hands.

"How was he weird?"

Richardson looked back up at me and shrugged. "I don't

know. I got the feeling he didn't like Mike. Really didn't like him."

"Why? What did he do? Say?"

"Well, when I told him I needed to see Mike, that he'd taken something of mine, and I needed to get it back right away, the guy said, 'Good luck. We'll never get back what he took from us.' "

"Did he say what Brewster took from them?"

Richardson shook his head, then rubbed the spot I'd hit with the dog bone. I didn't feel any remorse. My cheek was throbbing.

Although it was interesting to hear that Brewster had taken something from his next-door neighbor, what I wanted to know was what Steve Richardson did. "Okay, you arrived Saturday, Brewster's gone, you talk to the neighbor, and it sounds like Brewster's on a picnic or something. Then what did you do?"

"Nothing. That neighbor kept watching me, so I didn't dare break a window or jimmy a door. I did walk around the place. I tried to look casual as I tested the back door and slider. Not that it mattered. Both were locked. I hoped, since he had that For Sale sign in front, that I might find a key hidden under a rock or flower pot. But I didn't."

"So you just went home?"

"Not right away," he admitted. "I'm not sure how long I sat in my car, staring at the house. I couldn't get my brain to focus, couldn't believe I'd been so stupid. So trusting." Richardson sighed and licked his lips. "Finally, I gave up. Other neighbors were coming outside, and I was afraid someone might report me to the police. So I drove home. I was still trying to decide what to do next when Jill met me at the door and said some boat blew up on Lake Michigan, and the little boy they'd rescued looked like the boy we met at Mike's wedding . . . that the boy even had the same name as Mike's stepson."

Richardson paused again, but only for a moment, and then he went on. "At that point they hadn't identified any of the survivors or victims, so I spent the rest of Saturday and most of Sunday listening to the TV and radio and looking for information on the computer. I even called several hospitals, but, of course, they wouldn't give out any information. Ironically, it was my boss who called me Sunday evening and confirmed that Mike and Linda had been on the boat and as of then hadn't been found." His shoulders sagged, and he hung his head. "I know it's terrible, but I kept hoping Mike was dead."

"Considering everything, I don't blame you," I said.

"I went to work Monday morning afraid Mike had sent my algorithm to someone before he got on that boat, and that I'd see evidence of its usage in the market. I asked to be left alone, and I think my secretary, the boss, and the rest of our staff thought my despondent attitude was due to what had happened to Mike. I didn't say any different, but what I was doing was checking the software companies that sell algorithms to see if anything was being advertised that matched mine. I was also checking the stocks my algorithm was picking for buys or sells to see if there were patterns that might indicate someone else was using it.

"I was feeling pretty good by Monday night, but then I started worrying. 'What if someone found the flash drive Mike had put the algorithm on?' Or 'What if he'd loaded it on his computer?' I knew I had to get in his house and see, but as you know, when I arrived there Tuesday, the house was surrounded by the police."

"Sheriff's deputies," I corrected, remembering the moment I first met Steve Richardson. "And I, foolishly, told you I had Brewster's laptop."

He nodded. "You also told me your name."

His smile indicated that was another mistake I'd made, and I suppose he was right. There aren't too many P.J. Benson's in the phone book, and I'm sure my address would have come up if he searched for me on the Internet.

"It took me a while to find this place," he said, "and when I pulled into your driveway, I saw your dog outside and knew I wouldn't be able to just duck into your house and grab the laptop."

"So you came back later that night. And what? Were you going to break in? Poison my dog?" I looked at the bone I'd taken from him. It was still sealed in plastic, still had the manufacturer's label on it, but that didn't mean he couldn't have put something on it that would harm my dog.

I pushed the bone farther away from the edge of the table and out of Baraka's reach.

"No, I wasn't going to poison him. I don't know what I was thinking. That maybe the bone would keep him quiet and I could sneak in and get Mike's laptop before anyone knew. But he started barking before I even got close to the door."

"So you came back today."

He nodded. "Your car wasn't here. Your door wasn't even locked. I thought my luck was finally changing."

"Okay, I can understand why you wanted Brewster's laptop, but why take mine?" I glanced at the one I'd just purchased, its cover and screen now broken. "Couldn't you tell it was new?"

"It was the only one I saw, so I figured it had to be Mike's." He also looked at my damaged laptop. "It's not my fault it's broken. If your dog hadn't—"

I'm not sure what excuse he might have given because Howard interrupted him. "You *will* buy her a new laptop."

Richardson swiveled in his chair and looked back at Howard, who once again had a hand resting on the barrel of his shotgun. "Yes, of course," Richardson said.

"One just as good or better than the one you broke."

"Yes, but—"

"No buts," Howard said. "Or I'll find you."

The way Richardson swallowed hard, I knew he understood the threat. He looked back at me. "But if I'm in jail . . . ?"

I glanced at Howard. Just a slight nod of his head told me it was up to me, so I decided. Putting Steve Richardson in jail wasn't going to resolve anything. The man was as much a victim as he was a bad guy. My answer was simple. "You bring me a new laptop, and I mean today, not someday, and I'll forget you were here."

"I can do that. Yes, I can do that." Richardson cautiously stood, glancing back at Howard as he did. "Is it all right if I leave now?"

Howard didn't stand. In fact, he leaned back in the chair and smiled. "Just remember, if you could find out where she lived, I can find you . . . and your family."

"No need to do that," Richardson said. "I'll have a new laptop here in an hour or two. I promise."

Howard did stand after the broker left the house, and so did I. Together we stood by the screen door and watched Richardson get into his sports car, back around Howard's Ford, and onto the road. Only when the silver BMW was out of sight did I look at Howard. "Would you really have shot him?"

Howard chuckled and cracked open his shotgun. "No shells. I've got a box of them somewhere in my car, but darn if I could find them when I pulled into your yard."

I also laughed, and then I leaned against his side. "Thanks."

For a second Howard simply stood, rigid as a board, and then he wrapped an arm around my shoulders and hugged me even closer. "No problem."

My head was way too close to his armpit, and I knew he hadn't bathed in a while. Also his overalls smelled of dirt and oil, which reminded me of my car. As casually as I could muster,

I pulled away from his side. "I don't imagine you've had time to work on my car."

"Nope, got side tracked," he said and looked at my face. "Whatcha gonna do about that black eye?"

Although the throbbing in my cheek had lessened, I had a feeling there would be some bruising. "Is it turning black and blue?"

"You got any steak you can put on it?"

"Steak?" I laughed. "Have you seen how much they want for a steak?"

"How about a bag of frozen peas?"

That I had and nodded.

"Why don't you grab the peas, lie down, and put the bag on that cheek. The cold will help keep the swelling down. Maybe you won't look as bad as you did last time. Meanwhile, I'll go see to your car."

I wasn't sure if I should be insulted by Howard's comment on how I'd looked last time I was hit in the face, or just accept that black eyes weren't fashionable. The idea of lying down for a while sounded great. I was tired. It might only be mid-afternoon, but my body said it was time for a rest. "I'll do that," I agreed, and headed for my freezer, then remembered the map. "Later, Howard, could you bring me that copy of the map, the one I made for you the other day? Jason ruined the original."

"Will do," he promised. "And then we'll go on a treasure hunt."

CHAPTER THIRTY-THREE

I didn't merely rest. I swear the moment I stretched out on the couch I fell sound asleep. It was the smell of meat cooking that woke me. Not just meat, steak. It smelled like someone was broiling a steak.

Confused, I pushed myself up to a seated position. The bag of frozen peas that I'd had on my cheek had slipped off while I slept and now lay on the floor. I leaned down and touched it. The peas were no longer frozen, which told me I'd been asleep for quite a while.

"Wade?" I called toward the kitchen doorway, wondering when he'd arrived.

It wasn't Wade who stepped into view, but Howard, Baraka by his side. "He's not here," Howard said. "Just me."

I stared at him, my mind trying to put everything together—what day it was, what had happened, and why Howard was in my kitchen, obviously cooking something considering the spatula he held in one hand.

"What . . . ?" I asked and slowly rose to my feet, still feeling groggy, the left side of my face aching. "Is that a steak I smell?"

"Two steaks," he said and smiled. "I figured you might be hungry when you woke up, and I read somewhere that steak's supposed to be good during pregnancy."

"But I didn't buy any steak." Nor did I have any in my freezer or refrigerator.

"I had some." A ding from the microwave caused him to

glance back into the kitchen. "Excuse me. Got to check the sweet potatoes."

He disappeared from view and so did Baraka, which didn't surprise me. My dog liked to be close by when food was being prepared . . . just in case I might give him a bite. I had trained him not to lurch at anything dropped on the floor, and he didn't exactly beg, but I always found it difficult to ignore those big brown eyes of his, and he usually did end up with a treat.

I started for the kitchen, but paused next to the dining room table. There, laying beside two grocery sacks, was a laptop, its lid slightly discolored and scratched. "Did Richardson come back?" I called to Howard. "Is this the laptop that's to replace the one he broke?"

I heard the microwave start up again before Howard appeared in the doorway. "Nope. That's my laptop," he said. "Richardson called while you were asleep. He said he wouldn't be able to get a replacement for yours until tomorrow, so I thought you might want to borrow mine until then. Oh, and I put away some of your groceries," he said, pointing at the two sacks on the table. "But there are a few things left. I didn't know where they went."

I hadn't heard the phone ring or Howard come into my house. Hadn't heard him putting away groceries. Hadn't heard anything while I slept. "What about my car?" I asked, and stepped closer to my front door so I could see my driveway. There sat my gray Chevy, and right behind it was Howard's blue Ford.

"It was just a coil wire that had come loose. Purrs like a kitten now." Again he glanced into the kitchen, and then back at me. "How do you like your steak? Medium? Well done? Oh, and I hope you like spinach."

"Spinach and sweet potatoes? I don't remember buying either of those items."

Howard shrugged. "Ann, at the store, said they'd be good for someone in your condition."

"You told Ann I was pregnant?"

He looked away. "Sort of."

Oh, shit, I thought. If Ann knew, it wouldn't be long before everyone in Zenith knew.

"I wanted to buy something that would be good for a woman in your condition," Howard said. "So I asked her what she recommended, and that sort of led to me telling her you were pregnant."

A woman in my condition. I chuckled at the term. Well, no big problem. Being pregnant wasn't something you could hide forever.

I went over to where Howard was standing, and before he had a chance to move, I hugged him and kissed his cheek. "Thank you," I said. "And you win."

He reared back slightly, scowling as he looked down at me. "Won what?"

"You can hunt in my woods whenever you want."

He grunted, and then grinned. "Knew I'd win, one of these days. So, what about the steak? How do you like it?"

"Medium," I said and followed him into the kitchen.

While Howard handled the cooking, I set the table and fixed Baraka's dinner. My cell phone rang as I was filling water glasses. It was Wade. "I'll keep it short," I told Howard, when he pointed at the plates he was preparing.

"Hey," I said as I stepped out onto my front porch. "How it go today?"

"Better than I expected," Wade said and started to tell me about his meeting with his ex-in-laws. I stopped him before he'd said more than, "I think we've come to an agreement."

"Can I call you back?" Howard was bringing our two plates to the dining room table. "We're about to eat."

"We?"

A part of me wanted to make Wade jealous—after all, he hadn't reacted as I'd hoped when I told him I was pregnant—but I didn't have the energy to play games. "Howard had to fix my car today, and he's also fixed me dinner."

"Are you okay?"

I liked the concern I heard in Wade's voice. "I'm fine. I'll tell you all about my day and you can tell me all about yours when I call you back. Or are you coming here tonight?"

"Ah, that's, ah, why I called," he said. "I'm not going to be able to make it tonight. Will you be around in the morning?"

"As far as I know, I will."

"Good. I'll see you then." He paused before saying, "Tell that old geezer to mind his manners. No horning in on my girl."

"Yeah, right, I'll tell him that." I smiled as I clicked off my phone. At least Wade considered me "his girl."

As I pulled open the screen door, I noticed there were only a few boxelder bugs on the screen and none on the siding around the door. I also noticed the spray bottle I'd purchased at the grocery store now sat on the porch railing, about a third full of sudsy water. "You sprayed?" I asked Howard as I came back into the dining room.

"Just the screen and around the door," he said, standing and waiting for me to sit. "I figured you could finish up."

"Seems to be working." But even as I said that, a boxelder bug landed on the table.

"I think you brought that one in with you." Howard swished it off. "So what's up with lover boy?"

"I don't know. I told him I'd call him back later." I thought about Wade's warning to Howard and decided not to mention that.

"I talked to a couple buddies of mine," he said and began

cutting into his steak. "No one's heard of any contract out on Wade."

"I guess that's good." Except so far it didn't look like anyone would have wanted Wade's boat to blow up . . . other than Wade himself.

Howard must have picked up on my fears. "If they really thought he did it, they would have arrested him by now."

"And if they really thought he was innocent, I would have my computer back by now," I countered. "This whole situation feels like a cat-and-mouse game." And I didn't like being the mouse.

"You'll figure it out. As I've said before, you're a regular Jessica Fletcher." He nodded and stabbed a piece of steak. "Now eat up."

That my gruff neighbor even knew who Jessica Fletcher was or had watched *Murder, She Wrote* amazed me, but he loved telling me I was turning Zenith into a Cabot Cove.

I sure hoped not.

After dinner I did call Wade. "Sorry," I said. "Howard went to so much trouble fixing dinner I didn't want it to get cold."

"No problem," Wade said, but I could tell from the way he said it, he was a little upset. I wasn't sure if it bothered him that I'd cut his earlier call short or if he was upset because Howard had fixed me dinner.

"He bought the steaks because they told him at the grocery store they'd be good for someone in my condition."

I thought Wade would find that statement as funny as I did, but he responded with, "What kind of condition is that?"

"Pregnant," I said, deciding if anyone had a reason to be upset, it was me.

Wade grunted.

"Howard also stopped Richardson from taking off with my

flash drive, and—"

"Richardson? Who's Richardson?"

"He's the man I talked to at Brewster's house Tuesday. He worked with Brewster."

I realized then that I needed to tell Wade everything. Well, almost everything. I told him I ran into Ken at the grocery store, but I didn't mention having lunch with him. Wade's opinion of my computer guru isn't the highest. Mainly I told Wade that Ken figured the message on Brewster's answering machine was referring to an algorithm for buying and selling stocks, and that such an algorithm would be very valuable to a software company or another brokerage house.

Wade stopped me when I told him my car stopped running a mile from my house. "Yes," I said. "The car had gas and hadn't run out of oil." Just because I nearly ran out of oil a month ago, he's been harping on me to keep that checked. And I guess I need to. The Chevy does seem to have an oil leak.

I may have overemphasized my frustration with cars going by without stopping and my relief when Howard did stop and offer a ride because Wade interrupted with, "Okay, okay. How's this connect with that Richardson guy taking your flash drive?"

"I'm getting to that."

I decided to skip the part about my new laptop giving me problems, and how, since I couldn't load my files, I decided to go into the woods and see if I could find where my dad buried Nora's baby. "It was when I got to the house," I said, "that I found Richardson sneaking out the front door. He was after Brewster's laptop, and he thought the one I'd just purchased was Brewster's."

"But Howard stopped him?"

"Yeah." I saw no need to mention Richardson dropping and breaking my new laptop, or that I now had a black eye. I just said, "Richardson told us how Brewster drugged him last Friday night and stole an algorithm he'd created." I thought I'd better clarify that. "One that Richardson created. Not Brewster. Richardson's pretty sure Brewster copied it onto a flash drive. It might be on that flash drive Jason found Tuesday, when he and his grandparents went upstairs at Brewster's house."

"Jason has Brewster's flash drive?"

"No." I wasn't sure if I wasn't being clear or if Wade was being purposefully obtuse. "Your son gave the flash drive to Deputy Sawyer. So, can you find out if they've checked what's on it, see if it might be an algorithm?"

"I'll give her a call," Wade said.

"That flash drive may be evidence. Motive. You need to get it to Deputy Milano."

"Yes, Detective Benson."

I heard the sarcasm. "I'm just saying . . ."

I paused. What was I saying? Even if Richardson's missing algorithm was on that flash drive, what did it prove? That Brewster was a sneaky thief who didn't care if he hurt a coworker? Brewster's faults were becoming quite clear, but they didn't prove Wade innocent of murder.

I decided I needed to change the subject. "How is Jason doing?"

Wade chuckled for the first time during the call. "Ginny wore him out at the zoo. Wore herself out, too, I guess. Anyway, Jason's asleep on the sofa. They came back around four, we had dinner at five, and Jason was zonked out by five-thirty."

"You said your meeting with Linda's parents went all right."

"Went better than I'd expected. I think the shock of losing their daughter is wearing off. They're now focused on her funeral. I also think they're beginning to believe I might not be the one who planted the bomb. Not that that makes me innocent in their eyes. If it was someone with a grudge against me, that still puts me at fault. But I guess the fact that I haven't been arrested and tossed in jail, along with some of the things the Van Buren Sheriff's deputies have told them, have mellowed their opinion of me."

"Howard said he hasn't heard of any contract out on you."

"Oh yeah?" Again Wade chuckled. "Glad to hear that, and I'm not asking how he would know."

I glanced Howard's way. "That's good because I don't think he'd tell you."

Howard's smile confirmed that statement.

"Any chance I'll get my computer back soon?" I asked.

"I thought you said you bought a laptop."

"I, ah . . . I did, but there's something wrong with it, so Howard loaned me his until I can get a replacement."

"I'm beginning to wonder if that old coot has the hots for you. He's giving you gifts, fixing your car, cooking you dinner."

"And we're now going for a walk in the woods," I said, noticing Howard had moved over to the kitchen doorway and was pointing toward the woods behind my house, while moving his fingers as if walking. He held his copy of the "treasure" map in his other hand. "Call me in the morning. Okay?"

I hung up the phone feeling pretty good. For the first time this week I'd told Wade I was busy and didn't have time for him. And if he was just a little jealous of Howard, that was just fine with me.

CHAPTER THIRTY-FOUR

Howard suggested we take a shovel with us, and I agreed. I had no idea if that X on the map indicated something above ground or under, and simply getting to the spot—if we could even find it—was going to entail working our way through and around briars and underbrush.

In addition to the shovel, Howard grabbed an old, rusty machete hanging on the wall in the woodshed, and I picked up the pruning shears I'd bought earlier in the summer. We also doused ourselves with mosquito repellent. Evenings brought those pests out in droves.

Baraka came with us, following behind me once we left the trail. I wasn't surprised he let me go first. I was doing the same thing, letting Howard lead the way through underbrush that seemed intent on snagging and tripping us. The path Howard was taking wasn't the same as the one I'd traveled earlier in the day, but I trusted Howard's interpretation of the map more than Jason's or mine.

"How can you even hunt in this?" I called ahead to Howard.

"Come fall and a couple killin' frosts most of this underbrush will be gone." He gave me a quick glance. "A lot of times when you see me and Jake coming out of your woods, we've just gone for a walk."

"With a shotgun?" Whenever I did see him, he was usually carrying one.

"Never know what might pop out."

So far nothing had popped out in front of or around us, which surprised me. On my walks with Baraka, I've usually seen squirrels and chipmunks. This evening even the crows were silent. The only living creatures around seemed to be the three of us, the mosquitoes, and the deer flies. The repellent we'd applied were keeping the mosquitoes off me, but I noticed the flies were bothering Baraka.

I paused and wiped some repellent on his ears and over his body.

"Did you know my dad when he was a teenager?" I asked Howard as soon as I caught up with him.

"I knew him," he said and spat a wad of chewing tobacco onto the ground. "I was in the service, overseas when he was a teenager, but I'd watched him grow up. Not surprised he turned out the way he did. Even as a kid his love of adventure got him into a lot of trouble. His mother—your grandmother—had a fit when he climbed out his bedroom window using sheets tied together, and Mr. Halsted, who back then owned the farm the Sommers bought, wasn't too happy when he caught your dad riding his cows." Howard chuckled. "Your dad said he was going to be a bull rider and needed the practice. Don't think he ever did try riding Halsted's bull."

"He said he did," I replied, remembering the day Dad took me to the fair, and told me how he sneaked a ride on the neighbor's bull and ended up being tossed into a mud puddle.

"Your dad loved the woods," Howard added, using the machete to chop a small sapling down that was blocking our way. "He was always taking off and spending a day or two back here. That was before your grandfather turned it into his private junk yard."

One thing I noticed was the farther into the woods we traveled, the less junk we encountered. There was also less undergrowth, probably because not as much sunlight reached this area. Ten acres didn't make a forest, but I was glad Howard was leading the way. I had no idea where we were headed or even how to get back to the main trail.

"Do you have any idea where we're going?" I asked, hoping he did.

"I'm pretty sure I know where he buried the baby. There's a spot just up ahead where two boards have been nailed together. They form an X. I always thought that was curious since there's not a lot of other boards around, but now it makes sense. They're about where this map indicates." He paused and looked around, and then glanced back at me. "Never thought he'd knock up Nora. She wasn't his type." Howard chuckled. "She wasn't any man's type. Maybe she didn't realize she was queer, but I sure did."

"I heard her parents were really strict."

"Lordy, yes." He rolled his eyes. "I hate to think what they would have done to her if they'd found out she was pregnant."

"Do you think she aborted the baby?"

"No." He shook his head and started walking again, angling to the right rather than straight ahead. "I think she thought your dad would marry her. I know my dad said she was really upset when your dad married your mother. She joined the army right after that."

"I never knew any of this until last June," I said.

"I'm not surprised," Howard said. "I don't imagine it was something your dad would have wanted to talk about, but you can see why Nora has never liked you. If he'd married her, these woods would have been hers."

"Initially I thought she didn't like me because she was afraid I'd try to take Rose away from her." That was when the irony hit me. "But it was him, my dad, who ended Nora's relationship with Rose. What a cad."

Howard didn't say anything, and I stopped talking. There

were days when I wished my grandfather hadn't willed the house and farm to me, days I wished I could go back to a time when I idolized my father and considered him a hero. The truth isn't always easy to face.

I didn't realize Howard had stopped until I nearly ran into him, and I think, if he hadn't been leading the way, I would have walked right over or around the two boards lying on the ground, a tangle of brush almost totally covering them. "This is it?" It sure didn't look like a gravesite. "You're sure?"

"Sure?" He shook his head. "No, but it's the only spot I've ever seen with two boards nailed to form a cross or X. Years ago, it wasn't this overgrown, but maybe I'm wrong."

Baraka wandered on, sniffing the ground. I had no idea what he might be smelling, but he's not a cadaver dog, trained to sniff out dead bodies, and after thirty years, I wonder if there would even be a scent.

"Any idea if your dad put the baby in a coffin, or did he just dig a hole and bury it?"

"According to Nora, Dad was going to put the baby in a container that animals couldn't get to, something water and bugs wouldn't get into. He told her it would be like a real coffin, and that he would put a marker on the spot."

"And this preemie was how old?"

"Five months," I said. "Nora was five months along when she lost the baby."

Howard shook his head. "Wouldn't have been very big at that point. Maybe ten inches or so. Well, let's hope your dad did what he promised, put the baby in a container, otherwise, I doubt we'll even find bones." He gazed down at the boards. "You ready to see what's under these?"

I nodded, and he told me if I'd cut away the branches, he'd do the digging.

I did get several scratches across the back of my right hand as

I snipped away the branches covering the cross. Once I'd cleared the area, Howard used the tip of the shovel to move the boards aside, and then he carefully started removing dirt from where they'd been. It wasn't until the shovel hit something that made a clunk that Howard dug deeper and faster. And once the army-green metal container came into view, he hurriedly shoveled around it until it was completely free.

"It's an ammo container," he said, answering my unasked question. "They're pretty much water- and bug-proof."

He pulled it out of the ground, and I used my hand to brush away the dirt clinging to the container's surface. As I did, I could see a date and a name scratched into the surface. The date would have been one year before my dad married my mother. Over thirty years ago. The name was the one Nora had told me last June. *Timothy Archer Benson.*

My father had done exactly as he'd promised, put their baby in a container that animals couldn't get to, something water and bugs wouldn't get into, and he'd marked the spot. "Good for you, Dad," I murmured and looked up at Howard. "What should we do next?"

"That's up to you."

He stared up through the tops of the trees above us, and I followed his gaze. The clouds had parted, allowing a stream of sunshine to penetrate and illuminate the area where we stood. The effect was strangely mystical.

And then he looked back down at the ammo container. "We can open it and look inside, but after all this time, I doubt you'd find anything but liquid. Or we can call the sheriff's department and tell them what we found. Or you can simply tell Nora what we found and ask her what she wants us to do."

I knew calling the sheriff's department would create more trouble for Nora and more confusion for me, and I had no desire to open the container and see what was inside, so my decision was simple. "I'll tell Nora. Or rather, I'll talk to her lawyer. Maybe something can be worked out so she doesn't have to go to prison." I thought back to the various times Nora had tried to kill me. Did I really want her back in the neighborhood? "I'll talk to her lawyer."

CHAPTER THIRTY-FIVE

We put the unopened ammo container back in the hole, and Howard tossed the dirt he'd removed back over and around the container. I then placed the boards on top of the spot, roughly the same way we'd found them. We did leave the area around the cross clear, and it was obvious the ground recently had been dug up, but I didn't expect anyone other than Nora to return here in the near future. And if she didn't . . . ? Well, in a few years briars and brush would again claim the area, and Timothy Archer Benson would continue to rest in peace.

Using the machete, Howard marked a few trees as we worked our way back to the main trail. They weren't big marks, and I doubted if most people would recognize them as arrows, but they would help me find my way . . . if I ever wanted to go back to that spot.

Baraka was still in the woods, sniffing around a pile of junk, when Howard and I stepped onto the trail that led back to the house. Howard stopped and pointed ahead to the gate we'd left open. "What do you see?" he asked.

I saw crows. Two of them, one each perched on the fence's end posts. "Crows," I said, not sure if that was what he meant.

"I see an attempted murder."

"What?" I stared beyond the birds, past the end of the old farmhouse, toward the road. As far as I could tell, there was no one around, much less someone trying to murder another person.

Another crow flew down, landing on the lawn.

"Ah, now it's a murder," Howard said, and I understood. Now there were three, which made it . . .

"A murder of crows."

"Yep." He started walking again, and all three crows took off.

"You do like your crows, don't you?" Besides being a member of a group with CROWS as its acronym, Howard had often commented on the benefit of crows. I should have remembered a group of crows was called a murder.

"People don't realize how much they benefit farmers. Yes, they may eat the corn plants when they first come up, but they also eat a lot of the insects and larvae that damage the crops. They are our local garbage men. Well, garbage birds."

"So why is a flock of crows called a murder?"

"Not exactly sure why," Howard admitted. "I heard there was a folk story of crows holding court and when the verdict was guilty, they murdered the offending crow. But I think that's just a fable. However, in medieval times and even more recently, where there have been battlefields or mass execution sites, people have seen flocks of crows feeding on dead bodies. That may be what prompted people to call a flock murderers. Not that they killed anyone. As I said, they're scavengers. They don't murder animals . . . or people."

"Sometimes, the way the crows caw," I said as we returned the shovel and tools to the woodshed, "I feel like they're warning me . . . or accusing me of doing something I shouldn't. And one day, I would swear I heard one say 'Baraka.' Just like I say it when I yell for him."

"Could be you did. They are mimickers, and some in captivity have been taught to talk. Have you ever been dive-bombed by one?"

I shook my head.

"I have. They're very protective of their young. Probably

another reason why a flock of crows is called a murder. You get enough of them after you, you probably would feel like they were trying to murder you."

"Like in Hitchcock's movie, *The Birds.*"

"Exactly." Howard wiped his hands on the sides of his overalls. "You gonna be all right tonight?"

"I'll be fine. Thanks."

I hugged him. He wasn't prepared for it, and I could tell he didn't know where to put his hands or what to do. For a second he did nothing, then he gave a grunt and stepped back, forcing me to release my hold. "I'll be going home, then," he said and started for his car. "Put a cold pack on that eye of yours . . . and make sure you lock your doors."

"I will," I promised and chuckled. Wade might be jealous, but in my opinion, Howard was starting to sound like a parent.

Baraka came trotting up to my side as I watched Howard open his car door. I expected Howard to simply get in and drive the short distance to his place, but he paused and looked directly at me. "You seem to attract trouble," he said. "I don't want to hear about any more murders unless we *are* talking about crows."

"I'll be fine," I said . . . and crossed my fingers.

CHAPTER THIRTY-SIX

It was almost nine o'clock Friday morning when Wade and Jason arrived at my place. Although I'd tried to cover the bruise on my cheek with makeup, evidently I didn't do that great a job because the first thing Wade said when he saw me was, "What happened to your face?"

"I ran into something."

"Something like a fist?" He narrowed his eyes. "Did Howard do that?"

"No, not Howard."

"Then who hit you? What happened?"

I wasn't sure how Wade knew *someone*—rather than *something*—had hit me, but I decided I might as well tell him exactly what happened, how I hit Richardson on the back of his head with a dog bone, and how Richardson turned around and hit me with his fist. From Wade's expression, I knew it was a good thing Mr. Suave Stock Broker wasn't around or he might also be sporting a bruised face.

I hesitated, not sure if I should say anything about what Howard did—about the shotgun and Howard's threat to take Richardson out back in the woods and get rid of him—but when I did tell Wade, he laughed, nodded his approval, and hugged me close. "Good for him."

"The gun wasn't loaded," I added, just in case, at a later date, Wade reconsidered Howard's actions and didn't see it as funny.

"So did this Richardson guy buy you a new laptop?"

That was the negative. "If he did, he hasn't shown up with it." I leaned back in Wade's arms and looked up. "Which reminds me, did you call Deputy Sawyer about that thumb drive Jason found at Brewster's house?"

"He did," Jason said from the other room, where he was already playing with the toys he'd left. "They told Daddy all it has on it are games, but they won't give it back."

"As you can tell," Wade said releasing me from his embrace, "you're not the only one upset with the sheriff's department for keeping things that have no bearing on this case."

"So no algorithm on it?"

"Not on that one. I did call Sergeant Milano. I told him about Richardson and that Brewster took something of Richardson's. At least that's one more person with motive."

I didn't agree. "If Brewster didn't take the algorithm until the night before Brewster got on your boat, and Brewster didn't decide to go along with Linda and Jason until Saturday morning, how did Richardson get a bomb on your boat?"

"You're assuming the story Richardson told you is true. For all we know, Brewster took the algorithm before last Friday, and Richardson realized what had happened and put a bomb in one of those wine bottles they gave Brewster as a going-away gift. That Brewster opened the bottle while on my boat was simply my bad luck. That and . . ."

He didn't finish, which left me wondering what else he'd meant to say. "And what?"

"The propane tank," Wade said with a sigh. "Milano is convinced that Brewster and Linda might have had a chance, might still be alive, if that propane tank hadn't exploded."

"And he's blaming you for that?"

"He keeps asking me why I had such a large propane tank, why it was on the floor near the table."

"I hope you told him we picked the larger grill stove because we were going to use it as a regular stove, that it would be more useful than the smaller model, and that you needed the larger propane tank with that model."

"I did," Wade said, "but he's hung up on the fact that the tank was in the cabin, not out in the open."

Sergeant Milano was beginning to irritate me. "Where does he think it should have been? On the swim platform? You had it strapped in place. You know enough not to close up the cabin when we're cooking. You certainly didn't expect a bomb to go off in there."

"I told him that." Once again Wade wrapped his arms around me, drawing me close. "You know what's really bad? If I were in his position, I'd be asking the same questions and drawing the same conclusions."

"Maybe. Or maybe not. When we first met, you kept an open mind about me."

He chuckled, and I felt the rumble in his chest. "When we first met, I thought you'd killed a guy."

"Later," I said.

"Later, I thought you were crazy."

Like my mother. He was right.

"What I can't figure out," Wade said, again with a sigh, "is if Richardson didn't plant a bomb in that basket of goodies the company gave Brewster, and if Brewster's gambling debts didn't get him killed, what did? Why did my boat explode? Why are Brewster and Linda dead?"

"I don't know, Wade. I don't know."

We stood that way—our arms wrapped around each other, my head against his chest—for half a minute, saying nothing. I could hear his heart beating, steady and strong, feel his chest rise and fall with each breath. Felt his forehead touch the crown of my head. And then he grunted and straightened, releasing his hold on me.

I saw him touch the cut on his forehead. "Still sore?" I asked.

He nodded and looked into my living room. "As usual," Wade said, keeping his voice low. "I have a favor to ask."

I followed his gaze. Jason pushed a toy dump truck toward Baraka's feet, and Baraka reached forward with a paw and pushed the truck away. Jason giggled and tried it again. The game was on.

"They're going to raise *The Freedom* today," Wade went on when I didn't say anything. "I'd like to be there when they do. But I told Jean I'd meet with her at Brewster's house. She wants to see if there are some pictures she can use for Linda's funeral, and Jason said he knows where another pair of pajamas are packed. He sort of wet the bed last night."

I looked away from Jason and Baraka and back at Wade. So much for a day of work. I glanced at the laptop Howard had left for me to use. I wasn't even sure if my accounting program would work on his laptop, and there was no guarantee Richardson would bring a new laptop, as promised . . . or that I could get the accounting program working on it. As much as I didn't want to be with Jean Healy, I couldn't really deny Wade. "What time?" I asked. "What time are you supposed to meet her?"

"Eleven." He stepped back. "Only problem is, I'm not sure if the house is locked or not."

"No problem. I have a key." I'd forgotten to leave it at Brewster's house when I left Tuesday. I'd wondered how to get it back, or to whom I should give it.

Wade explained the situation to Jason, but Jason wasn't as easy to convince as I'd been. I could understand why the boy didn't want to be separated from his dad. He'd lost one parent; he didn't want to lose another. I also understood Jason's reasoning when he said, "I don't want to see Grandma. She smells funny, and she's always hugging me and touching my hair."

Jean Healy did wear too much perfume, and she was always touching Jason's hair. "We won't stay long," I promised Jason. "Then I'll take you out for a hamburger."

"At Chuck E. Cheese?" Jason asked, jumping to his feet, suddenly interested.

Wade cleared his throat. "I'm afraid you two are going to have to postpone that. I promised your grandmother she could take you to lunch."

Jason flopped back down on the floor next to Baraka. "I'm not going."

"Yes, you are," Wade ordered, and after ten minutes of Jason screaming, kicking, and sobbing, Wade left, saying he had to get to South Haven if he was going to be there when they brought up his boat.

I was prepared for a fight when I told Jason it was time to head into Kalamazoo. To my surprise, he didn't argue. He even helped me put Baraka in his crate. "I don't want you to eat my books," Jason told my dog as he closed the crate's door.

Baraka simply sighed and laid his head on his paws, those big brown eyes of his seeming to accept his fate.

Wade had placed the booster seat for Jason in my car before he'd driven off. Jason climbed in without an argument, and for the first ten miles or so was silent. It was only when we were on I-94, heading west, that he began talking. "Maybe Grandma will take me to Chuck E. Cheese. Can you ask her to do that, P.J.? I think she'd like it. Don't you?"

I couldn't quite see Jean Healy "liking" the kid-oriented restaurant with all the noise and games and children running around, but if she was smart, she would pretend to like it. "I'll ask her," I promised.

"Grandma says they're going to take Daddy away, and I'll live with her and Grandpa. I don't want to live with them, I want to live with Daddy."

"I don't blame you," I said. "That's why your daddy's doing everything he can to prove he's innocent."

"I don't think he killed Mama."

"I don't either."

"Mama could be mean sometimes. Like Grandma."

I said nothing.

"Daddy Michael got mad at her. He said she shouldn't believe what people said, that it wasn't his fault she killed herself."

I wasn't sure I'd heard him right. "Who killed herself?"

"I don't know. Some girl. Or maybe it was a lady. The lady next door said he was a bad man. Mama said he shouldn't play games on the computer, that he was going to get us all killed. Do you think he was a bad man? I liked him. He showed me how to play those games. He said I was good luck, that he won when I sat on his lap. That's when Mama got real mad at him."

I glanced in the rearview mirror. Jason was sitting straight and looking around. What he'd said bothered me, but it didn't seem to be bothering him. "Did your Daddy Michael ever touch you in a funny way?"

"He'd tickle me sometimes."

"I mean in other ways, ways that made you feel uncomfortable."

"No." Jason shook his head. "Grandma touches my hair all the time. Why's she do that?"

"I don't know." I kept my eyes on the road as I tried to make sense of what Jason was telling me. "You said someone died. Who died?"

"Mama died," Jason said, the laughter gone from his voice. "And Daddy Michael. I thought you knew that."

"Yes, I meant . . ." I realized I shouldn't have reminded him. "Never mind."

"That's a funny word," he said, laughing. "Never mind. But Daddy says I'm supposed to mind."

"It is a funny word," I agreed.

"Why do people die?"

"I don't know." I thought about the ammo container Howard and I had dug up the day before. Did it contain the remains of a five-month-old fetus? If that baby hadn't died, would my dad have married Nora? If so, I wouldn't exist. And if I didn't exist, my father would still be alive.

Or maybe he wouldn't be.

"Are you going to have a baby girl or a baby boy?"

Jason's question surprised me. I'd forgotten he even knew I was pregnant. "I don't know. I'm not even absolutely sure I'm going to have a baby."

"Mama was going to have a girl. Is the baby dead, too?"

"Yes, the baby would have died when your mother did."

"But I didn't die."

"No. You were lucky. You were on the front of the boat with your daddy."

"Yeah, I was lucky." Jason sighed. "Daddy Michael was glad Mama was gonna have a baby, but Mama said he'd better not touch it. Why wouldn't she let him touch it?"

"I don't know."

CHAPTER THIRTY-SEVEN

Jean Healy was already parked in front of Michael Brewster's house and standing on the lawn near the For Sale sign. I didn't see any sign of Frank Healy when I pulled onto the driveway. "He's at the funeral home," Jean told me when I asked. "Waiting for our daughter's body to be delivered. What happened to your face?"

"I hit someone, and he hit back," I said, hoping that would satisfy her.

It didn't. She frowned. "Wade hit you?"

"Not Wade." I didn't want her thinking that. "Just some guy who was trying to steal my laptop."

Jean Healy shook her head. "My daughter said you attracted trouble. She was worried about Jason being around you."

I didn't want to get into a debate on whether I was good for Jason or not, so I quickly said, "Speaking of Jason, I understand you two are going out to lunch after we're finished here. He would love to go to Chuck E. Cheese."

"Chuck . . ." She frowned. "I was thinking of taking him to—"

"Chuck E. Cheese. Chuck E. Cheese," Jason chanted, pulling the For Sale sign out of its post hole. "Where's the key?"

"I have it." I showed the house key to both of them. "Shall we go inside?"

"I wondered where it was." Jean Healy gave me a suspicious look, and then started for the front door.

I hurried to follow, but as soon as I reached her side, I wished I weren't so close. Although I wouldn't describe her perfume as yucky, as Jason had said, it was overpowering. I think it's one of those perfumes they advertise in *Elle* or *Mademoiselle*. Not cheap, but my stomach wasn't reacting well to the sweet smell. I swallowed back the taste of bile and hoped I could keep my breakfast of dry toast and ginger tea down. However, the moment the front door swung open, I knew that wasn't going to be possible.

The stench that came billowing out of the house hit me like a punch in the stomach. "Oh, god," I groaned and turned toward the nearby bushes.

"What is that smell?" Jean demanded, stepping back off the stoop.

I heard Jason say "Yuck" as I emptied my stomach on the ground. I wasn't sure if he meant the smell or that I'd thrown up. Not that it mattered.

"Here." Jean thrust something damp my way, and I realized it was a wet wipe. Using it, I cleaned around my mouth, then dropped it to the ground.

She handed me another. "What is that smell?" she asked, her voice muffled, and when I looked at her, I saw she had a wet wipe covering her nose and mouth.

"I don't know."

"Well, do something about it!" she demanded and took Jason's hand. "Call someone. I want it cleaned up by the time we get back from lunch."

"Me?" I said, still trying to convince my stomach to calm down.

Jean Healy was already walking away from the house, leading Jason to her car. "Yes, you," she called back to me, and mumbled something else I couldn't clearly hear.

"What's going on?" a woman's voice asked from my other side.

I looked the direction of the voice and saw Carol Dotson walking toward me. Brewster's neighbor had a different appearance from the first time I'd met her. Today the woman's flowered short-sleeved cotton blouse was wrinkled and stained, the left side pulled out of her tan Capri pants. As far as I could tell, she wasn't wearing any makeup, and her hair was mussed and ratty. All in all, she looked like I felt . . . but she was smiling.

"Something inside smells," I said, glad to see a friendlier face.

"And she left you to clean it up?" Carol shook her head and went right up to the door. There she stopped, made a face, and backed up so she was standing beside me. "That is terrible."

"Do you think there's a body in there? Someone or something dead?" I had a mouse die behind my refrigerator once. The smell was similar.

"I don't know. Give me a second."

I watched Carol suck in a deep breath, then hurry into the house. She was only inside a few seconds before she came hurrying out, expelled the air she'd been holding, and took in more air. She took several quick breaths before she spoke. "Meat. On the counter," she said, making a face. "Dried blood. Maggots."

"Oh, my gosh." I remembered seeing the meat on the counter when we were in the house Tuesday. "Nobody cleaned it up?" Which was obvious since it was still there. "I guess I *should* call someone."

"I'll clean it," Carol said, almost too quickly.

"You?"

"Sure. You just go do whatever you want, and I'll get it cleaned up in there."

"Really?" I couldn't believe my luck. I'd been tempted to

simply ignore Jean Healy's order and walk away from the house, leaving it as it was. After all, it wasn't my daughter's home. I didn't need anything out of it. She was the one who should be calling someone to clean up the place, not me.

"Sure. Go," Carol repeated, motioning with her hands for me to head for my car. "I'll take care of everything."

Strange thing is, if she hadn't been so eager to get rid of me, I would have left. But something in her tone of voice and her body language made me curious. It was as if she couldn't wait for me to leave.

I wondered why.

"I really shouldn't leave you to clean this up," I said, watching for her reaction.

"No, no. Go. I insist," Carol said.

It was the "insist" that got me. I wasn't sure why, but something didn't seem right. "Okay," I said, staying where I was. "Thanks."

"I'll go get some cleaning supplies," she said and hurried toward her house.

I didn't move away from the front of Brewster's house. I didn't want to go inside, not with that smell, but I wanted to know why a woman who'd told me once she didn't particularly like Brewster or Linda was willing to clean up their house. I pulled out my cell phone and punched in Wade's number.

He didn't answer, so I left a message. "I'm at Brewster's house," I said, watching for Carol's return as I spoke. "No one cleaned up the meat on the counter and the place stinks. Your ex-mother-in-law took Jason and left me to clean up. Brewster's neighbor has offered to do it, but I think I'm going to stick around. Not sure why, but something doesn't seem right."

I'd shut my phone and slipped it back into the holder on my hip by the time Carol came out of her house, carrying a garbage bag, a pair of latex kitchen gloves, and a jar of Vicks vapor rub.

"You're still here," she said, frowning as she came nearer.

"I decided to stay and help you. It doesn't seem right, asking you to do this on your own."

"No." She shook her head, scowling slightly. "Go. I'll take care of everything."

"I'm staying."

I said it firmly and waited, wondering what she would say or do next. To my surprise, she shrugged and handed me the jar of Vicks. "Then you'd better put a little of this under your nose," she instructed. "It will help mask the smell. We used it in the service when we had to handle dead bodies."

I hoped it would also help mask the smell of her breath. I had a feeling, while she was inside her house, she'd had a shot of something. Something stronger than wine. Not that I was going to say anything. I couldn't blame her if she felt she needed a little fortification before facing the mess inside. Besides, after throwing up twice, I was pretty sure my breath didn't smell that great either.

I rubbed a glob of the vapor rub under my nose, the smell reminding me of when I had colds as a child and my mother or grandmother put the menthol rub in a vaporizer. Carol did the same after I handed the jar back to her.

"I haven't been in this house since he got married," Carol said as she replaced the lid and slid the jar of Vicks into the pocket of her capris. "He actually invited us to his wedding. Can you believe that? He said he was eating crow, turning over a new leaf. Like that would make everything all right."

"Why was he 'eating crow,' " I asked.

"Because he was a bastard."

She headed inside, leaving me to ponder that statement. It wasn't the first time she'd called him that, and, considering the word spray-painted on Brewster's wall, I gathered she wasn't the only one who thought that way.

I followed her inside, hoping the Vicks would do its stuff and I wouldn't throw up again.

"By the way, what happened to your face?" Carol asked, not bothering to look back at me.

"I got into an argument with a man trying to steal my laptop."

"I hope he looks worse."

"I think I got the worst of it."

"Too bad." She stopped a few feet back from the kitchen counter with the rotting meat. "You take care of that," she said and handed me the gloves and the garbage bag. "I need to look for something."

"Look for what?" I asked, not moving any closer to the counter. I could see maggots crawling around the unwrapped roast.

"Some pictures." She motioned for me to go on into the kitchen area. "I'll help as soon as I find them."

"You wanted to come in here so you could find some pictures?" Her eagerness to clean up in here made more sense.

"I'll help," she assured me, going over to one of the tipped-over boxes and righting it. "Just as soon as I find what I'm looking for."

The contents in the box clattered as pots, pans, and dishes hit against each other. "What kind of pictures? Maybe I could help."

"Oh, they're just some pictures he took." She moved on to another box, righting it and looking inside. Again I could hear what sounded like plates crashing together.

"Stop!" I ordered. "You're going to break something, and I don't know what Mrs. Healy's going to want to keep."

"She can go to hell," Carol said and looked over the other boxes on their sides. "Actually, I don't think he'd keep them down here." She glanced at the stairway. "I'm going upstairs."

"No." Her behavior had me totally confused. "I think you'd

better leave."

She chuckled, totally ignored me, and headed for the stairs.

"I mean it," I said. Not that she seemed to care. She continued up the stairs.

I dropped the garbage bag on the floor and followed her upstairs. She went directly to the master bedroom. I stood in the doorway and watched as she started pulling things out of boxes, going from one to the next. I didn't say anything. Simply watched. Finally, she sank down on the rug, legs crossed and shoulders slumped forward. It took me a moment before I realized she was crying.

"What's the matter, Carol?" I asked and moved closer, placing a hand on her shoulder.

She shook her head, but didn't look up.

"What exactly are you looking for?"

"Pictures. My baby said he took pictures of them. She said she was sorry. But it wasn't her fault. She was just a child." Carol gulped back a sob. "Just an innocent child."

"Michael Brewster and your daughter?"

She nodded.

I stood next to her, unsure of what to say next. Finally, I decided. "You keep looking. I'm going back downstairs to clean up that mess."

Again she nodded, but she didn't move, and I left her like that, seated on the carpet, crying.

Back down in the kitchen, I slipped on the latex gloves and quickly shoved all the packages of rotting meat into the garbage bag and placed it outside. Then I went back inside and washed the dried blood and a few lingering maggots into the sink and down the drain.

Once the counter was clean, I picked the deflated Mylar balloons up off the floor and set them next to the card from his coworkers. The handwritten note inside the card read: Enjoy a glass of wine, a hunk of cheese, and a loaf of bread in your new home.

I remembered how Sergeant Milano had asked me if I drank wine. And Wade had said the sheriff's department thought a wine bottle had something to do with the explosion, that they'd found a shard of glass in one of the bodies. But how could a bottle of wine be rigged with a bomb? And why would Brewster's coworkers want to kill him? If what Richardson told me was correct, he didn't know Brewster was going to steal the algorithm when they gave him the basket.

My cell phone rang.

The moment I flipped it open, I recognized Wade's number. "Where are you?" I asked as soon as I answered.

"On my way back to Kalamazoo. What's up? Your message sounded strange, and I also received a call from Jean. Something about the police not doing their job and how we need to give back that necklace. Did you say something to her about the necklace?"

"No. I didn't have a chance. The moment she smelled this place, she was out of here."

"Pretty bad, huh? Well, I told her the sheriff's department had a lead on the necklace. That calmed her down a bit."

"Have they found it?" I hoped so. I was tired of the Healys accusing us.

"Not yet, but Lisa—Deputy Sawyer—said they've sent a notice to all of the pawnbrokers within a fifty-mile area. She'll follow up with some phone calls. If it's out there, she'll find it."

"I hope so."

"And what's up with you? Did you stay at Brewster's place or head home?"

"I'm at Brewster's." And I hoped Wade could answer a question I had. "You know how that Sergeant Milano kept asking about wine bottles? Was there anything special about the wine bottle that they think held the bomb?"

"He said it was green, but that's not uncommon."

I agreed. Most bottles for red wines were colored green or brown.

"Oh, they did find a trace of glue on one edge," he added. "Milano asked me why I used glue. The guy just won't give up."

"Glue?" I glanced over at the stairs. "Milano thinks the bottle was glued together?"

"No, not glued together. You don't glue wine bottles together."

"I saw one that had been," I said, remembering the one in Carol's bathroom, the one with another, smaller, bottle inside. "It didn't have wine in it, but—"

I noticed a brown sandal on the top visible stair. I had no way of knowing how long Carol had been there, or what she'd heard, but the thoughts racing through my mind scared me. "Wade," I said as quietly as I could, "Come here. To Brewster's place. Quickly."

"What's the matter?" he asked, but I didn't dare explain. Carol was on her way down the stairs.

I snapped my phone shut.

CHAPTER THIRTY-EIGHT

"I didn't find any pictures," Carol said, moving between me and the front door, her gaze never leaving my face. She pulled her own cell phone from the holder clipped to her waistband. "I'm going to call my husband and have him come over and help me look."

Although what she was saying sounded reasonable, the way she was looking at me made me nervous. If she was responsible for the bomb on Wade's boat, I needed to get out of this house . . . and quickly. "Well, I've done about all I can do," I said, hoping she didn't notice the slight tremor in my voice. "And I'm getting hungry, so I think I'll just leave."

"Oh, why don't you stay for a while longer?" She smiled. "We can all get something to eat at my place."

"That . . . that won't be necessary," I said, hoping I didn't sound as nervous as I felt. "And just because I'm gone, you don't need to leave. Stay as long as you like. I . . . I do need to go see my mother." I flipped my cell phone open again. "In fact, I'm already late. I think I'll call and let her know I'm on my way."

I managed to push nine-one-one before something slammed into my arm. My fingers automatically opened, releasing my cell phone. It and the jar of Vicks vapor rub—the one Carol had placed in her pocket earlier—crashed onto the tile floor near my feet. The lid popped off, and some of the jar's contents spilled out.

"Hey!" I stared at her. She was looking directly at me, her eyes narrowed and her cell phone up by her face.

"Get over here," she said, "and bring Matilda. We have a problem."

"No problem," I said, trying to keep the panic from my voice.

My thoughts scrambled. *Who was she talking to? Did my nine-one-one call go through? Who was Matilda?*

A glance back at the floor didn't give me much hope. My phone was now in two pieces.

"Glad to hear there's no problem," Carol said as she slid her phone back into its holder. "My husband will be over in a minute."

Her words didn't calm me. The set of her jaw and her rigid stance said we had a *big* problem.

"Wade's coming," I said, hoping he'd heard me. "He'll be here any minute."

"I hope he's speedy," she said, flexing her shoulders and smiling. " 'Cause you won't be here very long."

"Oh yeah? Where am I going?"

"To your mother's. Right?" Her smile was way too sweet.

I glanced toward the back of the house. The sheriff's deputies hadn't cleaned up the mess from the vandalism, but they had closed the sliding door. Closed it and placed a wooden stick on the track to stop future vandals from getting in that way.

I wasn't sure how long it would take me to remove the stick and open the door. Probably longer than it would take for Carol to grab me. And even if I did succeed in escaping from the house, I'd have to run around the side yard to get to the street and possible help. The front door seemed like the best option, even though Carol now partially blocked that exit.

"You know, I wasn't sure if it *was* the bottle we gave him," she said, backing up closer to the front door. "But I guess it was, wasn't it?"

I moved forward, closing the distance between us. She stood like a wall, smiling. Taunting me to go through her.

"Why did you do it?" I asked, hoping if I got her talking, she would relax her guard a little. "Why kill Michael Brewster?"

"Because he raped our daughter, that's why. Raped her, got her pregnant, and then made her think it was her fault. Told her . . . Told us . . . she came on to him, that she was the one who made him do it."

The anger in Carol's words turned her face ugly. "She was fifteen years old," she ground out. "Fifteen. A child. She thought he loved her. He told her he loved her."

"You're right. He was a cad," I said. I wondered how many other people Brewster hurt in one way or another.

"You can't imagine what it's like," Carol half sobbed, her face twisted with agony. "Alan found her. He blames himself, but he wasn't to blame. Michael was to blame. And he was going to get away with it. He was going to live in California, was going to have a good job, a beautiful wife, a stepson, and a daughter."

She closed her eyes, tears sliding down her cheeks, and I made my move. I ran straight for her, hoping a shove would push her off balance and out of my way. And I might have succeeded if her husband hadn't stepped into view just at that moment, holding a shotgun in his good hand.

He shouted, I hesitated, and Carol punched me in the stomach.

I went down on my knees, pain and panic coursing through me. As I gasped for a breath, all I could think was, *My baby*.

"What are we going to do?" I heard Carol ask her husband. "She knows. And Linda's ex-husband is coming. They're looking for a wine bottle that was cut in half and glued together. She saw the one in our bathroom."

"When? How?" he asked.

"Tuesday, when she came into the house to use the bathroom."

"You never should have let her into the house."

"What was I going to say? 'No, you can't use my bathroom because you might see something you shouldn't?' "

They were talking about me as if I weren't there. The front door was only a few feet away—wide open—but both Carol and her husband blocked any chance I might have to escape through it. The sliding door still wasn't an option, but there was a door on the other side of the refrigerator, one I'd never seen open or tried opening. My guess was it led to the garage.

Would it open easily?

And if I made it through there, would I be any better off in the garage?

I'd caught my breath and the pain in my midsection was gone, but I wasn't sure how fast I could scramble to my feet and run.

Silently I counted to myself. *One. Two. Three.*

I used my right hand on the floor to push myself up, half turned in a crouch, and ran toward the living room. I planned on veering left, toward the door, before they realized what I was doing.

Carol stopped me before I could make the turn. All she caught was the edge of my T-shirt, but that was enough to pull me off balance. I stumbled back a step, twisted away from her, and lunged to my right. The change in direction was enough to loosen her grip. The moment I felt her let go, I dashed for the stairs.

I had no idea where I was going, only that I had to get away from them. Behind me I heard her swearing. Her husband yelled for me to stop.

Like hell I would.

I knew one of them was right behind me, but I made it clear

to the top of the stairway before a hand looped around my left ankle. I tried countering the pull by kicking back, only to have gravity take over. My hands hit the landing before my chin. Pain radiated up my right arm, and I tasted blood. Hands pushed down on my legs, and then jerked me back. My body dropped down to the next step. Another pull. I reached to the side and grabbed the railing with my left hand.

I needed to get on my feet, get free of the hold on my ankles.

Keeping a tight hold on the railing, I twisted and kicked. The carpeted edge of the step pressed into my stomach, hampering my breathing. Hurting. I tried to push myself up and off the step using my right hand.

A knife-like pain traveled from my wrist to my elbow.

I cried out.

He yelled up to her. "Do you have her?"

"I've got her."

She tightened her hold on my ankle. Pulling. Not letting up. She was breathing hard. I was breathing hard.

One thought ran through my head. I had to get free. I had to.

I screamed as loud as I could. Screamed and yelled for help.

"Shut up!" Carol demanded, twisting my ankle even more and pulling down.

My fingers slipped off the wooden railing bar, and I thumped down another step before I grabbed the next polished cylinder. Bile rose in my throat, fear mixing with pain. I screamed again.

I thought I heard Wade's voice just before something hit my head.

CHAPTER THIRTY-NINE

I don't know how long I was out. I was still lying on the stairs when I realized no one was holding my leg and Wade was saying my name, asking if I was all right.

"Fine," I said, though I didn't feel fine. My head hurt. My wrist hurt. My stomach hurt.

"I've called for backup," he said. "And an ambulance."

I turned my head and looked in the direction of his voice. Wade was standing in the entryway, the front door open behind him. He had a gun in one hand and his cell phone in the other.

Alan Dotson stood near the stairway, on the other side of the railing, his face almost even with mine. I didn't see Carol, but I could hear her, hear her sobbing. She was somewhere behind me, still on the stairs.

I also didn't see the shotgun.

"He has a gun," I said, looking at Alan Dotson as I twisted myself into a seated position, being careful not to put any weight on my right wrist.

"Not anymore," Wade responded and slipped his phone back in its holder. "Stay where you are, P.J. Wait until I have backup before you come down here."

The way I felt, I wasn't sure my legs would hold me up, so following his order was no problem. I also understood his reasoning. Carol Dotson was sitting on the bottom step, tears sliding down her cheeks. She no longer looked threatening, but if she did grab me as I went by, she could use me as a shield.

No sense in taking a chance.

"They're the ones who made the bomb," I said, to help Wade understand why they'd attacked me.

He frowned and looked at Alan Dotson. "How did you get the C4 in the bottle? Connect a detonator without getting it wet?"

"It was a bottle inside a bottle," Carol answered. "I created it."

She sounded proud.

Her attitude made me angry. "You could have killed Wade. Killed his son. You did kill Jason's mother. She had nothing to do with the death of your daughter."

Carol looked up at me. "She was a bitch. I tried to tell her what he'd done, but she called me a liar. Said my daughter was a nut case."

Just like you, I wanted to say, but stopped myself. "Brewster evidently got their daughter pregnant," I told Wade. "Their daughter committed suicide."

"He raped her," Alan Dotson said. "Raped my baby. He deserved to die."

The anger in the man's words was reflected in his face, and I knew no one would ever convince this couple that Brewster's death wasn't deserved.

"He wasn't supposed to open that bottle of wine until he was in California," Carol said. "We told him that. We told him he should open it when they were in their new home, that we'd made it special for that occasion." She shook her head. "He shouldn't have taken it on your boat. He shouldn't have."

"But he did," Wade said, and I saw no pity in his eyes.

I heard the sirens then and Wade looked behind him, out the door. Carol jumped to her feet, glanced at her husband, and then started up the stairs, by me. I'm not sure where she thought she was going, but I wasn't about to let her get away. I grabbed for her legs, catching one ankle with my left hand and crying out in pain the moment I moved my right hand. In spite of the pain, I held on. I wouldn't have been able to do so for long, but it was enough to put her off balance.

She stumbled and fell forward, and Wade yelled for her to stop. "Now!"

With a defeated sigh, she lay on the steps next to me. I released my hold, and babying my right arm against my chest, I eased down a step, then another and another, leaving her above me. Only when I reached the bottom of the stairs did I stand, and only then for a second.

A veil of black swept over my eyes, my stomach churned, and my head felt very light and funny. My legs seemed to melt under me, and I knew I was going to fall, but there was nothing I could do to stop myself.

I do remember giving a cry of pain when my arm hit the floor.

And I remember Wade calling my name.

Everything after that was pretty much a blur. Deputies arrived, then paramedics. I was going to add a couple things to the explanation Wade was giving the deputies, but when the paramedic working on my wrist said, "This might hurt," he wasn't kidding. I think I passed out, because the next thing I remember was being in an ambulance, a light being shined in my eyes, and being asked if I knew what day it was.

By the time Wade arrived at the hospital, I was in a semi-private room, and I totally understood how he'd felt when he had a concussion. I just wanted to go home. But, unlike me, Wade didn't give in when I insisted on being released, and when he said I needed to stay so they could make sure the baby was all right, I gave in.

The fact that he seemed concerned about the baby made me feel good.

I missed Linda's funeral on Saturday. I can't say I'm sorry. I've always hated funerals. Funeral homes can call them a "Celebration of Life," but giving the service a different name doesn't change anything. The person's dead. Gone.

I did feel sorry for Jean and Frank Healy. Linda was their only child. I may not have liked how Linda treated Wade and acted around me, but I'm sure she had a good side; otherwise, Wade never would have married her to begin with, and Jason wouldn't be such a neat kid.

"The bomb wasn't intended for her," Wade told me when he came to pick me up from the hospital after the funeral. "But they're so full of anger, I don't think they cared who died."

"I still don't understand how they did it," I said as we waited for the doctor to release me. "How did they set it off?"

"They didn't. Brewster did." Wade sketched out a picture for me. "From what he told me, the C4 and detonator cap were sealed in the smaller bottle. Wires attached to the detonator were connected to the cork in that bottle. Another wire was attached to the cork that went into the neck of the larger bottle. Once the smaller bottle was placed inside the two halves, and they were glued together, wine was poured into the larger bottle. Being a red wine, the smaller bottle wasn't really visible, and since it was a fairly large bottle of wine, I don't think Brewster thought anything about the weight."

"So when Brewster pulled the cork on the large, outside bottle, he also pulled the cork on the smaller bottle?"

Wade nodded. "And that created the shockwave that detonated the C4."

"How did he get the C4?" I was pretty sure something like that couldn't be picked up at a local hardware store.

"He's not telling, but Milano said there were calls on Alan

Dotson's phone to a buddy who still has access to explosives. He's guessing that's the source."

"So Milano no longer thinks you had anything to do with the explosion?"

Wade smiled, looking more relaxed than he had in a week. "I'm no longer a person of interest."

"What about the Healys? Are they still going to try to gain custody of Jason?"

"I think they've dropped that idea. Jason wore Jean out Friday afternoon. And I promised them I'd make sure they got to spend time with him. But, just to make sure they don't change their minds, I suggested they keep their grandson with them this afternoon and all day Sunday. I told them I'd pick him up Sunday evening." His grin was devious. "I think, by then, they'll realize how much energy it takes to keep up with a six-year-old."

A nurse showed up then with a wheelchair and my discharge papers, so I didn't get a chance to ask Wade anything more about the Healys until we were on our way back to my place. That's when I asked about Linda's necklace.

"Lisa found the necklace and called the Healys. They've talked to the pawnbroker. It's going to cost them quite a lot to get it back, but I think they're going to pay the pawnbroker what he gave Brewster. Frank said he has to sell some stock first."

"Did they say how much Brewster got for it?"

"No, but the way Frank talked, I think he plans on suing Brewster's estate for the money. I know he's already hired a lawyer."

"Good luck on him getting anything from the estate." From what I'd surmised, Michael Brewster was deeply in debt.

We hit a bump, and Wade glanced my way. "Sorry about that. How are you feeling? How's the arm?"

"Sore." My right arm was wrapped from the palm of my hand to my elbow and resting in a sling. "They said it might take a while before it's back to normal, but nothing was broken. Just badly sprained."

"And the baby?"

He hadn't said anything about the baby since picking me up, which had bothered me. I looked his way, watching his expression. I needed to know how he felt. Truly felt.

"The doctor said the baby's fine, that I'm probably seven weeks along. I'm to keep the appointment I made with my doctor, but they did give me some vitamins to take, and something for the nausea."

I took a deep breath.

"I didn't mean to get pregnant, Wade, but now that I am, I'm not going to do anything to harm this baby. Don't feel you have to marry me, or have any responsibility. I know you didn't want any more children, and that we're still sort of getting to know each other, but—"

"Getting to know each other?" Wade looked my way. "Don't you think we're a little past that point?"

"Well, maybe, but . . ." I didn't know how to explain.

"But I've been acting like an idiot." He sighed and steered the car over to the side of the road, bringing it to a stop. For a moment he closed his eyes. When he looked at me again, he shook his head and reached over and took my good hand in his.

"I'm sorry, P.J. I've been so worried that I'd end up in prison, I haven't been able to think of anything else. I know you didn't mean to get pregnant. And I know you're worried that you'll end up like your mother. But don't you realize I'm way past the 'getting to know you' stage? I love you, P.J., and I want to marry you. I want to be your husband, to be with you when our baby is born."

I stared at him, not sure I'd really heard what I thought I'd heard. "Wade Kingsley," I asked, my heart in my throat, "did you just propose to me?"

He leaned back, his gaze never leaving my face, and then he smiled that lopsided grin of his. "I guess I just did."

ABOUT THE AUTHOR

Born and raised in California, **Maris Soule** majored in art at the University of California Davis, and was working on a masters at the University of California Santa Barbara when she met a redhead with blue eyes who talked her into moving to Michigan—for just a couple of years.

She's still married to that man, has two grown children, two granddaughters, and still lives in Michigan (Florida in the winter). Soule (two-time RITA finalist) began writing romances in the 1980s, and had 25 published. Ultimately she switched to mysteries: *The Crows* and *As the Crow Flies,* published by Five Star.

The Rhodesian Ridgeback in her books is no accident. Soule has owned several. In 2013 she said goodbye to Zuri (the Ridgeback on her Facebook page), who was more like family than a pet.

For more about Soule, go to *http://marissoule.com.*